I0745233

PRINCE OF A THOUSAND WORLDS

STEFON MEARS

Thousand
Faces
Publishing

Also by Stefon Mears

Cavan Oltblood Series
Half a Wizard
The Ice Dagger
Spells of Undeath

Spells for Hire
Devil's Shoestring
Zombie Powder
Spirit Trap
Dragon's Blood

The Rise of Magic
Magician's Choice
Sleight of Mind
Lunar Alchemy
Three Fae Monte
The Sphinx Principle
Double Backed Magic

The Telepath Trilogy
Surviving Telepathy
Immoral Telepathy
Targeting Telepathy

Edge of Humanity
Caught Between Monsters
Hunting Monsters

Power City Tales
Not Quite Bulletproof
No Money in Heroism

Sects and the City
Prince of a Thousand Worlds
Longhairs and Short Tales: A Collection of Cat Stories
Devil's Night
Portal-Land, Oregon
Stealing from Pirates
Fade to Gold
With a Broken Sword
Twice Against the Dragon
The House on Cedar Street
Sudden Death
On the Edge of Faerie
Confronting Legends (Spells & Swords Vol. 1)
Uncle Stone Teeth and Other Macabre Poems
The Patreon Collection, Vol. 1-5 (Vol. 6, coming soon)
The 30-Day Novel and Beyond!

Published by Thousand Faces Publishing, Portland, Oregon

http://1kfaces.com

Copyright © 2020 by Stefon Mears

Front cover image © Wisconsinart | Dreamstime.com (File ID: 132102861)

All rights reserved.

The characters and events in this book are fictitious. Any resemblance to real persons, living or dead, is coincidental and not intended by the author.

No part of this book may be reproduced in any form or by any electronic or mechanical means, including information storage and retrieval systems, without written permission from the author, except for the use of brief quotations in a book review.

ISBN: 978-1-948490-24-5

PRINCE OF A THOUSAND WORLDS

1

I knew Uncle Karl was dead before anyone told me.

I woke up out of a sound sleep, half-convinced I was in the middle of some raging medieval battle scene. Arrows flying everywhere. Cascading clashes of steel. The screams of horses and humans. The smell of mud and blood and offal still in my nose as I sat up, sweating through my cotton sheets.

Still half-asleep — or so I believed — I could see that mounted knight still. Burnished golden armor, coated in a panoply of reds from those he'd already killed. That unicorn horn spiraling out of his helm, just above his closed visor.

His mount — a giant of a horse — bore matching gold barding and a matching golden unicorn horn. And just as many red stains.

The battle around me faded faster into dreamland than the knight. The sounds and smells of battle receded to faint echoes. But I could see that knight still, vibrant as ever and superimposed over the sliding door of my closet, just across the room.

Much the same way, I wasn't quite sitting in my bed. I was also half-lying in the mud. My side screaming from a wound so great it'd torn through my mail.

A chunk of something broken hung out of my side. I stared at it, but it didn't make sense. Too thick for a spear or an arrow…

My life bled out in torrents across grasslands already muddy and bloody from the battle. My heart fluttered frantically.

No. It pounded. Strong, but terrified.

No. It was weak. Fighting for life, but only able to manage a flutter. A thready hint of its past self.

My dry lips cracked with the effort of trying to spit defiance at the knight. I knew my sword lay somewhere near at hand, but I couldn't find it. Couldn't feel my hand reaching for it.

The knight tossed aside his now-broken lance.

Oh. So that was what was in my side. The rest of his lance.

The knight hefted a great ridged mace in both hands. Spurred his steed to charge.

Hooves pounded the bloody mud and carpeting between us.

He swung for my head.

I tried to move, but my body wouldn't respond…

"Vol!"

Diane's voice, coming from far away. That pounding of hooves. Not hooves at all. Her snapping fingers.

"Vol!" she called again, and this time the world snapped into place.

No battlefield.

No knight.

I wasn't dying.

I was sitting on my bed in my little college apartment. I wasn't smelling a battlefield. I was smelling my laundry pile across the room in the open closet. A closet where no mounted knight sought my death.

Diane was next to me. Pretty Diane, with those worried green eyes and her bottle auburn hair almost as wet with sweat as my own matted blonde locks.

No. That wasn't fair. She wasn't nearly as sweaty as I was.

"Can you hear me, baby?" she asked, gently touching my face. Wiping my long hair away from my eyes.

I managed a shaky nod.

"You had me worried there, for a second. I had to call you four times before you answered."

She pulled me into her arms. I tried to object. Muttered something about being gross and sweaty. She hushed me and pillowed my head on her breast.

She rocked me gently, making hushing sounds, while I pulled myself together. Got my heart rate under control. Let my sweat gel instead of continue streaming down my face.

"Must've been some dream," she said at last.

"Yeah," I said, then sat up next to her, both of us leaning back against the cool drywall, and told her about it.

"At least you woke up before you died," she said. "Dying in dreams is no joke."

Diane loved dream stuff. Didn't matter if it was psychological or folkloric. Lucid dreams, so-called prophetic dreams, or strange, spirit animal guided dreams. She read it all and formed her own opinions somewhere in the middle ground between the various extremes.

"Wasn't me," I said, knowing I was right, but not knowing how I knew. "It was Uncle Karl dying in that dream."

"The great adventurer," she said with a smile. She'd only met my uncle once, but she'd been as taken with him as everyone was.

I might've been jealous, except, well, Uncle Karl just had that effect on people. And it wasn't as though she started flirting with him or anything.

"Have you heard from him lately?" she asked.

"Not since my birthday," I said. I nodded toward my closet. "That new suit of custom armor."

"That's right," Diane said, smiling as though she'd put everything together. "He's the one who got you into western martial arts, isn't he?"

I nodded. "Back when I was a freshman in high school." I chuckled. "He always told me, 'You, your father and I, we're the sons of kings. And princes like us should be able to use swords.'"

"See?" she said, triumphantly. "It all comes together now. You're worried about finals, you haven't heard from your uncle since January. It all just jumbled together in your head and came out a wicked dream."

"Maybe so," I said, but I didn't mean it. I knew. I didn't know how to explain it, but I knew.

That dream. It *was* about Uncle Karl. And whether it was a metaphor or not, I knew that my uncle was dead. I just felt that cold certainty settle into my stomach.

But then Diane smiled again, teasing now. Walked her fingers up my chest.

"So," she said, looking at me sideways. "You're descended from kings, huh?"

"That's what Uncle Karl says," I said, and I could feel a ghost of a lopsided smile managing to make an appearance. "Dad says there's not a kingdom in this world that would claim *our* bloodline."

"That's too bad," she said, and leaned in closer. "Prince Volner has a nice ring to it."

"Doesn't sound bad."

"And you're your dad's only son," she said. "So I guess that would make you Crown Prince Volner."

Her distraction was working. I managed a chuckle.

"Well, both Dad and Uncle Karl would be in line for the throne before me. And Karl's the older brother, so technically he'd be the crown prince. I'd just be a prince."

"Prince Volner," she said, savoring the words. "And here, my family doesn't have any royal blood at all. Mutt peasant stock, all the way back."

"You could still be my princess."

Diane shook her head slowly, her eyes and fingers roaming over my sweaty chest now.

"No," she said, smiling, then cocked an eyebrow at me. "Not tonight, anyway. Not after the night you've had."

She tilted her head forward, and looked up at me with flirty, hazel eyes. Fluttered her lashes. Spoke in softer, more yielding tones now.

"A peasant girl like me could never be a princess. But I could be your chambermaid. If you'll have me. My prince."

No way I was going to argue with that offer.

THE NEXT MORNING, I CONVINCED MYSELF THAT IT HAD JUST BEEN A dream and nothing more. That maybe Diane had a point, that my worries about finals came out weird in my sleep. And it was true that I associated Uncle Karl with knights and battles, and had ever since he got me into western martial arts.

Maybe before then, too. I think it was Uncle Karl who got me into fantasy novels, when I was a kid. Mom and Dad never cared for them.

Part of me still whispered that Uncle Karl was dead. But I managed to convince myself that it had only been the three o'clock hour making those words sound true.

After all, three in the morning, that's an easy time to convince yourself of almost anything. As long as it's bad.

All the same, I called home after classes that day, but Dad hadn't spoken to Uncle Karl since mid-March. And it was common for us to go months at a time without hearing from him.

I never knew how Uncle Karl made his money, but he had a lot of it. And he traveled pretty much nonstop. I didn't even think he owned a home. Just a scattered series of post office boxes.

Worries about Uncle Karl had to go to the back burner, though. It was the last week of the last semester of my senior year, and I had one remaining set of finals to live through.

After false starts in three different majors, starting with Biology, I settled on cobbling together my own degree, out of classes scattered across History, Anthropology and Religious Studies.

Officially, my Bachelor of Arts would be in Metaphysics, with an emphasis on post-Renaissance Europe. Unofficially, it was a degree in magic.

Oh, far as I could tell, none of those spells really worked. Not that

I hadn't tried. And I freely admit that it wasn't a major that brought in job offers by the bushel.

Here was the thing, though. I'd gotten to Cal — the University of California at Berkeley to most people — intending to major in Biology. But I flamed out something fearsome during the fall semester of my sophomore year.

I just had this complete break with science. Wasn't that I didn't believe in it, or anything foolish like that. It was just ... I had this sudden realization that I could devote my entire life to studying a theory, only to have some new discovery turn my entire life's work into an obsolete footnote.

I just couldn't handle that idea. That I could work hard my whole life, only to watch my accomplishments go up in flames.

At least, anything I wrote on the topic of magic couldn't get disproven like a scientific theory could. No matter how strange I got with my ideas, at worst no one would care.

And hey, at best, maybe fifteen minutes of fame on the talk show circuit while something I wrote became a fad.

Even if that happened, though, it wouldn't last. Figured I'd end up teaching. Maybe become the weird old professor that everybody liked. Even if they all thought he was slightly insane.

Maybe even write fantasy novels on the side, under a pen name. If I could find anyone crazy enough to publish them.

On the plus side, what I was doing was obscure enough that I had an easy time getting scholarship money for a doctoral program at UCLA, in the Anthropology department.

Sure, good grades probably helped, but I doubt there was much competition.

Now, while I was doing all this, Diane had been working as a house cleaner while putting herself through community college at night, a class or two a semester while preparing to transfer to a four-year school.

She had more serious aspirations than I did. She had her heart set on becoming a clinical psychologist. Part of the reason my parents loved her, I think.

Dad was a surgeon, and Mom was a research psychologist. If I weren't going into medicine, they liked the idea of me at least *dating* — Mom was being good so far about not bringing up the "m" word — someone in the medical field.

Of course, Mom's avoidance of the "m" word might change, when I brought Diane home from college with me. Which was what I planned to ask her about the night after my last final exam.

That very night, when she got home from work.

I'd been feeling so good that day. I'd even nailed the essay questions about the influence of Vatican internal politics on the religious policies of the Roman Catholic Church in the time of Pope Alexander VI.

I'd whipped home on my bicycle with the wind at my back, making every green light. The sun was shining. The bluebirds were singing. And the air was just cool enough that I could ride home hard the whole way without breaking a sweat.

I swear. I even smelled more fresh grass and elm trees than I did oil and asphalt that day. But let's be honest, that was more about my mood than the packed, major streets of Berkeley.

I'd felt on top of the world as I hopped off my bike and unlocked the gate to our little eight-unit building. No mail waiting that day, so I carried my bike up the floating concrete steps to the one-bedroom apartment I shared with Diane.

I was just asking myself if I had time to surprise her with lasagna for dinner as I unlocked the front door.

That was when I heard her crying.

I tossed the bike down next to our ratty old hide-a-bed couch. Barely remembered to throw the door closed behind me.

I hustled across the thin carpet to the bedroom.

There she was. Slouched forward on the edge of our creaky old bed. Still wearing her work clothes: green scrubs bearing the words "Masterclean, the best for your mess."

She didn't even look up when I came in. Might not have heard me. She'd been crying long enough and hard enough that her face had gone blotchy.

I wanted nothing more than to take her in my arms, but I knew better. I stopped for a tissue first.

I dropped to my knees in front of her and handed her the tissue.

She didn't stop crying. She didn't give me a smile, or even a thank you. Which meant whatever it was, it was really bad.

She took the tissue and blew her nose, then threw the crumpled remains in the general direction of the wastebasket.

I realized I was still wearing my backpack. Shucked it off, to thump on the floor. I slid onto the bed beside her.

Took her in my arms. She didn't resist, but she didn't snuggle in.

"Diane?" I asked softly. "What's wrong?"

She shook her head against my chest. Still crying enough that my Giants tee shirt was growing damp.

I stroked her hair and held her tight.

"I'm here," I said. "And I'm ready to listen when you're ready to talk."

I just sat there, holding her for a while. Rocked her just a little bit, the way she liked. Not sure how long we were like that.

Eventually, though, her tears stopped.

"Tissue?" she asked.

I had to stop holding her to get it, and when I handed it to her, she insisted on sitting up on her own instead of letting me hold her.

I have to tell you, that was kind of worrying. I could feel my stomach twist at the thought that I'd done something wrong without even knowing it.

"Diane, you're scaring me," I said softly.

That made her look at me. The weight of sadness in her eyes was overwhelming.

"I'm sorry, baby," she said, just as softly. She reached out and gripped my shoulder, before her hand dropped back down to her own lap. "It's not... It's just..."

"What's going on?"

She took a couple of deep breaths before she answered.

"One of the houses I clean — my team cleans — was robbed.

Some seriously valuable jewelry. Maybe worth more than the company has insurance."

"They couldn't think *you* did it," I said, already angry on her behalf.

The anger in my voice brought a wisp of a smile to her lips before it faded.

"I think they know better, but it doesn't matter." She looked around. "Police'll probably be here soon. Search the place."

I shrugged. "So we cooperate fully. Think someone on your team did it?"

"Doesn't matter," she said, shaking her head. "Vol, I..." She drew a deep breath. "Vol, I've already been fired. The insurance company insisted on that part."

"Those bastards!" I said. "After all you've done for them. Three years of hard work, for—"

"That sucks, but that's not the worst part." Diane shook her head. "They're suing me. The family."

"They're suing *you*?"

"Well..." She shrugged. "They're suing the company, but they've attached me as team lead, and the rest of the team as well. And since I've been fired, the insurance company won't cover my representation."

"But..." That was just too unfair to be true. "They can't do that. Can they?"

She shrugged again. "Maybe. Maybe not. Nothing I can do about it either way. Not like I can force them to do the right thing."

"This is bullshit," I said.

"I'm fucked, no matter what happens." She shook her head. "Gonna look great on future job applications when I have to admit to being fired for cause."

Tears started trickling down her cheeks again.

"But there's no cause." I was getting flushed with fury at all the indignities. "I mean, California's an at-will state, so they don't need one. But they can't fire you for cause when *you didn't do anything wrong.*"

"It happened on my watch." She shrugged again. "That's what Cecilia said."

Cecilia. The owner/operator of Masterclean, and right then, the person I hated most on this earth. Anyone who could make my Diane sound so defeated…

"There has to be something we can do," I said, digging into the pocket of my cargo shorts for my phone. "I'll call—"

"No," she said firmly, snatching the phone out of my hand. "You won't."

"What are you talking about?" I said. "We need to—"

"No. *We* don't."

"I don't understand."

She gathered herself through another breath and sat up a little straighter.

"I know you're ready to go to the mat for me," she said, and stroked my cheek. "And I love you for it. But I'm not going to let this drag you down with me."

"Diane—"

"I mean it, Vol," she said. "You're due to go home next week anyway." A sad smile creased her lips. "I know you were planning to ask me to come with you. And I wish I could. But I have to stay here and deal with this."

"So I'll stay here too, until it's done."

"No," she said, voice firm again. "This is likely to drag on for months, maybe a year or more. And you know it. Probably barely be started before you head south for grad school."

"But—"

"No buts, baby," she said. "I'm not letting you put your life on hold for this. And I'm not letting any judgments against me spill over onto you." Her eyes got fiery for a moment. "I *won't*."

"But I want to fight this with you, Diane. I love you."

Tears started running down her cheeks again.

"And I love you," she said. "Which is why I'm telling you to go."

"What?"

"Pack your stuff. And go tonight." She was crying harder now. "Just. Go."

I kissed her then. Hard. And she got frantic as she kissed me back. Then we were both tearing off our clothes and making furious love one last time.

We were still naked and entwined in the afterglow when police pounded on the door.

THE ARRIVAL OF THE POLICE BROUGHT A WATERFALL OF COLD REALITY crashing down on us both. They let us throw on shirts and sweats, but had their warrant, and they did their damnedest to find some trace of anything that *might* have been on the list of jewelry they were looking for.

Probably the only time Diane ever felt grateful not to own any nice necklaces or earrings. Fanciest thing she had was a thin gold chain with a little golden Seal of Solomon, which I'd given her.

Two officers did the searching. A pair of detectives in plain clothes. Two men, both of them African American. One, the older one, maybe in his mid-forties, wore a navy blue suit so clean and crisp he might have donned it just before coming over here.

The other, the one still in his twenties, wore a rumpled brown suit with a mustard stain on his dark red tie, but perfectly polished shoes.

They were kind to us in their search. They didn't just rip things open and throw them around, the way I'd expected from watching occasional cop shows. Instead, they conducted a very orderly, but very thorough search of apartment from top to bottom.

Hell, they even found my DVD copy of *Re-Animator*, which I'd thought was lost. Turned out it had fallen down behind the couch.

I wasn't part of their warrant, so when it came time to search cars, they could search Diane's little pickup truck, but they couldn't just search my old Dodge Charger.

They asked to search it anyway, of course, saying it would look better for Diane if I let them.

That part was barely out of the older detective's mouth when I was already agreeing and tossing them my keys.

Obviously they didn't find anything in my car either.

When they were finished, the older detective returned my keys, straightened his jacket, and smiled at us.

"For whatever it's worth, Ms. Rhodes," he said in a gentle voice, "I don't think you had anything to do with it. Soon as we can clear you, we will."

"And idea about how long that could take?" I asked. "She's getting sued in civil court over this."

"It'll take as long as it takes," the younger detective said, looking eager to be on his way.

"We'll do what we can," the older detective said. "Might not help you much, though, with the lawsuit. Civil court is a different kind of animal altogether."

"You mean even when you prove someone else did it," I said, unable to keep the disbelief out of my voice, "she might still get sued?"

"It's the American way," the older detective said. "I wish you luck, though. Now if you'll excuse us."

"This is so unfair," I muttered, while Diane was thanking the detectives as they left.

Then they were gone, and silence settled between us so heavily it slowed our steps back up the stairs.

A heavy AC Transit bus rumbled past, setting off car alarms in its wake. Life was going on even as my world fell apart.

Once our apartment door was closed behind us, I tried to start the argument again, but before I said three words, Diane cut me off.

"Please, Vol." Diane shook her head, arms crossed over her stomach. "Please don't argue. Please. Just go."

"How can you expect me to just ... abandon you at a time like this?" I asked, sounding almost as tired as she did. "What kind of asshole would I have to be, to run out on you in your hour of need?"

Her nostrils flared. She wouldn't look at me. Studied the cheap linoleum of our little kitchen. Maybe noticing how badly it needed to be swept.

"Vol," she said softly, "I love you. But you don't have a practical bone in your body."

I straightened like she'd slapped me.

"What's that supposed to mean?"

"It means..." She shook her head. "You and me, we always had an expiration date. This ... this just moved it up on us."

I wanted to ask what she was talking about.

No.

I wanted to scream those words loud enough to express the pain she'd just jolted through me.

I couldn't scream at Diane, though, and I couldn't get the words out any other way. So I stood there. Blinking. Mouth slack. Trying to talk and failing.

Diane must've heard my unspoken question.

"I couldn't move home with you anyway, Vol. Even if you didn't leave until next week, you'd still be leaving without me."

That jarred at least one pained question loose.

"Why?"

"Where would this lead, Vol?" She looked up at me now, and the pain in her eyes had an undercurrent of anger that I couldn't parse. "Even if, by some miracle, I get cleared of the crime tomorrow and the lawsuit gets dropped the next day. Where did you see this going? Did you expect me to move south to L.A. with you, too?"

"Why not?"

"I'm almost done with community college. This fall I'll be applying to four-year colleges to get my degree."

"So?" Maybe it was just reflecting the hints of anger I heard in her tone, but I was starting to get mad now, too. "What? UCLA's not good enough for you?"

"I'm not good enough for UCLA!"

Those words hit me so hard all the anger flew right out of me. All the sadness, too. I had a moment of pure, uncomprehending numbness, as I started to ask what she meant.

Diane didn't wait for the question. And anger burned brighter than sadness in her eyes now.

"I'm not *you*, Vol. I'm not so smart I can just ... make up a major at one of the most prestigious universities in the world. I can't just make grant money show up when I snap my fingers!"

"That's not..." The denial died on my lips. Truth was, I didn't know where my scholarship money was coming from. It just showed up when I formally declared my major. Same way the grant money showed up when UCLA accepted me.

Instead, I just told her another truth that she didn't seem to understand.

"Diane, you absolutely could handle UCLA, or any other university."

She gave me a wistful smile, but shook her head.

"Look," she said, and blew out a breath. "I'll be fine. I'll get into a good state school. San Jose, maybe, or San Francisco."

"But what about us?" I asked, realizing now that she had to have been preparing for this talk for weeks.

"You'll go off to UCLA, get your degree," she said. Then gave me a quirked little smile and added, "And you'll probably find some new spin on some old idea, and end up getting rich and famous. Meanwhile I'll get my degree and set up a little practice somewhere, making my friends jealous with stories about how I was the great Volner Ulfson's college girlfriend."

I closed the space between us. Whispered my next words to her lips.

"You're more than just my 'college girlfriend.'"

She met my eyes with an expression that brooked no argument.

"No, Vol. I'm not."

DIANE LEFT THE APARTMENT WHILE I PACKED. DIDN'T TELL ME WHERE she was going, and I didn't think asking was a good idea. I left her everything we bought together. Kitchen stuff, mostly, but also towels, sheets and the like. Figured she needed that stuff more than I did.

I wrote her a long note, then tore it up. I tried again, and it didn't go any better. I finally settled on a short note:

Dear Diane,

Please remember that I love you.

Vol

There was so much more I wanted to say, but I figured at least this one, she'd read.

Then there was nothing to do but leave.

I'd like to pretend I didn't cry on the fifty-minute drive from Berkeley down to Long Pine City, but if I start lying to you now, you'll never believe me when I get to strange parts of my story.

So, yeah. I cried. I was a freaking mess when I got home, and for the next couple of days, too.

So what say we just skip past that part?

Now, Long Pine City is just about as stereotypically suburban a town as you're likely to find.

It sits smack dab in the middle of the peninsula, just about halfway between San Francisco and San Jose. Never a very big place, but it was on the old Wells Fargo route, back in the gold rush days.

It was big enough to have its own downtown theater showing live plays and musicals. It was small enough to have only one movie theater and no more than three or four Boomer's Coffees.

It was so middle class that some of our neighbors were among the hills tried to pretend they were a separate township.

Oh, they didn't file any formal paperwork. They just started putting "Crystal Hills" on their addresses instead of Long Pine City. Post office didn't care, because the street address itself, and the zip codes, didn't change.

We're talking about rich folks who probably wished they'd bought into one of the wealthier communities like Forest Grove or Pinewood.

My parents never put on airs like that.

Our house started life as a little two-bedroom. But as my parents' respective careers took off, they added on.

When I got home from college, the house I got back to was two stories tall, and stretched back into half of what had once been a huge backyard. They decorated with they bought when Dad was stationed variously throughout Central and South America, and over in the Middle East. Back before I was born, when he was a doctor for the Army.

Most of what they'd brought back was fancy looking stuff like the dining room table and the china cabinet, but all of it was much less expensive than most would guess.

My mom could spot a bargain at two hundred paces on a foggy day.

In fact, that was how she'd paid "next to nothing," but gotten our kitchen remodeled from something she'd considered "unworkable" into an elegant arrangement of granite and oak over a floor tiled in the Mediterranean style.

She would have ditched our old, round kitchen table in the process, but Dad fought hard for it. Insisted that it reminded him where they came from.

Even Mom had to admit, it was a good-looking table, beneath the hated countless scuffs and scrapes. It was some kind of purple hard-wood, with intricate scrollwork patterns etched along the sides.

Dad was sitting at it, when I walked into the kitchen that Saturday morning, while Mom stood at the sink, slicing tomatoes.

Dad isn't quite as tall as I am, but he'd kept his body fit and mili-tary trim as long as I've been alive. He kept his blond hair the same way.

Mom was one of those women who couldn't put on weight if you shoveled cake into her mouth. She was barely five feet tall, and prob-ably weighed no more than one of my legs.

"It lives," Dad said, smiling at me from behind the newspaper. "We were starting to wonder."

"Now, Alvin," Mom cautioned him, wiping her hands on a tea towel as she turned to me. "How you doing, honey?"

"Hungry, mostly," I said, to avoid another unwanted conversation about Diane. A topic I could deflect from further by asking about the other issue that had been in the back of my mind. "Any word from Uncle Karl?"

"None," Dad said, while I popped a couple of chocolate Pop 'Ems in the toaster. "But I wasn't expecting to hear from him before maybe June."

"Why so worried about Karl?" Mom asked, while I filled a glass with tap water.

Might just have been my imagination, but Mom sounded too casual. Made me suspicious. Did she know something?

"Had a dream about a week ago. A big medieval battle scene. A knight in golden armor killed me, but I wasn't me. In the dream." I shrugged. "I woke up certain that I'd been Uncle Karl in the dream, and that Uncle Karl was dead."

I expected them to laugh, but Mom and Dad shared a significant look.

"What?" I demanded.

My Pop 'Ems popped up. I swear my parents held a silent conversation while I put my breakfast on a paper towel and joined Dad at the table.

"I ... had the same dream," Dad said through a sigh. And from the look on his face, he really didn't want to admit this.

"The same dream," I said, skeptically. I mean, yeah, on some level it felt right. But it also felt as though Dad might be humoring me, after the breakup.

He nodded.

"He woke up in a cold sweat," Mom said. "Clutching his side. Here."

She tapped her stomach right where I'd dreamed Uncle Karl had been run through with the lance.

"What did the knight have on his helmet?" I asked.

"A unicorn's horn. Bloody as his armor. His horse had the barding done in the same style."

I forgot all about breakfast. Cold creeps rushed all over me until I shivered right there at the breakfast table.

"You think..." I couldn't let the sentence finish.

"I didn't want to," Dad said. "But if you had the dream too..."

"Lynn didn't," Mom said, referring to my little sister, who was off to Ireland on an exchange program for her senior year of high school. "Or if she did, she didn't say anything when we talked the other night."

"Did she ask about Uncle Karl?" I asked.

Mom nodded as she sat, before saying, "But she always asks after Karl."

"I hate to say this," Dad said. "But Lynn wouldn't have had the dream."

"Why not?" I asked, still not knowing why *I* had had the dream — let alone why Dad had — and seriously hoping to move the conversation that direction.

Dad drew a deep breath. Folded the paper.

"No," he said. "You're still too young for this."

He stood up as though the conversation were over and he was going to go play tennis at the club.

"Too young for what?" I asked, standing now too and trying to cut him off from reaching the garage and his racket.

"Alvin," Mom started, standing up too, but too slowly to stop me. If she'd been planning on it.

Dad realized he couldn't cut around me.

"No," Dad said. And even though he was looking at me, he was answering Mom. "He's too young yet. If Karl really were dead, that'd be one thing—"

There was a knock at the front door.

2

———————

It was weird. Seeing my own frown reflected back at me from Dad's face as we stood there in the kitchen. Me blocking him from reaching the door to the garage. Mom only a pace behind Dad, to his right, looking just as puzzled as we were.

None of us were expecting anybody.

We didn't get door-to-door religion salesmen. In our part of Long Pine City those people actually respected our "no solicitors" sign.

All of our neighbors would have knocked on the door behind me, because my parents kept the garage open pretty much all day. When they were home.

"Irene," Dad said, "would you?"

Mom nodded and moved off to see who was at the door.

"Your pastries are getting cold," Dad said, and he was right. The smell of their chocolate was already fading.

But I had another priority.

"Too young to know what, Dad?"

"A question I'll be happy to answer," Dad said with infuriating patience, "when you're old enough."

"I'm a college graduate. Or will be, after the formal ceremony in a couple of weeks. I'm old enough to vote. Old enough to drink. Old enough to join the military. Hell, I could run for office. I think I'm old enough to hear whatever you're keeping from me."

"And yet—"

"I'm old enough to get my heart shattered."

That took the flippant wind out of Dad's sails. He patted me on the shoulder. Gave my shoulder a squeeze.

"Still. And I'm sorry. But you're not ready for this."

"Alvin," Mom called from the other room. "Volner. I think you'd better both come."

Mom was standing over our glass, two-layer coffee table, hands twisting as though torn between wanting to offer her guest something and wanting to ask a thousand questions.

The guest in question was a woman. Maybe twenty-five years old. Long, shimmering black hair. Tanned skin. Gorgeous enough that even in my heartbroken state, I couldn't help noticing.

Though I admit I only noticed in a clinical way. That she'd be easy to pick out of a crowd, because of her smooth skin, high cheekbones, and bright brown eyes.

She sat with perfect posture on the edge of our old, white leather couch. How she managed to sit so neatly on a couch that could suck an entire football team into its recesses, I didn't know. I was impressed, though.

She wore worn, brown leather pants over the kind of low boots that made me think of scouts sneaking through the woods. Her pants matched the soft leather gloves that didn't extend an inch up her wrists.

She wore a heavy cotton work shirt, a faded red, and a vest of the same brown leather as her pants and gloves.

There was a golden symbol high on the left panel of her vest, but I didn't want to risk looking long enough to tell what it was.

In her gloved hands, she held an ornate box a dozen shades of blue. It looked to have been carved out of some kind of shell, or maybe very delicate stone, with small, subtle images graven all about it.

She looked up at Dad and me as we came in, and something

about the way her attention shifted seemed to say, "the important people have arrived."

I was immediately angry on Mom's behalf.

"Tiksdottir," Dad said, "isn't it?"

"I wasn't sure you'd remember me, sire."

Sire?

Suddenly all the anger I'd been working up got twisted around in a fit of confusion.

"So," Dad said with a sigh. "I take it this means it's true? Karl's dead?"

"Fallen in battle, far from home." She made the words sound reverent, and almost like a chant. "Will you and yours attend the funeral?"

"No," Dad said with a single shake of the head. "I loved Karl, but I haven't changed my mind. I'm not going home again."

"The—" Tiksdottir glanced at Mom and me. "Your parents miss you."

His *parents?* But Mom and Dad always told me...

"Wait," I said. "Gramma and Grandpa Ulfson aren't dead?"

"Go to your room, Volner," Dad said without looking at me. "We'll talk later."

"No," I said. "I want to know what the hell is going on."

"Later," he said. "Irene, can you give me a hand?"

Mom put a hand on my chest as though she'd push me down the hall toward the stairs. But it had been many years since Mom could move me by force when I didn't want to budge.

"Dad," I said, but he wasn't talking to me.

"I know what you have there," Dad said to the woman, Tiksdottir. "But I have forsworn it. You can take it away."

"With all due respect, sire," Tiksdottir said, "I do not bring this for you, but for Prince Volner."

Prince Volner?

"He rejects it," Dad said quickly.

"You cannot reject it for him," Tiksdottir said, and now she stood.

"Please, Volner," Mom implored, shoving pointlessly with both hands. "Trust your father. We'll explain all this later."

"It can't go to him," Dad said. "Not while I'm still alive."

"That would be true," Tiksdottir said. "But you have withdrawn yourself. Which means your son is the next in line."

"He's ineligible," Dad said. "If I am, he is."

Tiksdottir shook her head. "You are not the first to reject ... your family. Precedent has been established. Your son is eligible."

"Fine," Dad said. "Give it to me, then, and I'll see that he gets it."

The look of utter disbelief Tiksdottir gave Dad then managed to stay respectful, but barely.

"I am to present it to him myself."

"I can stop you," Dad said. "I haven't been away so long that I couldn't."

Tiksdottir stopped. Her lower lip curled in as she frowned and she narrowed her eyes. She lowered her center of mass, knees and elbows bent as though she'd fight if she had to.

She looked dangerous.

"Prince Volner," she said.

"No," Dad said.

"I accept," I said. "Give it to me."

"No!" Dad shouted.

I cut around Mom, who lost her balance and tumbled into an armchair.

Dad lunged for Tiksdottir. She spun like a halfback and cut around him.

By the time Dad turned it was too late. He could only watch helplessly.

Tiksodottir dropped smoothly to one knee, bowed her head and offered me the box.

"Prince Volner, I present your legacy."

The moment my hands touched the box, I felt a tiny jolt of electricity through my fingers, followed by a frisson up my spine. I smelled something musky, and heard a rustle of fur.

The air gained a ... clarity it had lacked a moment before. I could see dust motes floating in the space between myself and Tiksdottir. I could feel the warmth of the spring day everywhere on my skin.

"You should find your answers within, sire," she said. "As well as the means to contact me when you are ready for your first Journey."

I swear. I could hear the capital letter attached to that last word.

"Damn it," Dad muttered.

***

When Tiksdottir left, I was tempted to run upstairs to my room, rip open the box, and finally find out what the hell was going on.

But Dad stepped in front of me and said, "Kitchen. Now."

Something about the way he said that. It was what I thought of as his *this-is-serious* voice. It was a voice and expression that warned me that if I didn't listen this time, I'd regret it for the rest of my life.

I hadn't been able to deny that voice when I was a kid, and I couldn't do it that day either.

Then Mom, Dad and I were seated at the purple hardwood of our kitchen table again. I kept one hand on the box, but with the other I started in on my cold, chocolate Pop 'Ems.

"All right," Dad said, then sighed and shook his head. "That's what I get for trying to protect you."

Honestly, I think he wasn't done talking there, but I cut in through a mouthful of chocolate and pastry.

"Tha's wha' 'oo geh 'or..." I swallowed. "For not trusting me."

"Oh, son," Dad said. He shook his head with a pained grimace. "It's not that I didn't trust you. Never that. It's just that—"

"Alvin," Mom said quietly, "maybe you better begin at the beginning."

"Why don't I just open the box and find out?" I asked.

"No. Your mom's right." He sighed. "I was born—"

The front door burst open.

"Sire!" Tiksdottir's voice. "To arms! They're coming!"

"Who?" Dad called, voice ringing with an authority I'd never heard before.

Mom immediately ran to the fridge and started shoving food into a plastic sack.

"The Nulac," Tiksdottir said, reaching the doorway to the kitchen. "Three of their assassins."

It was the weirdest thing. She held her right hand as though holding a sword. Except she wasn't holding one.

Or was she? I couldn't decide. One moment, her gloved hand was empty. The next, there was a shining silver rapier *almost* visible in her grip, but not quite.

"I can handle three," Dad said.

"I can—" Tiksdottir started.

"No," Dad said. "They're here for Volner. Get him to safety by any means necessary. I'll take care of the assassins."

"But sire," she said, hesitating. "You've rejected—"

"I've got this, and you have your orders. Go!"

And just like that, she nodded. Then even the ghost of the sword was gone as Tiksdottir strode into the room.

Mom shoved that sack of food into her hands.

Apparently I was the only one entirely flat-footed here.

"But," I said, though even I wasn't sure where the rest of that sentence was going.

"Please, sire," Tiksdottir said with a quick bow of her head. "We must away."

"But if there's danger," I said, "I should help."

"You are unready for this fight," she said. "Now please, come with me."

I shook my head. Ran for my room and my sword.

I didn't make it to the stairs. Tiksdottir brought me down with a shoulder to the lower back.

I slammed into the soft, thick carpet, but even before I could find my air, she was pulling me to my feet and dragging me through the library toward the back of the house.

I could finally breathe again as we passed the pool table. She tore open the heavy, sliding glass door as though it were a maple leaf.

I tried to turn once more back toward the front of the house and the fight my dad had coming.

But his voice boomed out something in words that didn't quite make sense. As though he were speaking a language I had learned in a dream, but lost upon awakening.

Then, I heard the deep, ringing howl of a wolf. If that wolf weighed maybe a thousand pounds. And I could feel the air that direction sparking with ... something.

Magic?

Was this why Dad never fought me on my major?

Tiksdottir yanked me through the open sliding glass door...

...but not into my backyard.

We fell, tumbling onto a hill of thick, stiff purple grass under a green sky. A blue sun shone brightly through wisps of yellow clouds.

My head kept whipping around, looking for something, anything, that made sense. But even the nearby tree was too bizarre.

Its narrow trunk was covered in what looked more like brown crystals than bark. And its branches all grew downwards, as though stretching for the grass instead of the sun.

Its leaves all looked like broken slivers of black glass.

My stomach roiled. Rejecting what I was seeing. This was impossible. Where was my backyard? Where was the sky? What was I lying on?

What was in those Pop 'Ems this morning?

Even looking at Tiksdottir was no help. She was dressed more or less the same way as she had been, but the cut of her clothing was different. I'd've sworn that faded red work shirt had had machine stitching the last time I looked. But now, hand-stitching. And the cut of her vest was slightly different now. A little more form fitting. Plus, that bag of food was now a leather knapsack.

Oh, and she was wearing a rapier at her belt now, as well as a long knife on her other hip.

"All right, sire?" she asked, while scanning the area and tying back her hair with a leather thong. "We should be safe here, at least—"

I ... I interrupted her by puking all over the grass.

Gods, why did I decide honesty was the best policy in telling you this?

Anyway, she let me get rid of what breakfast I'd had. Then gave me a moment to compose myself from the sweaty, heart-pounding mess I'd been a moment before to a ... well ... standing and vaguely coherent heart-pounding mess.

"This is your first Journey, I take it, sire?"

I nodded.

She sighed and shook her head. I would have sworn she wanted to say a couple of things about how my dad should've prepared me better. And if she had, I would have agreed with every one of them.

On the other hand, Dad might very well have been fighting for *my* life while I was standing there, wondering where the hell I was that had purple grass, a green sky, and a blue sun.

Maybe she thought of that as well. Or maybe she just chose not to speak out against the decisions of a prince. Either way...

"Come on," she said, and I noticed that Tiksdottir was sweating a bit herself, and sounding a little winded. "I can manage one more, I think, and you look like you could use some food."

"Right," I said, tucking my box under one arm.

"Wait," she said with a frown. "Before we do that, you need to open the box."

"Here? Now?"

"You won't have time for everything," she said. "Certainly not for the letters. But there's one thing you need before we go any further."

"All right," I said.

I opened the box.

WE MOVED OVER TO STAND NEAR THE ... SAFETY, I GUESS ... OF THE brown crystal tree.

I sat on stiff, purple grass, wondering for a moment if I should feel good or bad about the fact that the breeze was warm, and smelled like anise.

I think I was just too numb to decide. Too much had happened in too short a span of time, for me to properly appreciate the little details of what appeared to be *an entirely different fucking world altogether*.

All right. Maybe I wasn't quite *that* numb.

I did wonder flittingly what Diane would think if she found out that, apparently, I actually *was* a prince. But thinking about Diane hurt.

And Uncle Karl. It hadn't been just a dream. My beloved uncle really was dead. Thinking about that hurt too.

Much better to focus on the box, and maybe even get some concrete answers to what the hell was going on.

I opened the box with a soft *click*.

Inside was a sheaf of three letters written on old fashioned parchment, sealed with wax, and bound together with thick red thread.

The only other thing in the box was a golden disc, maybe three inches across on a chain of heavy gold. A seal of some sort, and I was pretty sure it was the same symbol I'd seen — but not really looked at — on Tiksdottir's vest.

"Put the chain around your neck," Tiksdottir said. She wasn't looking at me, though. She stood with her back to me, her sword in one hand and her knife in the other. Watching all around us for threats. "Look at the seal. Try to look through it, if that makes any sense."

I set the box on my crossed legs, and picked up the golden seal. The device graven into it was a ring, circling a howling wolf. Facing up and to my left. To the dexter. Wasn't that what they called it, in heraldic-speak?

I couldn't remember what a twolf symbolized. But then again, my name was Ulfson. Son of the wolf. So maybe worrying about heraldry was overthinking it.

I slipped the chain around my neck. It wasn't as heavy as I

expected, which made me think it was gold plating over something lighter.

I held the seal in both hands, and stared at it. Into it. Tried to look through it, even though that wasn't physically possible.

Then again, neither were purple grass, a green sky, a blue sun and a brown crystal tree. So what the hell, right?

For a moment, I felt silly.

But then I felt the urge to say my name.

"I am Prince Volner Ulfson," I said, because including the title felt right.

The wolf turned and looked at me. His eyes were amber now. And growing.

Growing.

Growing.

Soon I was falling into a world of gold and amber.

I landed on a pile of old bones at the mouth of a cave. The air was warm, and moist. I smelled a resin of some kind. And hints of old smoke. There was a tanginess to the smoke, as of burned meat.

The bones clacked and shifted under me as I worked my way to a standing position. There was no dirt under my feet. Just rock, the color of smoky amber, same as the cave itself.

I spotted a skull among the bones. A human skull.

The shapes of the rest of the bones resolved themselves. They were all human bones. Every single one. The remains of hundreds of people. The only whitish-yellowish-brownish things in this world of amber and gold.

I heard soft feet padding toward me from the darkness of the cave. I wanted to turn away, but I didn't dare.

Glowing amber eyes in the darkness. Eyes the size of my fists. Eyes that grew bigger as they approached.

Terror tried to seize me, but I fought it off enough to grab a femur in each hand. Ready to fight, if need be.

Then the great wolf stood before me.

I could be twice as tall and still not reach its shoulder. Its fur was all in shades of honeyed gold.

But oh, its teeth were bigger than the femurs I dropped out of sheer pointlessness.

This wolf could devour me in a single gulp. Those femurs, they wouldn't even stick in its throat.

The wolf regarded me, and the power of its gaze seemed to squeeze me from all sides.

"I am Prince Volner Ulfson," I said, hoping it was the right thing to say. "Son of Prince Alvin Ulfson and..." — did Mom have a title? — "and Lady Irene Ulfson nee Collinsworth."

The wolf's regard sharpened. Intensified. And I don't just mean the squeezing pressure I felt coming from every direction at once.

It was as though I was seeing into the wolf, as I looked back. And in those eyes I saw vast power and ancient intelligence.

What I saw felt so alien that the wolf might have been a mask worn by a creature of shifting silicon and plasma.

And yet...

And yet there was something familiar in those eyes too. Something that seemed to reverberate inside me.

As I stared back into those eyes, that resonance, that reverberation, it grew stronger.

And stronger.

Then my bones seemed to hum with it. My blood began to sing with it. My muscles and tendons all throbbed with it.

My skin began to itch all over.

I could ... *feel* my hair. Itching. And not just on my scalp. Every hair on my body. Arm hair, underarm hair, facial hair, chest hair, pubic hair, leg hair — all of it itched, while everything inside me started vibrating in what I hoped was harmony with...

...with whatever that wolf was. Because this might have been a real creature. A real experience. And it might just have been a metaphor, taking place in my mind.

I just didn't know anymore. And I wasn't sure which I wanted it to be.

Either way, what was happening felt ... valid. Significant.

The one thing I knew — and I knew it with such certainty that knowing carried a terror of its own — I knew that, at least in *some* way, this was really happening.

This wasn't madness. This wasn't a dream.

This was...

This was a test.

Yes. That was what this was. And the moment I recognized that I was being tested, a kind of confidence washed through me.

Prince or not, I was Volner Ulfson. Tests were something I ate for lunch and asked for seconds. And I had the academic track record to prove it.

That boost of confidence changed something between the wolf and myself. I wasn't just seeing into the wolf, now. I was projecting who I was right back at it.

The great wolf's eyes gained depth. Dimension. Pull.

Those eyes swallowed me whole.

***

I tumbled through a sky of blazing amber.

Heat seared me. Inside and out.

My bones. My blood. My skin. Every inch of me scalding. Broiling.

Even my throat, as I cried out.

Even my nostrils, with every breath.

I came apart as I fell, endlessly.

My skin sloughed off of me, then blackened and turned to ash. And even the ash burned away to nothingness.

My organs, one by one, were next, while the rest of me kept falling. Followed by my veins. Muscles. Tendons. Until every bit of meat and gristle was gone.

Then my bones disjointed and fell away, one by one by one. Each burning, in its turn, into less than ash.

Until finally, nothing was left of me to fall, except ... except whatever was left *within* me. My awareness. My mind. My soul. Whatever it was that formed my essential nature.

That part of me remained.

But that part of me was burning as well.

This fire felt different, though. This was not destructive fire. This was ... transformative fire. My essential nature was not being burned away to sheer nothingness.

I was being heated in a forge. Or perhaps a crucible.

But even sensing this on some deep level didn't help. Even transforming fire burns, and this heat, this pain, it was beyond imagining.

The heart of a supernova would not burn with the intensity of the fires I found inside the world of that wolf's eyes.

It turned out that even my essential nature had some ... inessential elements. At least, I hope that was what I felt burning away.

Or maybe it was just that even my essential nature had elements it could be separated into, and that was what was happening.

I know that ... I felt as though I were being organized. Or that parts of me were being categorized, maybe.

To this day, I'm still not quite sure how to explain it.

I do know this. What I'd said before about something in that great wolf resonating inside me — that part of me came to the fore.

And the moment it did, the experience began to shift.

That part of me, it didn't just become the core around which everything else was assembled. It became ... holographic, in a way. As though everything I was — every part of me, body, mind and soul — was reassembled out of tiny reflections that contained the entirety of that core, reverberating element.

It took an infinity of time, there within that amber sky. An eternity of being burned and boiled away, followed by a second eternity of evaluation, then a third eternity during which I was assembled once more.

Time had lost all meaning. Space had lost all meaning.

In the end, I knew one thing, and one thing only.

On some level, I was the wolf.

3

———

I SAT CROSS-LEGGED ON STIFF, PURPLE GRASS UNDER A GREEN SKY, beneath the questionable shade of a brown, crystal tree. I smelled anise on the warm breeze.

My body felt as though it were ringing. As though I'd stood too close to a two-ton bell when it sounded, and its vibrations were still working their way out of my system.

In front of me, Tiksdottir stood guard. Both weapons still drawn.

I no longer held the golden seal in my hands. The chain was gone too.

No. Not gone. They were within me now. Part of me. As the wolf was part of me.

That knowledge didn't trouble me. In fact, I felt calmer, more at peace, than I could ever remember feeling before.

I wasn't numb. I could still feel the heartbreak of losing Denise, the grief of losing Uncle Karl, the worries about my parents. But I was calm because those feelings were not immediate needs. They required no action from me, not right now.

I had other things I needed to do. My father was off at home, battling assassins to save my life. Possibly my mother was well. I couldn't honor their fight by wallowing in my own pain and fear.

Even the hunger rumbling my stomach was more urgent than my grief and heartbreak and worry.

I stood up.

"Everything all right?" Tiksdottir asked, not yet turning around.

"I'm ready to go," I said, tucking the box under one arm.

She sheathed her blades and turned to look at me. I wasn't exactly dressed to impress. A Cal tee shirt and gray sweats. Hadn't even had time to grab shoes before we fled.

And hey. My clothes now looked as though they'd been hand-stitched, not machine-stitched. And the Cal logo was embroidered, instead of being ... whatever it was on most tee shirts.

Even dressed as I was, though, Tiksdottir did a double-take as her eyes tracked over me, slower on the second viewing. She shook herself.

I remembered people looking at Uncle Karl just that way.

"Definitely an Ulfson," I heard her mutter, but, louder, she said, "I think I can handle one more Journey now, but then we'll need to hunker down someplace and rest. And you need food, sire."

"Then let's go," I said.

She looked around, though from our vantage point, I couldn't tell what she was looking for. It was purple hills in pretty much every direction. Though some directions had more of the brown crystal trees, while other directions had crystal trees in shades of red and yellow.

And off in the distance, was that ... a sea of deep red-orange?

"This way, I think," she said, and started off toward a pair of low hills between a small, brown crystal forest.

"You're not sure?" I asked, as much to make conversation as anything else.

"I'm not of the Wolf, sire," she said. "My ability to Journey is limited."

"Tell me how it's done, then," I said. "I'll take us."

"Too much risk right now," she said, looking over her shoulder. "I may have left a trail, and you don't know how to avoid leaving one."

"So tell me," I said. "I learn quickly."

"Sire," she said, turning to face me and clearly fighting not to give voice to the frustration in her eyes, "if Nulac assassins catch us right now, I might not be able to keep you alive. So please, let's leave the questions until we're someplace safe."

I gestured for her to lead on. And as we started walking, I said, "One condition. Call me Volner?"

"No, sire," she said. "That would be inappropriate."

"Why?"

She gave me a flat look.

"Right. Later for the questions, then."

"Can you run?" she asked, but she sounded as though she knew the answer. I told her anyway.

"Try me."

She started jogging at a quick pace. Matching her would've been easier if I'd been wearing good running shoes, but I'd run barefoot before.

Of course, I'd never run barefoot on stiff, purple grass before. And we hadn't gone three hundred yards before the grass was taking its toll on my feet.

I slowed. She noticed.

"Oh, the River. You're bleeding. Why didn't you say something?"

I didn't know how to answer that, just dropped onto the purple grass along the decline leading to what I could see was her goal now. A cave tucked into the space at the foot of those two low hills.

Tiksdottir pulled a pouch from her belt. Stripped the gloves from her hands, which were both heavily scarred. Enough that I wondered if there was a category beyond third degree burns.

She dumped some ground herbs into one palm. The herbs were shades of browns and greens, and looked to have little ground seeds scattered within them too.

She spat into the mix. Rubbed it between her palms, while muttering words I could almost understand. Something about blood and sap and bark and skin.

She smeared the paste onto my feet — which I didn't think were all that bloody — and rubbed it in.

The skin of my soles not only closed over where it had broken open, it calloused as though I'd been running on broken glass three times a week for the past six months.

I'm pretty sure she smiled then because my look of utter bewilderment was, shall we say, unprincely.

"Old field trick," she said, slipping her gloves back onto her hands, and re-tying the pouch to her belt. "Sucks to lose a boot in battle, let me tell you."

We both stood, and I might as well have been wearing the same boots she was, little as the grass bothered me now.

We started running again.

"You've been in battles?" I asked, as we made our way between those low hills, toward that cave.

"Only once," she said, "but believe me. Once was enough. I'm much happier as a royal messenger."

"Why do I think that sounds even more dangerous than soldiering?"

"Because you're smart," she said, shooting me a grin. "Sire. But I prefer my kind of danger to the sheer chaos of a battlefield."

We reached the cave mouth then. Didn't look like anything special. I mean, for a cave made of matte black rock in the side of a purple hill.

"Why here?" I asked.

She didn't answer me.

Well, that's not entirely true.

Tiksdottir did not turn and explain in words why she had led me to this cave mouth.

She did, however, turn toward the cave and show me.

There was no chanting or incanting of any kind. No grand gestures or sweeping hand movements.

Instead, it was as though she turned inward for a second. And as she did I could almost hear a wolf howl.

Something flared within her.

Power.

I wasn't surprised when I felt a resonance of that power within me.

Sweat broke out on Tiksdottir's forehead, but she held onto it. That power. Wrestled with it as though it would escape. Fought it to a standstill between her shaking hands.

In fact, all of her was shaking with the effort.

She lowered her gathered hands. Pulled them back by her right side. Her legs trembled as she stepped closer to the cave mouth, at the right-hand side.

With a sharp cry of pain she shoved that power at the edge of the cave mouth.

The power connected. Limned into the visible spectrum, at least to my eyes, where it coruscated brilliant reds and ambers, as it whirled around the edges of the cave mouth, coming back along the ground to meet the starting point. A completed circle.

The moment the circle completed, I felt it click in my head. The faintly visible red and amber power sheened across the cave mouth.

"Come on," she said, grabbing for my hand without looking back. "I can't hold it long."

I took her hand, and together we jumped through.

<hr>

WE PASSED THROUGH THE SHEEN OF POWER INTO ANOTHER PLACE entirely. This time, we landed in a small, wooden cabin. Dimly lit, thanks to a late afternoon overcast sky visible through a few windows of runny glass.

The smell of sea air was strong, and chilly.

We landed on our feet this time. Or I did, at least. Tiksdottir tumbled down onto what looked in the shadows like a bearskin rug.

She lay there, panting as though she'd run marathons back to back, and would have been murdered if she lost either one.

I stood there, trying to let my eyes adjust, but Tiksdottir said, "Fire," and pointed past her head.

I set the blue box down at my feet, and made my way between the shapes of wooden furniture to a rounded stone hearth. A bucket of split wood on one side, and a bucket of kindling on the other.

I half expected to dig around for flint and steel — all the while trying to remember the lessons Dad had taught me on camping trips in my youth — but there was a fireplace clicker in with the kindling.

I had the fire going in no time. The hearth had been well designed, and starting fighting the chill immediately. And winning.

With more light now, I could take a better look at the cabin.

Regular wood this time, not crystalline wood. Orangish, and something about the logs made me think of driftwood. Their smoothness, maybe. They were held together with what looked like iron nails, and a mortar made from a brownish paste that I didn't think was mud.

A high, arched ceiling had been done the same way, with a platform loft that took up half the cabin and a rope ladder for access.

The furniture was, indeed, all wooden. And the same kind of wood. A pair of armchairs, and a little couch. Tiny end tables, instead of a coffee table. Also a series of lockers, along two walls.

Tiksdottir, though, looked pale and soaked with sweat. And had yet to catch her breath.

"Anything I can do?" I asked, hoping the question wasn't an insult.

She started to shake her head, then said, "Candles."

I realized then that on the end tables and two of the lockers sat thick, yellow beeswax candles in iron holders. I lit one from the fire, and used it to light the others.

Soon, the glow inside the cabin was almost homey. And Tiksdottir had stopped panting and made it to a sitting position, leaning against one of the armchairs. Though her head still hung forward.

I could finally forestall the question no longer.

"Are you all right?"

She gave a breathless chuckle, but nodded.

"Not supposed to..." she cleared her throat. "Not supposed to do that twice in one day. Not supposed to cover that much distance either. But the blood. They'd track that. Blew my first stop."

"Sorry," I said.

She shook her head hard enough that her ponytail bounced off each shoulder. "Not your fault. Sire. Mine."

"Hardly," I said. "I—"

"You had shoes. In the living room. I should've grabbed them."

"You spotted those?"

She smiled enough to show teeth. "I'm ... a messenger."

"Which means you're a spy."

"Knew you were smart, sire."

"Are you also an assassin then?"

She drew three deeper breaths, and sounded more normal as she answered.

"I'm whatever the Crown needs me to be," she said, but her eyes made the answer clearly "yes."

I chuckled. "Remind me not to cross you, then."

"I would die before harming you, Prince Volner," she said with a formality that gave me chills. There was that chanting quality to her words again.

This time, under the chant, I could feel power. Not compulsion. Nothing was making her say that. But saying those words the right way, and meaning them, there was power in it.

Initiations, I realized, as my schooling of the past four years came to the fore. This woman had been through initiations of her own form of magic, to train and become who and what she was.

The power I heard in those words, that was the power of an oath freely sworn, reflected in her words.

The corollary hit me like a ton of bricks. Paled my skin and stole my breath.

Me.

This woman had sworn oaths that applied to *me*, and before today I hadn't even known she was alive.

And there were others. There had to be. No one had only one messenger-slash-spy-slash-assassin.

Also, she'd fought in a battle. For the Crown.

There were armies. They'd probably sworn oaths too. Oaths that included me.

There was a whole world out there that knew about me. A whole world to whom I mattered.

A world of strangers. A world I didn't even know *existed* until that day.

Yeah, about that not-telling-me thing, Dad. Gotta say, you blew this one.

"What troubles you, sire?" Tiksdottir asked.

"Just ... realizing things about myself that I never knew before."

"Prince Alvin truly told you nothing of who you are? Where you come from?"

I shook my head.

"What about Prince Karl? I know he visited you frequently."

That was true. Uncle Karl. He hadn't just gotten me into fantasy novels. He'd told me fantasy stories himself.

And maybe they weren't just stories...

How did they go?

"Once upon a time..." I muttered, hoping the key phrase would bring back Uncle Karl's stories.

The words came back slowly.

"Once upon a time, there was a wizard named Emerlaine. He united an island kingdom of his world. What was it called?"

"Lonava," Tikstdottir said, in a quiet, prompting way.

"Yes. Lonava." I settled onto the wooden couch across from her. "And Lonava knew peace under its king. But Emerlaine continued his magical experiments. Pushed his knowledge and mastery. In so doing, he learned that there were other worlds."

"Worlds in conflict," Tiksdottir said.

"Right," I said, nodding. It was coming back, slowly, but Uncle Karl had told me these stories so long ago, I could remember only a shorthand version of the tales at best.

"Emerlaine dreamed of bringing peace to those worlds, as he'd brought peace to Lonava."

"But they rejected him," Tiksdottir said.

"His Twenty Proposals of Peace, right," I said, nodding. "Emerlaine grew furious, and brought them peace through conquest."

I shook my head, awe in my voice now as I realized this was a true story.

"World after world, Emerlaine spread his rule. Conquering even those who were at peace when he found them. He grew to love the conquest, and the power of ruling, even as he loved the power of his magic."

"They say he conquered more than a million worlds in his lifetime," Tiksdottir said.

"He founded the Empire of New Lakoshanty."

"Nulac O-Shantí," Tiksdottir corrected me.

"Nulac O-Shantí," I repeated. "And established himself as Emperor Emerlaine, the first of the sorcerer-kings."

"What about his fall?" Tiksdottir asked.

"Many chafed under his rule. Assassins failed. Coups failed. Centuries passed. He remained."

"His fall," she prompted softly.

"Each world still had a form of its own governance, under the rule of the emperor. And it was in the world of Aesgarr, in the kingdom of Vol Halá that King Ulfgar rose up, beginning the Great Rebellion."

I shook my head. "King Ulfgar. I was sure Uncle Karl had made that up."

"Go on."

"The Great Rebellion. A hundred and fifty years of bloody war, across a thousand, thousand worlds." I shook my head again, trying to grasp the scope of what I'd always thought was just a fanciful turn of phrase. "So that really happened?"

"It did. Go on."

"In the end it came down to Ulfgar himself, locked in battle with Emerlaine. And Ulfgar emerged triumphant."

"This is why your ancestor is known as King Ulfgar the Liberator."

"My ancestor," I said. And in that moment, I realized that Dad had been right after all.

Oh, I still felt he should have told me the truth about our family.

But he had been right that he couldn't just *tell* me. Not until I'd met the Wolf.

But sitting there, worlds away from home. Having seen, having felt, having *used* real magic, I could not doubt that everything in this story was true.

"What did King Ulfgar do then?" Tiksdottir asked me.

"There were twelve sorcerer kings and queens who'd rallied first to his call. The allies without whom, the Great Rebellion would have died in its crib. And so he parted out the Empire. Split it among the twelve."

"Not all of it," Tiksdottir said.

"No," I said. "He kept a thirteenth part for himself. Perhaps the richest worlds of them all."

"Difficult to say," Tiksdottir said, "but what of the Council? Did Prince Karl tell you of the Council?"

"Yes," I said, remembering suddenly. "The Council of Twelve. Composed of ministers from the twelve great kingdoms, that they could keep watch on each other, to ensure that an Emerlaine never arose again."

"Why twelve?" she asked. "Why not thirteen?"

"Because..." I confess, I'd paid more attention to Uncle Karl's tales of battles and rebellion than the politics that followed. "Because the Council met in ... Aesgarr? In Vol Halá?"

"Why there?"

"Oh!" I said, remembering. "Because the twelve had named Ulfgar High King Over All."

"Not their emperor," she said, raising a finger to emphasize the point. "He couldn't give them orders. But they acknowledged him as high king and gave him power to rule over disputes among the twelve, as well as the right to patrol the border worlds, and send armies where they were needed."

"And," I added, "because Ulfgar was the mightiest of them, they wanted to keep an eye on *him*."

"Of course," she said, smiling.

"The assassins," I said. "You said they were Nulac assassins. As in, from Nulac O-Shantí?"

"The kingdom of Nulac O-Shantí, the crowning jewel of the ancient empire, was destroyed in the Great Rebellion."

She looked at me expectantly, though I wasn't sure whether she expected me to already know this part, or just to figure it out.

Well, I didn't know it. So I guessed.

"What was the sigil of Nulac O-Shantí?"

She smiled as though I'd asked the right question. "Twin crossed staves, with lightning flowing between them."

"And that sigil has been seen again. Maybe from the borderlands of the most distant kingdoms?"

"Three worlds belonging to the outermost border kingdoms have been attacked in the last five years. Each invading army bore the twin staves crossed by lightning."

"And the assassins. They bear that sigil right there?"

I pointed to her left breast, where the Ulfson sigil marked her vest.

"That's right, sire."

"So who's leading them?"

"That's the real problem," she said. "We don't know."

***

TIKSDOTTIR AND I DINED IN THE CABIN THAT NIGHT ON WHAT MOM HAD packed for us. Cold fried chicken, a block of sharp cheddar cheese, and a bunch of grapes.

To drink, we had water. I'm pretty sure Mom had put plastic bottles of water in the bag, but now they were glass, stoppered with corks.

Outside, it rained heavily, pounding the wooden roof above, and chilling the area near the windows, when I went to look at the cliff edge outside, and the deep black sea beyond.

But the rest of the cabin stayed pleasantly warm, from the fire. I didn't recognize the wood, but as it burned it smelled somewhat like spiced cherries and nutmeg.

We ate, each of us sitting in a wooden armchair, with the food spread between us across the two small end tables. And as we did I asked a couple of other questions that had been bothering me.

"Why are my clothes different? And I *know* Mom shoved this food into a plastic bag, not leather. And the bottles were plastic too."

"Not every world allows for the same things," Tiksdottir said. "Plastic. Machine stitching. These things were not possible in the world of purple hills. Part of the power used in Journeying adjusts things as necessary."

"What if the world wouldn't allow for us to breathe?"

She started to answer, then closed her mouth and frowned. Thought about it as she ripped half the meat off of a chicken leg.

"I don't think I could take us to a world like that. I'm not sure about you, though. Your superior magic might tailor your lungs and so on, as needed."

She shrugged.

"Wouldn't recommend trying it. Not unless you had no other choice."

"So how do I—"

"Please, sire," she said, raising one chicken-greasy glove. "I'm not the one to teach you this."

I hated asking the next question, but I couldn't *not* ask it.

"So what do I do if something happens to you?"

I may have felt bad about asking, but Tiksdottir took the question in stride.

"It shouldn't," she said, looking around. "At least, not while we're in here. More than Journeying guards this place."

She pulled a wound cord out of her shirt, and from it dangled a small clay disc. It was heavily inscribed, but I couldn't read the writing from where I sat.

I could feel its magic though.

"Even knowing about this place," she said. "Even having been here before. I could not have brought us here without this."

She slipped it back under her shirt. She nodded at the box as she finished that chicken leg.

"And if something happens to me after we leave here, well, I expect your answers are in there."

"Three letters?" Amazing, when I think about it, that I could sound skeptical after everything I'd seen and done that day.

In fact, it was a wonder I wasn't falling down tired. I almost started wondering about that, but Tiksdottir distracted me by addressing my question.

"Doubt they're just letters, sire."

I wasn't ready to open them, though. Not until we were done eating.

"So," I said, swallowing a slice of cheese, "if you're Tiksdottir, who's Tik?"

"Tik Garrison. The high king's constable," she said, proudly. "He runs the royal palace in the capital city. He has six sons and six daughters, and all of us serve the Crown."

"So you do have a name other than Tiksdottir then?"

"Of course, sire," she said, "I am Ulna Tiksdottir."

"And I'm guessing it would be inappropriate for me to call you Ulna."

"It would, sire. It is important to maintain distance between the royal family and we who serve you."

That near-chanting quality again, to her voice.

Under those words, I could almost hear a second sentence. *My death may buy your life, but not if you spend your life trying to save mine.*

I didn't like it. But I'd have to accept it. At least, for now.

We finished dinner in silence. The topic of death seemed to drive out other conversation.

I'm not sure what Tiksdottir was thinking about. I was thinking about Mom and Dad. Wondering if they were all right.

The only real problem was that, the more I wondered, the less I could think of anything else.

Except, and this is the weird part, I think I could have. Thought of something else, I mean. Just shoved that worry to the back of my mind. That was part of the legacy of the Wolf, to keep current matters current, and allow other matters to wait.

But damn it, we were talking about my parents, here.

They might be dead. And that was not some minor worry to shove aside.

Finally, I had to ask.

"When can we find out if my mom and dad are still alive?"

"Of course they're alive, sire?" Tiksdottir said, blinking in astonishment. "Well, I cannot swear that your mother is alive. But I know this. When your father dies someday, you will know it as surely as you knew when Prince Karl died."

That seemed obvious enough that I felt stupid for not having realized it.

"What about Mom?"

"Alas, you would not know if your mother died. She is not of the royal blood." Before I could object, Tiksdottir stilled me with a raised glove. "But your father gave up everything for her. His rank. The family. All of it. There is no way she died while he lives."

I nodded, feeling better. My shoulders and jaw even relaxed tension I hadn't realized I'd been holding.

"So he couldn't marry her," I asked, "and stay a prince?"

"He was not required to surrender his rank for her. He chose that for reasons of his own." She shook her head. "And no, sire, I do not know them."

We were popping grapes through that part of the conversation, and I finished the last grape with a sweet, crunchy pop.

At last, though, dinner was done.

It was time to open the box and see about those letters.

I sat on the bearskin rug, before the crackling fire. Its smell of spiced cherry and nutmeg almost a dessert after that simple dinner in the cabin.

Tiksdottir still sat on one of the wooden armchairs. She looked exhausted, but curious.

I turned my back to the fire, so I'd have its light to read by. A little brighter here, than near any of the candles.

I opened the box.

There they were, just as I had seen them before. Three letters. Aged parchment, sealed with red wax and the imprint of the wolf sigil of...

...of my house. I'd have to start thinking of it that way. Maybe when I'd woken up this morning, I'd just been Volner Ulfson, new college graduate and soon to be doctoral student.

But now I knew the truth. I was Prince Volner Ulfson of Vol-Halá.

And these three letters, they held to key to exactly what the hell that meant.

The three were bound together by a thick, red thread. I thought I'd have to cut it apart, but when I touched the knot it loosened and fell away.

I picked up the first letter. I read my name and title, written with black ink in a swoopy, formal, possibly calligraphic hand.

I broke the first seal, full expecting some kind of spark of power, or gust of wind, or maybe a wolf's howl.

Some kind of magic.

But it broke apart like perfectly ordinary wax.

I'd like to think I concealed my disappointment from Tiksdottir.

I pulled out the letter from within. Unfolded it.

And unfolded it.

And unfolded it again.

Finally, what I was holding was an ornate family tree, running back six generations.

At the top, I was not surprised to see my ancestor, High King Ulfgar, the Liberator. Apparently he married a Queen Delfina, though it didn't say what kingdom — or queendom — she'd come from.

"Hey," I said. "Ulfgar's last name was Ulfson. But I thought he was our..."

I couldn't even finish the question before I knew my answer.

We were, all of us, sons and daughters of the Wolf. Hell. Literally, so far as I knew.

At the bottom of the tree, my own name, son of Prince Alvin and Irene (cm). Next to Dad was Uncle Karl, who apparently hadn't married or had children.

On Dad's other side was a sister: Rikka.

I had an aunt, and no one had told me?

She had married a Prince Tigor, and they had two daughters, Lyfsana and Stazja, and a son, Baros.

Wait. Why wasn't Lynn listed as my sister?

I noticed something then, going back up the tree. There were three places where a wife or husband was tagged (cm). And in each case, the only children listed matched the sex of their parent with royal blood.

What was up with that?

"Tiksdottir?" I asked.

"Yes, sire?"

"CM means commoner, right?"

"That is correct, sire."

"But why is my sister not listed on this family tree?"

"When a member of the royal house marries a commoner, the magic denies the commoner's blood. Since your father is a prince and your mother a commoner, your sister does not inherit the magic."

"But," I said, "simple genetics says she and I have the same bloodline."

"Scientifically, yes," Tiksdottir said with impressive patience. "Magically, you do not."

"But she should still inherit the title," I said, firmly. "She should still be acknowledged as a princess."

Tiksdottir shook her head. "It is the magic in your blood that makes you royal, sire. Lacking that, your sister has no claim to title or inheritance."

Before I could object again, she added, "This is not just the rule of Vol-Halá. All the great kingdoms have insisted on it."

I frowned.

"Wait," I said. "What if birth doesn't reveal someone's true gender? I've known—"

"This has happened," Tiksdottir said. "If the magic acknowledges them, they are listed as the appropriate gender on the family tree."

"But how does the magic decide?"

"Difficult to say," Tiksdottir said. "From what I have been given to understand, it has to do with sincerity. The magic of the Wolf cannot be tricked. If the son of a royal princess and a commoner plays at being a girl in an effort to claim the birthright, the magic will deny him. If, however, she truly should have been born a girl, the magic will acknowledge her and assist the transition."

I looked over the family tree again. Goodness, it was wide. High King Ulfgar had sired twelve sons and eight daughters. Poor High Queen Delfina must've needed a wheelchair by the time the eighteenth kid came out.

Shock wove through me, though, as I realized something.

This family tree. It *was* wide. But it wasn't very deep.

I was only the sixth generation of this royal line.

These stories I'd recounted for Tiksdottir, they'd sounded like things that had happened thousands and thousands of years ago.

And yet, between myself and High King Ulfgar were only *four generations.*

"How long do we live?" I asked. "My family?"

"So far as I know," she said calmly, as though these words were no big deal, "if you aren't killed, you won't die."

"Won't die..."

"This," Tiksdottir said, "is why those rejected by the magic are not listed. Your sister, Lynn, she will live only a normal span for the world of your birth."

I reeled at these revelations for a time. I'm not even sure how long. I know that by the time I was next aware of myself, I was still staring at the family tree. And realizing that, of the dozens of names on it, only a handful were listed as dead.

High King Ulfgar was not one of them.

"High King Ulfgar is still alive?" I asked.

"And may he never die," Tiksdottir said, the words coming automatically.

"I don't understand," I said. "When Uncle Karl died and you showed up with the box, I kind of thought that meant I was now next in line for the throne or something."

"An argument could be made that direction," Tiksdottir said, and leaned in closer. I realized that she smelled woodsy, in a good way.

She pointed to a dead names, farther up the tree. My great-grandfather Torin.

"Now..."

And then she went into an explanation that probably made perfect sense. If I already was well-versed in family history and the inheritance laws of Vol-Halá. Or maybe knew these names as something other than names on a list.

The long and the short of it was that, according to one interpretation, my great-great-grandmother should be next in line for the throne. Except that she was deemed ineligible after she Journeyed out across the worlds some long time ago. No one's heard from her since.

According to that interpretation, with great-grandpa dead, the next in line would be Grandpa Larsek.

With him as crown prince — again, according to one of about eight interpretations of the law of succession — Uncle Karl would've been second in line. Since he had no sons, Dad was third in line, but Dad recused himself.

Which made me third in line. No. Uncle Karl was dead. So that made me *second* in line. And the second in line to the throne — even if the position was subject to a great, great deal of debate — couldn't live in ignorance of who and what he was.

I was still absorbing this when Tiksdottir said, "You have two more letters, sire."

I was now officially exhausted. Too many revelations in too short a time span. I didn't know how to deal with them. All of them. Maybe any of them.

I couldn't parse it. Couldn't make it all make sense in my head. As soon as I thought I might be grasping that, according to one way of viewing things, *I might be second in line to inherit a vast kingdom spanning many, many worlds, and the responsibility to oversee a dozen other such kingdoms...*

No. I couldn't even pretend I had a grip on that.

But during those moments when I thought I could almost jiggle the puzzle together and make it all make sense, some obstinate part of me insisted that it just wasn't fair that Lynn wasn't a princess.

It wasn't right that I should get all this cool stuff, and she should get left out of it. Just because I happened to be born male while she was born female.

"I'm going to do something for her anyway," I said. "Give her something."

I was still sitting on the bearskin rug, before the fire. Tiksdottir had found and broken out a bottle of wine for us, though I hadn't touched my cup yet.

"I beg your pardon, sire?" she asked, from her place in the wooden armchair.

"Lynn. If I can't make her a proper princess of Vol-Halá, I'm going to find a way to do *something* for her, at least."

"Very noble of you, sire." She gestured to the letters on the rug near my knees. "But you still have two more of those. And you need to open them before we leave in the morning."

I refolded the family tree and put it back into its envelope. I picked up the second envelope. Broke the seal. Took out the letter inside.

Once more, it unfolded and unfolded and unfolded.

But this time, it didn't unfold into a broader sheet of parchment.

This time, it unfolded into a trunk.

The trunk was about two feet wide by three feet long, by two feet tall. It fit easily into the space between the chairs and the sofa.

The trunk was made of purple hardwood, same as the table I'd eaten breakfast at all my life. Even had the same scrollwork along the edges

It had no locks, but two latches.

"Ah," Tiksdottir said. "Of course. Good."

All right. So this was good. Glad to hear it.

I think I was getting too tired to appreciate any more surprises that day. But even in my exhausted state, I had to admit that a piece of paper that unfolded into a trunk was pretty darned cool.

I undid the latches and opened the trunk.

The inside was a lot bigger than it looked.

A lot bigger. Three, four times the size. Easily.

In the top of the trunk was affixed an array of weapons. Swords and short swords. Spears and daggers. Maces. Warhammers. Axes. Even a hooked net and a couple of whips.

In the bottom of the trunk, smaller boxes, that I quickly determined contained clothes, money (paper and coinage), food, books, and more. And the trunk was only maybe a quarter full. If that.

I was so stunned by everything that had happened that day that I started rambling.

"It's lovely, really," I said. "I particularly love the bigger-on-the-inside part. I've always loved that idea. And I could certainly use the clothes and a good sword. And maybe some money. But, I mean, we're not carrying this thing with us."

Tiksdottir was smiling at me now.

"Close it, sire. Affix the latches."

I did.

The box faded into nothingness.

"Whoa," I said. I waved my hand where it had been, but it was gone. Not invisible. Just ... not there.

I shook my head. Steadied my breathing. Then smacked myself in the forehead.

"Wish I'd grabbed some shoes before I'd done that."

"Call it, sire," she said. "Call your locker."

I frowned at her, but figured I should listen. I opened my mouth.

"Not with words, sire," she said. "With your mind."

All right.

I felt like an idiot — a tired idiot — but I did as she asked me.

The locker appeared in front of me again.

"It is part of you now, sire," she said, and I could hear pleasure in her voice. "No matter where you are. No matter what your circumstances. Your locker is always available to you."

"All right," I said, smiling, despite myself. This was magic. And I already had command of it *"That's* cool."

I called the locker and sent it away again a couple of times, just to make sure I had it down. It was pretty easy to do, really.

Its letter, of course, was gone. But that was all right.

Spent and tired as I was, I'd gotten a burst of giddy energy from the coolness of the locker. I sat on the bearskin rug again, eager to open that last envelope and see what else was waiting for me.

I broke the wax seal and opened it.

The last envelope only held a letter. I admit, I felt a little disappointed. At first. Then I sensed a kind of lingering magic about it. Something that waited to be triggered.

I quickly opened the letter and started reading.

Dear Prince Volner, I read, *I regret that I must be the one to officially inform you of the death of your uncle, Prince Karl...*"

The letter went on to cover a lot of what I'd already discussed with Tiksdottir. About the royal family, and my place in it. The letter presented that there were three primary interpretations of the laws of succession.

In the first listed, I was second in line for the throne. That was, assuming anything ever happened to High King Ulfgar, which I already considered highly unlikely.

According to the logic of the second, I was seventh in line for the throne. The logic of that one seemed to hold together a little more for me than the first, but then, I wasn't sure at all that I wanted to be high king.

According to the third, I was about thirty-eighth in line for the throne. And to be honest, that was just fine with me.

I got to the end of it, and saw that the letter had been signed by my grandfather, Prince Larsek.

It wasn't until I finished the letter that I realized something else. Every sentence had been written in a different language. And yet, I understood them all.

I held the letter up so Tiksdottir could see it, a look of puzzlement all over my face.

"You are a prince, sire, with magic in your blood that will carry you to thousands of worlds. And have your clothes, your weapons, your food, perhaps even your body tailor to suit your destination." She shrugged. "Did you think languages would be a problem for you?"

***

AFTER TIKSDOTTIR TRIED FOR THE THIRD TIME TO EXPLAIN TO ME HOW and why I could now recognize, understand, and communicate in pretty much any language I ran across, it became clear that I was just too tired to absorb any more new information.

I was ready to just curl up on the wooden sofa and call it a night, except for two things.

First, there was a perfectly good bed up in the loft, waiting for me. Also, Tiksdottir made clear that she wouldn't hear of me giving her the bed and my taking the couch. Rank and all that.

Felt impolite to me, but I was too tired to argue.

Second, she insisted that, before I went to bed, I dig out clothes and weapons for tomorrow. She wouldn't let me just take them out of my locker, either.

"The trunks along the wall are kept here for just this purpose," she said. "You'll find good traveling clothes that fit you, and a wide selection of weapons."

I think I stared at folded piles of clothing for ten minutes before I managed to dig out good, strong pants with several pockets, and a collarless long-sleeved shirt with a couple of more pockets.

I wasn't sure what material they were. They were stronger than jeans, but softer than an old cotton tee shirt that's been washed within an inch of its life. The pants were a dark brown, and the shirt a muted gold. They even had underwear and socks that fit me.

I found boots that matched the pants and reminded me of the ones Tiksdottir was wearing. Though they were less worn than hers.

"Grab a cloak, too, sire. Best to be safe."

The cloaks seemed to come in two varieties — showy and subtle. I went for one of the subtle, dark gray cloaks.

There were pouches full of gold and silver coins, so I took one of those as well, planning on tying it to my sword belt.

The sword belt and sword were next. They had a number of options, but I went with a longsword that was lighter than I expected, but still comfortable.

In my western martial arts class, I usually paired my sword with a shield. But I didn't want to carry one around, so I settled for a main gauche — a long dagger used for parrying — for my offhand. I wasn't as good with the main gauche as I was with a shield, but it felt more practical. I took a pair of smaller daggers for my boots then, and felt as loaded out as I was willing to get.

Tiksdottir raised an eyebrow as she looked over the assortment.

"You've used a sword like that before, sire?"

"In training and in tournaments, but never for real."

"Good that you know the difference," she said. "With luck that will still be true when we reach the royal castle."

I started to set my new clothes and armor on one of the chairs for the night, but Tiksdottir shook her head.

"They should be in the loft with you, sire, ready—"

Before she even finished the sentence I pulled out my locker and put the new finds into some empty space and put my locker away again. I raised one hand to forestall any objections as I turned back to her.

"I promise," I said. "I'll take them out as soon as I'm in the loft."

Tiksdottir smiled. "Of course. Good night, sire."

"Good night, Ulna Tiksdottir," I said, then climbed the rope ladder to the loft.

The loft had more space than I expected, height-wise. I'd been figuring I'd be bent the entire time I was up here. Instead, even though the roof sloped, enough of it was under the higher part of the peak that I could stand straight, unless I went out of my way.

There were two wooden nightstands, both of the same orange wood, and both with two drawers I was vaguely curious about, as well as another trunk along the wall.

Each nightstand had a smooth, white stone the size of my fist sitting on the inside edge. I could feel magic from both, and I suspected that they could light up the dimness. If I wanted them to.

But right then, I didn't care about light, or what was in those nightstand drawers, or even what was in the trunk.

No. Right then the most important thing was between the nightstands.

The king-size featherbed with four, big pillows and a soft, sea-foam green comforter.

It was all I could do to bring myself to call back my locker and dig out my fresh clothes and weapons. But I did, and laid those things out on the floor beside the bed. Then I stripped off my current clothes, tossed them into the locker, and put it away.

Finally, with every muscle in my body singing pleasure at the notion and the action, I dove under those covers and fell straight asleep.

The last thing I remember was the sweet smell of violets, and then I was out.

4

I was dreaming something about a field of wild violets when suddenly, in the dream, there was a two-ton woodpecker beating the holy hell out of a giant redwood tree that hadn't been there a moment before.

My eyes unwillingly dragged themselves open.

Okay. The smell of violets, that was from the sheets.

I was in that soft, soft featherbed in the loft of that cabin by the sea. Maybe my first princely decision should be that I needed more sleep...

"Sire!" Tiksdottir cried out. "To arms!"

The pounding. That was someone hitting the cabin door with something a lot bigger and heavier than a fist.

I shook myself awake. Realized that Tiksdottir had already thrown the rope ladder up onto the loft floor.

"Up!" I yelled, hoping that would be enough and rushing to the edge of the loft to see what was going on. I noticed that no light was coming in through the windows, so it was still somewhere before dawn.

Tiksdottir stood, weapons ready, facing the door.

I yanked on underwear and pants.

The people at the door didn't wait for me.

The door broke open with a crash.

The first one through was so big he could have played offensive line for the Forty-Niners.

I don't mean an offensive line position, like a guard or something. I mean the *whole* offensive line.

He looked human enough, though his skin was so red he looked like he'd slept all day on the beach in August. He wore oiled leathers of dark gray, with a symbol at each of his shoulders.

His size didn't help him. He came through with a crashing blow from a maul big enough to shatter engine blocks.

Tiksdottir was there and ready, slashing right though the corded muscles of his thick neck.

The spray of his hot blood reached even into the loft.

He fell to one side, shoved by someone behind him.

Then, sword and long knife weaving together, Tiksdottir fought to keep at least two foes from entering. I saw their gray leathers and the curve of their scimitars as they pressed Tiksdottir back away from the door.

She met their attacks with her own blade. Not really attacking yet, so much, as trying to keep them back. While steel rang out on steel like a drummer going manic on his splash cymbal.

These two were big, but not as big as the first one. They were built more like running backs, beneath their armor.

They fought with an odd synchronicity. Two big men, each with long scimitars. They looked as though they should have been in each other's ways, fighting nearly shoulder to shoulder as they pressed Tiksdottir back from the doorway and into the cabin.

But something about the way they wove their attacks worked in harmony. Never in each other's way.

And she was in trouble.

Fear sang in my muscles. But if I did nothing she would die.

I grabbed my sword and main gauche and leaped down, feet together and aiming for the far assassin. He had a red patch on his cloak, so I designated him Red and the other one Gray.

As I came down, I felt a cry well up within me and gave it voice.

I howled like a wolf, with bloodcurdling intensity.

The two assassins looked up just in time to see me slam my feet into Red's face. He had a hard jaw, but my feet were still calloused from that — spell, poultice, whatever — Tiksdottir used on them yesterday.

He went down hard, spitting blood and teeth.

His partner cut for my head.

Tiksdottir knocked that blade wide with her sword, and cut for Gray's neck with her long knife. He managed to duck out of the way, taking the cut off his armor and spinning to one side.

I landed on my butt, but the landing wasn't bad. Most of my momentum had gone into an assassin's face.

My target, Red, rolled with the blow, but crashed into the wooden sofa.

I hopped to my feet while he tried to untangle his from the bearskin rug.

Heart pounding and mouth dry, I thrust for his belly.

Red tried to parry with his wrist alone. Knocked my blade just off-line enough that I slashed his side instead of spitting him like a pig.

My blade was sharp though. It cut a dripping red line through his armor.

He snarled at me. I snarled right back.

"Down!" Tiksdottir yelled.

I dropped to a crouch, head tucked.

Gray toppled over me to land hard on the orange wood of the floor. Red had his feet again. One hand pressed to his side, he came at me. Scimitar high and weaving.

Tiksdottir. Where was Tiksdottir?

Normally, a foe like this one — with a single weaving sword — I'd shield-bash him to buy a moment then take him down with my blade.

Couldn't do that, though, and the main gauche would offer no protection if I tried to use it as a shield.

So I moved backwards, cautiously, while Red advanced. And

when the weave of his sword brought it moving past my right shoulder, I spun with it.

I hit the blade hard with my main gauche, held vertical.

I continued the spin into a slash with my sword across his gut. Opposite from where I'd cut him once.

His recovery was almost fast enough to parry. But my cut had slowed him.

I came in under his scimitar. Slashed across his side, with all my muscle and momentum behind the blow.

He cried out as he punched me with his pommel.

Stars flashed as pain exploded from my jaw outwards.

I staggered backwards, trying to blink the world into sense again. My blades automatically came back in line to defend.

A howl rose up in me again and I gave it voice.

Pain abated. The world steadied. I found my feet.

I saw the opening as Red made a wild cut for my throat.

I ducked his blade and lunged.

Resistance met the tip of my blade. First from his leathers, then from his flesh. Muscle and sharp steel won out.

I gutted him. Spilled his life and his innards right there on the floor, followed by my last night's dinner, as I threw up all over his dying body.

Shaky and sweaty, with a dull, steady ache from my jaw, I looked up to see that Tiksdottir had finished off Gray. She was looking at me with an odd mixture of sympathy and impatience in her eyes.

"Sire," she said. "They'll have sent word that they found you. We must leave at once."

"AT ONCE" TURNED OUT TO NEED A FEW MINUTES, WHILE WE FISHED down the cabin's rope ladder and I finished getting dressed.

Funny, how having something mundane to do under urgent circumstances — getting dressed in a rush so we could leave before more assassins arrived — helped me shove to the back of my mind the fact that I'd just killed someone.

Yeah, the guy had been actively trying to kill me. Still. That moment. The lunge. The sensation of my blade penetrating first his armor and then his body. The smell of blood and guts as I cut my way out. The sight of the light going out of his eyes just before he fell to the cabin floor.

These were things that would come back to me many times over the years.

In the moment, though, I could focus on simple enough yet important enough things that I could shove my emotions about it all to the back burner.

Which meant I was sweaty and shaking, with my heart still pounding like that maul had been going at the door and my jaw throbbing with every beat.

But I could act.

I finished as quickly as I could, and hustled back down the rope ladder to find that Tiksdottir was ready and waiting. With a pack on her back, likely full of food.

She tossed me a hard roll and a surprisingly fresh apple. "This will have to break your fast, sire," she said. "We must away."

Something about the way she stood, though, looked less certain than I liked. Also, she seemed pale, and fresh perspiration dripped down her neck.

"Are you all right, Tiksdottir?" I asked.

"I'm nervous, sire. Two Journeys yesterday, and I'm not nearly rested enough for another."

"Then tell me how it's done," I said. "I'll lead us."

"Would that it were that simple, sire," she said.

"Maybe it's like that howling thing," I said. "Whatever that was."

"Later, sire," she said, waving one hand in what was probably supposed to be a respectful, but calming gesture. "I promise to address that later. But for now, I shall have to lead us. But be ready when we arrive. If the Nulac are waiting for us, I may not be much good to you."

"How did they find us here?" I asked. "You seemed certain that—"

"I was, sire," she said, shaking her head again. "And I'm afraid I don't know. Nor can we take the time to figure it out here and now."

"Right," I said.

"They'll expect us to Journey straight from here," she said. "It would be safest and easiest."

"So we won't?"

She shook her head with a feral smile and extinguished the last candle in the cabin.

"Put up your hood, sire. Wouldn't want you to get wetter than you have to."

I realized then that she'd taken a gray cloak as well. And the two of us, hooded, went out the front door together.

The winds whipped us immediately, cold and smelly with sea spray. Rain threatened from dark clouds overhead. The night still so dark it might as well be pitch.

I was immediately impressed by the weatherproofing of that cabin. I had no idea conditions were this harsh out here.

I could make out Tiksdottir beside me, and the dark, umber rock of the cliff we stood on. But only barely.

"Um, Tiksdottir," I said, raising my voice over the violent crashing of the waves below, but she shushed me.

She shut the door, and though the latch was broken, she got it to stay closed with a short incantation that, if I heard right, I recognized now as Thelassian.

The door stayed closed, though.

"It will open now only for one of the royal blood," she said, staggering a little and shaking her head against the storm. "No matter how they batter it."

I thought about asking why we didn't do that last night. I decided against asking, though, in case the answer was that they'd burn it down with us inside.

"What will we do for light?" I asked instead.

"Nothing," she said, then touched one gloved finger to her lips to discourage me from asking more questions. She took my hand — her left hand, leaving her sword hand free — and led on.

We were heading for the cliff's edge.

I'll tell you. Says something about how much I'd come to trust Tiksdottir in the last day that I let her lead me toward the edge of a freaking cliff on wet rocks in the darkness. Especially since I had been given no reason to believe that she could see any better than I could.

I could say that it was the way she'd just literally fought to preserve my life. I could say that it was the fact that Dad trusted her enough to send me off with her, even when I had no idea what was going on.

I don't think it was either of those things, though, really. I think what it came down to was the way she'd said those words the night before.

I would die before harming you, Prince Volner.

The simple honesty of it. The chant-like quality of the words as she spoke them.

I firmly believed that I could trust this woman with my life. And that, more than anything else, was why I let her lead me along those slippery rocks, right up to the edge of the cliff itself.

Down below me I could hear the steady crashing of the waves. But, it occurred to me then, that maybe that was a ruse. Some kind of magic, hiding an escape route so well that none would suspect it of being anything other than a rough seaside cliff.

"What now?" I asked. "Jump?"

"No!" she said, and grabbed me with both hands to make sure I didn't just do it. But she seemed to understand my confusion. "It's every bit as fatal as it looks, sire. So trust me, move slowly, and follow my lead."

It turned out that she'd led us to narrow stairs cut into the cliffside.

Narrow, *wet* stairs. Saying this didn't seem safe was kind of like saying that jumping out of an airplane without a parachute didn't seem safe.

Nevertheless, Tiksdottir, took my right hand and put it to the cliff-side. She took my left hand in her left hand, and began to lead the way down those stairs.

I had no choice but to follow her.

My head was almost below the cliff's edge when I was blinded by a flash of yellow light, back near the cabin. It lit up the whole top of the cliff, including scraggly vegetation I hadn't realized surrounded the cabin.

Before the flash faded, blinding me completely, I'd spotted at least a dozen armed people.

I ducked my head and squeezed Tiksdottir's hand in pulses to get her attention.

A moment later I felt her warmth beside me. I was still blinking away spots when she said, her words hot breath in my ear, "We'll have to hurry. Be careful."

Be careful. What a lovely idea.

Of course, my idea of being careful didn't involve blindly descending wet, narrow stairs above a sea, crashing on rocks.

But going back up top seemed like an even worse choice.

One hand on the rocks and one gripping the other's hand, Tiksdottir and I went down those stairs.

Slowly.

***

FIGHTING FOR MY LIFE WHEN I WAS STILL WAKING UP, THAT WAS something I'd thought was stressful. Maybe a little scary even.

Yeah. That fight had nothing on descending those wet stairs under cover of darkness.

First of all, it wasn't just the stairs that were wet. I was wet from sea spray. Wet from sweat. And wet from sprinkles that seemed to become an essential part of the threatening skies above.

And that smelly sea air, it didn't just ruffle my hair. Oh, no. It whipped, slashing me with icy cold and trying to find enough purchase to yank me down off those narrow stairs to the waiting, crushing arms of the crashing waves below me.

Not to mention numbing my face and hands, which made this next thing even trickier.

The rocks of the cliffside, they weren't just wet with sea spray and rain. Oh, no. There were patches of moss or lichen that were so slick that my numb fingers slid hard right off them.

How hard? Hard enough that I started slipping off the stairs.

Four. Freaking. Times. That happened.

Each time, my heart surged like it was trying to flap wings with every beat.

Each time, my mouth defied the prevailing conditions by drying out like high noon in the Mojave.

Nerves jumped all over my body, while my muscles gave up trying to make any sense of this madness and settled for locking up on me.

If Tiksdottir didn't have such a strong grip, I probably would've crushed her hand quite by accident.

But she did have a strong grip. And either she could see better than the next-to-nothing shapes I could make out, or she'd made this descent before. Because she seemed to stay calm, cool and collected.

And every one of those four times I started to slip, she found a rock to clutch with one hand while she steadied me with the other.

She didn't ask if I was all right, of course. That would've been a stupid question. I wasn't. Obviously. She just steadied me until we could resume our descent.

Even so, it was slow going. The stairs were narrow, but their angle wasn't very steep. We were probably covering ... say ... a hundred feet horizontally for every maybe forty feet we descended.

And we had hundreds of feet to go, from the top of that cliff.

Not that I had any way of telling how far we'd gone, or how far we still had to go.

One benefit of the icy wind and sea spray. My jaw numbed to the point that it stopped complaining about having been hit hard by the pommel of a scimitar.

My stomach roared complaints as fully as it could, but its efforts were nothing to the thundering crash of the waves on those rocks below.

Nevertheless, while I couldn't hear my stomach's rumbling, I felt it. And I thought longingly of the bread and apple tucked into pockets in the lining of my now-soaked cloak.

Funny. All the power this family's magic had, and no one could've left me a waterproof cloak?

I'd like to think I laughed at that. If so, I couldn't hear it.

That descent felt endless. A constant, slow-motion replay of the same pattern.

I'm facing the cliff's edge. My right hand on the cliff wall, my left hand holding Tiksdottir's left hand.

This meant that she was facing the ocean, not the cliff. I didn't know why, but couldn't take the time — or risk the volume — to ask.

She might've been keeping her sword hand free. But if so, she considered it a possibility that we'd have to fight our way down.

Far as I was concerned, that sounded like a death sentence for all involved.

Anyway, my left boot was on a lower step, and my right boot on the step above it.

My left boot would slide down from the edge of one stair onto the stair below it. My right boot would follow. I would stabilize in my new position, then on to the next.

Over and over.

Hundreds of stairs. Thousands of them maybe.

No way of knowing. And I wasn't sure I'd want to ask, even if I could. I thought I might be better off *not* knowing.

I mean, for all I knew, it was now sometime after dawn. We just couldn't tell because of the rolling storm clouds overhead. But what good would that information do me?

My world was moving down one step with one foot, then another step with the next. Making sure I was safely in place, with my hands where they were supposed to be, before I repeated the movement.

I tried not to think about those assassins up on the cliff above. There had to have been at least a dozen more. Too many to fight.

If they found this staircase, well, I didn't like their chances of catching us. No way they could descend fast enough, safely enough to do that.

But these stairs were pretty straight. No switchbacks. No curves. I mean, they followed the cliff face, but I wasn't sure that would be enough to save us if, say, someone rolled a big rock down at us.

That was the kind of thought that made me turn my head once in a while. Check backward, just to see if I could see anything. I mean, last time, there'd been that flare of yellow light…

Nothing, though. Not that I looked often. It didn't seem like a good idea to split my focus. But when I did look, things were just as dark up above, as they were down below.

At once point, I did hear what I thought was thunder crashing. Until I realized I hadn't seen a flash of lightning.

An explosion, then. Back up at the top of the cliff.

Had to hope they couldn't blow up the cabin. Not because I cared so much for the cabin, itself, as because I devoutly hoped they'd have to waste more time on the cabin and less chasing us.

Finally, after I don't know how long, Tiksdottir squeezed my hand three times. Which was a signal though, in our hurry, she must've forgotten to tell me what it was a signal *for*.

I assumed it was a signal to stop.

Turned out I was right.

Now, I'll tell you. That may seem like a little thing. But in the middle of all that cold, wet, threat of death, correctly recognizing that signal swelled in my chest like an accomplishment of world-shaking importance.

Or maybe that was just hope that we were done with these thrice damned cliffside stairs.

She pulled with just a hint of gentle pressure. Two steps later, we were on a flat space.

She touched one gloved finger to my lips, then gently placed both my hands on the cliff wall.

I was puzzled, but shrugged and stood there, hands against the wall, half-expecting to get searched.

Instead, long seconds passed, and then she took my hand again.

We were walking into the cliff now, and almost instantly the wind was only at my back and no more spray hit my face.

A dozen steps in, she pressed a leather pouch into my free hand.

"Open it," she said, "but keep it close to your body."

It was weird to hear her voice now. To hear anything, really, except the whistling of the wind and the crashing of the waves. But in here, both of those were subdued enough that Tiksdottir barely had to shout for me to hear her.

I needed both numb hands, and fumbled with the drawstring, but I opened the pouch, right up close to my chest.

A warm, yellow glow emitted at once.

I realized it was like those rocks on the nightstands, back in the cabin. Round and smooth, but much smaller. Only maybe the size of the last joint of my thumb.

But the light it shed was enough for a dozen candles, at least.

I kept the stone in the pouch, and turned the opening forward like a flashlight.

Tiksdottir, now visible in gray tones, just outside the light's beam, smiled at me.

"Clever," she said. "And it should keep the assassins from spotting our light from up above."

I could see that we were in a cave of many colors. The sea had worn the umber rock to a variety of pinks and greens. Or maybe it was more lichen, or just the stratification of the rocks over some geological span of time.

Pretty, though, and I reveled for the moment in colors that weren't shades of gray where they weren't pitch blackness.

The cave itself wasn't very big. No more than a dozen feet tall at its peak, and maybe twenty feet wide at its widest.

"Wait," I said. "The cave mouth. Couldn't you use that for our Journey, like you did in the side of the purple hills?"

"I could, sire," she said, sounding exhausted, "but they would be more likely to see the energies from up above. There's a better place deeper into the cliff."

I was so tired and stiff from descending that cliffside that I felt as though I hadn't had any sleep at all. I ached all over.

But I started thinking about was how much worse off Tiksdottir must've been. I wasn't sure she'd slept even as little as I had. And I knew she couldn't have slept as well. I'd had that feather bed, and she'd had to make do with that wooden couch.

Plus, she'd had to handle two Journeys yesterday. And I didn't yet know exactly what kind of toll that exacted, but I got the impression it was rough.

And here she was talking about handling another. On short sleep. After fighting. And likely little, if any, breakfast herself.

These were the things I thought about as we made our way through that cave of many colors, with my glowstone lighting the way like an irregular flashlight beam from its place in that pouch in my left hand.

And it was truly a cave of many colors. The pinks and greens had been joined by browns more vibrant than I'd expected, along with purples and blues.

The cave itself wasn't all that regular. It narrowed in places, before widening again. And it curved, following patterns that didn't make much sense to me, rising sometimes and descending others.

And through it, Tiksdottir and I trudged along.

The smell of the lichen in here grew stronger than the sea smell, even. A kind of decay of vegetation smell.

There were humps in the cave, as well. As though bits of stalagmite had started to form, but couldn't be arsed to come to a point.

Then the cave split into two passages. Before I could even ask, Tiksdottir turned down the left passage and continued on.

I followed without a word. This didn't seem like a time for conversation. The way was narrower now, and sometimes we had to go one before the other. But the floor was smooth enough.

Finally, though, we came to our destination.

An iron door, set into the end of this passage.

"All right," Tiksdottir said, and stretched her arms and twisted her body to loosen some of the kinks she had to have been feeling herself.

"Now," she said, "I'll open the way. But when I do—"

"Stop," I said.

She frowned, jaw set, and I could hear her wanting to argue with me. But all she said was, "Yes, sire?"

"We're not going anywhere right now."

"Sire, there are assassins on our tail."

"You said they'd likely try to follow from the cabin, yes?"

She nodded, a sudden, jerky movement, but her lips clamped shut. Likely to avoid saying something insulting.

"And we left no sign that we went this way, yes?"

Same nod, this time with extra suspicion in her eyes.

"We are now thousands of feet away from that cabin," I said, "and deep inside the cliff beneath it. Many turns from the edge. Hell, many turns from the split back there."

"I've done the best I can to get us to safety, sire—"

"My point entirely," I said. "We are, right now, as safe as we're likely to get anytime soon." I held up a hand to hold off her rejoinder. "They're going to assume we left by Journeying, right? Which means this world is the last place they'll look for us?"

"They'll leave a contingent up top, in case we double back, but otherwise, yes, sire."

"Then we're going to stop and eat," I said firmly, "and then you are going to get some shuteye."

"Shuteye?"

"Sleep. You've had less than I've had."

"Sire, if you need sleep—"

"No," I said. "Well, I do, but I'm fine for now. You, on the other hand, need sleep and food before you even consider another Journey."

"But—"

"Check me on this," I said. "Journeying takes a lot out of you, yes? More than it would me, if I knew how to do it?"

"A good deal more, sire," she said, "than it will when you are ready."

"Which means you're going to be in pretty bad shape, when we arrive wherever you next take us, correct?"

"Yes, sire," she said, then sighed. "And let me apologize for—"

"No apology," I said sharply, cutting off what she was saying and making her blink at me in confusion, for a change.

"Look at it this way," I said. "Your job is to get me to the royal palace intact, right?"

She scowled, but nodded.

"And in your current shape, you can't take me there in a single Journey, can you?"

Tiksdottir hung her head forward, as though this were a failure, but muttered, "No, sire."

"Then you need food. And rest. And as your prince, it is my responsibility to see that you get them." She might have objected, but I didn't let her. "So we're going to eat. And then you're going to sleep. And that's an order. Understood?"

"Understood, sire," she said.

But she was smiling when she said it.

***

Lunch was strips of dried beef, seasoned to a tangy flavor that went well with my crisp, sweet apple. The roll I'd been carrying in my cloak wasn't so hard as I'd feared, and it had a rich, walnut-laced flavor. We drank fresh, clean water from a canteen made of some kind of light metal that didn't feel or flavor the water the way aluminum could.

Considering that Tiksdottir and I were hiding from people who wanted to kill us, it was a fairly restful lunch.

I also realized two things as we ate.

First, I wasn't as bad off as I'd thought. My jaw had stopped hurting. Entirely. Poking at it with my fingers didn't even suggest that I'd have a bruise. My butt didn't hurt at all from my rough landing after jumping into that assassin's face.

In fact, after just five minutes of sitting, I realized that none of my muscles were as stiff and sore as I'd expected them to be.

The other realization was that I was much, much drier than I expected to be, too. I was pretty sure I'd been soaked to the bone by the time we reached the bottom of those cliffside stairs. But as Tiksdottir and I sat in that many-colored cave, right in front of the broad, iron door, I felt positively warm and dry.

Tiksdottir caught me fingering my cloak for wetness and laughed with pleasure.

"The material is *tlikswul*, sire," she said. "Same as that of your clothes. It dries rapidly on its own, and the process is warming."

"That's why you wanted me to take clothes from the trunks, and not my locker."

"I couldn't be sure what the material would be, for clothing in your locker, sire."

I poked my boots. They were wet. But my feet felt dry, and even warmer than the rest of me.

"The boots will dry faster, because of the socks," she said with a nod.

"I don't feel as tired or sore as I expected either," I said. "Is that the *tlikswul* too?"

"No, sire," she said with a quirked smile. "You have met the Wolf, and your magic is coming alive inside you. Expresses itself, at times, with a howl." She nodded. "It will continue to grow within you, over time."

I nodded slowly, not sure I understood exactly what that entailed, but needing to ask a different question.

"Can you see in the dark?" When she laughed, I continued, "I mean, I couldn't see *anything* out there."

"Please excuse me, sire," Tiksdottir said quickly, catching control of her laughter. "I don't mean offense."

"Don't apologize for laughing when I say something funny," I said, smiling. Truth was, I liked to hear her laugh, but wasn't sure I should admit that. "I would appreciate an answer, though."

"I see in the dark no better than you do, sire. I have trained in the art of blindfighting, which is an aid. But I knew the route to safety because I've been here before. I know the number of strides from the cabin to the stairs, and the number of stairs to the bottom."

"You were counting all that way? Had to be thousands of steps."

"There's a trick to it, sire," she said with a shrug. "As there is to most such things."

Around that point, we'd both eaten about as much as we wanted. So I indicated with gestures that it was time for her to sleep.

Tiksdottir moved over to a spot along the cave wall. She spread her cloak across herself like a blanket, used the pack of food for a pillow, and fell asleep with a speed and ease that impressed me.

I sat for a few minutes. Watching her sleep, and listening to the crash and roll of the waves in the distance, as well as the soft whistling of the wind.

How strange it was to me that this woman who had never met me before yesterday was so willing to lay down her life for mine.

But all of this was so strange.

Dad. He'd hidden so much from me. Had he really grown up in Massachusetts or was that a lie? Was that why he didn't tell me stories of his youth there? Because he'd grown up in a different world entirely?

How could the man who'd taught me to hit a baseball and look for a job be the same man who'd howled with power as he readied himself to face three assassins on his own.

Three.

Tiksdottir and I had struggled with three assassins, and Dad had faced down three on his own?

Mom was a "commoner," according to the family tree. But did that mean she was just what she seemed to be? I mean, a normal human being, as opposed to part of some magical bloodline or something? Maybe a secret ninja?

She'd never shown any particular interest in fighting or combat arts. Then again, Dad hadn't either. Even in the Army, he'd been a doctor. Not some kind of green beret.

Wait. "*I've* got this," he'd said. "Not *we've* got this." So Mom wasn't doing any fighting.

On the one hand, that was good. On the other, could Dad really take on three Nulac assassins by himself?

He must have.

I mean, Tiksdottir said that I'd know if Dad died, the way I'd known with Uncle Karl. Which meant Dad had beaten those assassins.

Which meant that Dad was a certified badass.

That would take a little getting used to.

And I had a lot to absorb. Uncle Karl was dead, but my grandparents on Dad's side were alive. I wasn't sure how to react to either of those bits of information.

Then there was the whole, I'm-a-prince-with-magic thing. I wasn't ready to start thinking about that, though. Not with another, more urgent topic rearing its head now that I'd found a moment's quiet.

I'd killed a man.

I thought back over it. The fight. That thrust. The sensations. The way the light went out in his eyes.

I'd always thought that was just an expression. But I could really see the instant he died. It was when his eyes dulled as he fell.

In the moment, I'd thrown up. And I'd assumed that was just a natural, human reaction to having taken a life for the first time.

But as I sat there in that cave while Tiksdottir slept, I didn't feel guilt or remorse over taking that man's life. It had been necessary. Simple survival. Him or me.

I even realized that the regurgitation had been from stress. A tension release, of a kind. Not horror at what I'd done.

I'd never been so practical before in my life. Hell, outside of class and tournaments, I hadn't been in a real *fight* since tenth grade, when Jimmy Rodriguez misunderstood something I'd said.

Sitting there in the cave, I wasn't sure what exactly I *had* said that day, but it sure hadn't been anything bad about Jimmy Rodriguez's mother.

He'd thought it was, though, and jumped me right there in the hallway between classes.

It was a stupid thing to do. He was a year older, but six inches shorter and maybe thirty or forty pounds lighter.

He got in a good shot, but hit my ribs instead of the lower, soft tissue.

I caught him under the jaw, with a proper pivot. A punch that started from my legs and my core.

That was that.

Jimmy was down on the tiles and needed dental work. And with a dozen witnesses saying he started it, Mom and Dad didn't even have to pay for that dental work.

I'd felt terrible, though. It was a misunderstanding. And he was so much smaller. I felt as though I should've found a gentler way of stopping things than throwing the most devastating punch I could throw at a pretty good target.

I wanted to feel that guilt again, sitting there in the cave. Guilt over having killed a man.

But I didn't.

I wanted it to scare me that I felt so ... practical about taking that assassin's life.

But it didn't scare me, either.

If this had been a needless killing, perhaps I would have felt differently. I'd like to think I would have.

But I had awakened the Wolf within me. And the Wolf told me that I had killed to survive. Nothing more.

The Wolf also told me I would have to do so again.

5

―――――

As Tiksdottir slept in the cave of many colors, I stretched my muscles. Walked a little. But mostly I kept nearby and made sure she slept all right.

I'd left the glowstone on the rocky cave floor, its edges rolled back so that it's light spread out to about thirty of forty feet, but wasn't visible from around the closest bend.

I knew, because I'd gone to check with sword in hand. Hadn't seen or heard anything but crashing waves and whistling wind from back toward the entrance. And that direction was just as dark as it ever got. I started to wonder if the sun ever rose in this world, or if it hid behind a perpetual layer of clouds.

We seemed to be safe enough, though, so I'd put my sword away and contented myself with moving about, stretching my muscles, trying to see if I could feel the magic that was supposedly within me (I couldn't).

I checked on Tiksdottir every so often, but she seemed to be sleeping soundly. I hoped that the sea air would be salutary for her likely tired and sore muscles.

Thoughts of the sea air made me start inspecting the broad iron door. I was doing that when I heard Tiksdottir stir.

"Problem, sire?" she asked, and from the rustling sounds she made, I was sure she was getting up.

"No," I said. "Well, perhaps. This looks and feels like iron to me. But it can't be. There's way too much salt in the air down here. Iron would rust."

"It isn't iron, sire," she said. "Or rather, it is. But not iron as you think of it." She stood and stretched as she spoke. "It is a pretense of iron, developed in a laboratory several worlds away."

"Why?" I asked.

Tiksdottir gave a hopeless smile and shrugged.

"Because King Ulfgar ordered it, and there might be some who know his reasons, but I alas, am not among their number, sire."

"Fair enough."

"Thank you, sire, for the rest," she said, shaking out her hands and feet. "It helped in more ways than one?"

"What do you mean?"

"I'd been planning on a long Journey, getting you as close to the Vol-halá as I could manage in a single move. I might even have managed the courtyard of the royal castle." She shook her head. "That's not the right move, though. I see it now."

"Explain."

"Of course, sire," she said with a small bow that was so automatic I wondered a little if she knew she'd done it.

"The Journey I had in mind, especially in the state I'd been in, would likely have killed me. But with assassins on our tail, my only thought had been to complete my assigned task of bringing you to the royal castle."

I started to object to her just pissing away her life like that — even though I knew that wasn't how she'd see it — but she asked for patience with a raised, gloved hand.

"My task had been a simple one. But Nulac has sent assassins. This changes the situation." Her eyes grew determined. "I will bring you to the royal court. Oh, yes, sire. But first I must see to your safety. And not just immediate safety by way of a safe house."

"So where are we going?"

"Someplace I couldn't have reached from the purple hills," she said, donning the food pack and straightening her cloak. "But someplace I *can* reach safely, now, from here. From this door. And thanks to the rest, I shouldn't even pay too high a price for doing so."

"What kind of price?" I asked.

"Nothing even crippling, much less fatal," she said, dismissively. "And now, sire, allow me to escort you home in style."

Before I could say anything else, she turned to the iron door.

Once more I felt her call up her own power from within herself, and gather it together between shaky hands. She immediately started sweating and breathing hard from the effort.

This time, I could see the power she struggled to contain and direct. It was the color of ripe plums, and it fought her. Hard. She gritted her teeth with effort.

She was going to fail.

I wasn't sure how I knew, but I knew. She hadn't rested enough. Hadn't eaten enough. Journeying simply took too much out of her, and she'd done it twice yesterday.

She wasn't ready to do it again, no matter what she claimed.

She started keening softly in pain as she struggled to hold her power together.

Damn it. She was doing this for me. There had to be some way I could help her. She kept calling me "sire." Well, damn it, feudal ties went both ways.

She was my responsibility. Mine to protect and aid.

That thought surged power within me. Power that cried out into the night in a wolf's howl that felt as though it shook the very mountain around us.

With my right hand I grabbed the back of Tiksdottir's neck, as though she were a cub I would pick up and take from danger.

Power from within me reached into her through that clasp. Steadied her. Strengthened her.

She immediately contained the power she'd called, pulled it back near her right hip, and thrust it into the frame of the iron door.

The power glowed brightly this time, with its red and amber

colors swirling together around the frame and across the rock below to complete the circle.

I released her neck and picked up the glowstone pouch.

Tiksdottir touched her hand to the iron door.

"I am Ulna Tiksdottir, sworn into the service of King Ulfgar the Liberator, and acting on his direct orders."

She pulled the door open. Within was a sheen of bright red and amber energy.

She was smiling as she reached for my hand.

"Come, sire. A world awaits."

Together we took that Journey.

I'm not sure where I was expecting Tiksdottir to take us from that iron door, deep, deep under the cliffside below that cabin.

A forest, maybe. Or a castle. Hell, maybe even a Viking longboat or something.

I sure wasn't expecting a spaceship.

We arrived in a round room where every surface gleamed. The dark grays of the floor beneath us. The cobalt blues of the walls and ceiling. And, of course, the bar-shaped lamps that edged the space between walls and ceiling.

It was an empty room, but there was a door ahead of us. A dark orange door, without any visible means of opening.

The air was temperate, maybe a little on the cool side. And it tasted almost suspiciously fresh. As though it had been imported directly from the hills of Sweden, just after a snow melt.

"Where—" I started to ask, but the door opened.

Two men entered. At least, I presumed they were men, from the shape of their armor.

They wore articulated, cobalt blue body armor. Full body stuff. The helmets didn't look attached, but panels hung down to cover their necks, and dark, polarized faceplates covered their faces.

They were carrying black rifles. Sleek things. Thin. And their lack of magazines made me assume they were energy weapons.

Both soldiers pointed those weapons at Tiksdottir and me. And worse than that — well, for certain values of worse, at least — I see movement that indicated two more soldiers in the hallway.

"Identify yourselves," the soldier on the right said, and despite the cut of her armor, her sharp, commanding voice was clearly a woman's.

"This is Prince Volner of Vol-Halá," Tiksdottir said, "and I am Ulna Tiksdottir, messenger acting on orders from King Ulfgar himself."

"We weren't told of any royal visitors coming," the lead soldier said. "I apologize, sire, but I'll need proof."

"Your wolf," Tiksdottir said softly. "Unbutton your shirt."

I wasn't sure how unbuttoning my shirt would help, but I did.

I realized then that the golden seal I'd absorbed yesterday was now visible on my chest as an amber tattoo of the royal sigil, over my heart.

How had I not noticed that before? Had I just been so busy that...

Yeah. That sounded about right.

The lead soldier removed the gauntlet from her right hand. Her skin was dark-complected, but smoother than I expected from a soldier.

From the way her head moved, I thought she looked at me for permission, though I couldn't see a thing through her lowered faceplate.

I nodded anyway.

She touched the sigil while muttering something softly.

She yanked back her hand as though the wolf in the sigil had bitten her.

She was nodding rapidly as she donned her helmet. "He's royal family, all right," she said to the other three soldiers. To me, she added, "And do you confirm the identity of Ulna Tiksdottir, sire?"

A suspicious part of my nature wondered, for a moment, but I quelled it by reminding it that she'd been carrying the package that was obviously from someone in the royal family. And that Dad had recognized her.

"I do," I said.

The lead soldier raised her faceplate then. She had strong features, emphasized by what looked to be a narrow burn scar on her right cheek, taking part of the ear as well.

She bowed to me and said, "My apologies for the greeting, Prince Volner. We were only following protocol for an unexpected arrival. Welcome to the King's Fury."

"No apology is necessary," I said. "The procedures are there for a reason."

Yeah, I know. I felt like a pompous ass, pretending I knew all about this ship's procedures and such when I had no idea where the hell I was. Or what universe I was in, for that matter.

But I kind of felt like I owed it to these people to at least *act* the part of a prince. Even though I wasn't sure yet what my new role entailed.

The lead soldier raised her head, looking into the distance. Gave me an exasperated half-grin.

"Confirmed, bridge. And thanks for the spare eye, Sulek. The royal messenger has already arrived. And she's brought a prince of the blood with her."

The response was loud enough that she winced.

I was too fixated on a turn of phrase I wasn't used to. "Thanks for the spare eye."

I realized then that we weren't speaking English, but Aarwolish. And I wondered how I could know the language's name, or that its core ... location, since I didn't know if that was a city, country or planet ... was Aarwol.

"Sire," the lead soldier said, still gritting against what had likely been sharp pain in her ears, "I've been asked to invite you to meet with Captain Foardanna on the bridge. Unless you would prefer to see your quarters first."

I glanced at Tiksdottir who gave me a tiny shake of her head.

"The bridge will be fine," I said.

The other three soldiers put up their face shields and bowed to me as the lead soldier led the way. The other three were men, and all of them looked to have seen some combat in their day.

They fell into a box formation, and led us out of the empty, cobalt landing room and down an equally shiny corridor. The walls out here weren't cobalt, which I appreciated. Combined with the guards, that would have been too much.

The walls were pale gray over a dark gray deck, with more light bars edging the ceiling. The deck, whatever it was made of, rang out like some kind of metal under our boots.

Well, to be honest, it rang our under the boots of the four soldiers. The boots Tiksdottir and I were wearing barely made a sound as we walked.

Technicians in white jumpsuits kept out of our way. Some of them bowed, as though recognizing me. Though that was impossible. Wasn't it?

Then again, I was one of two people walking through the halls of a spaceship while visibly carrying a sword and not some kind of energy weapon. Not to mention that I wasn't wearing cobalt blue armor or a jumpsuit. So maybe the safe assumption, from the technicians, was that I was someone to bow to.

The soldiers led us between the opening doors of an elevator, which whisked us up a dozen floors — or decks, I guess I should say, since I knew by then that I was on a ship — and over a handful more.

I lamented the fact that there was no ship schematic on the wall of the elevator. Not even a you-are-here silhouette. I really wanted to know what the ship looked like, from the outside, so I could picture it properly.

I blame my upbringing for that. I'd grown up watching *Star Wars* and *Star Trek* and *Babylon 5* and other such shows like so many kids of my generation. And now I was actually on a starship? Or at least a spaceship, since I didn't know if its travel was interstellar.

The cognitive dissonance of it made me dizzy to the point that I almost started giggling. I mean, I was just getting used to the idea that magic was real and that there were other worlds. Along with that whole prince-of-the-blood thing.

But there were spaceships too? And energy weapons of some kind? And cool, shiny, articulated armor?

I was starting to wonder if this was all some kind of fever dream.

But then I remembered taking that assassin's life. The feel of my blade cutting through his leathers and then his flesh. The sights and smells of him dying before me.

Yes, it had been necessary. No, I didn't feel guilty.

But I damn sure couldn't doubt that *that* had happened. Even in my weirdest, wildest dreams, I'd never had an experience like that before.

An affectless male voice said, "bridge" in four languages, as the elevator came to a halt.

Excitement mounted in my stomach. I was about to step onto the bridge of an actual freaking spaceship.

I hoped I didn't make a fool out of myself.

THE BRIDGE ITSELF WASN'T AS BIG AND ROOMY AS TELEVISION SHOWS had led me to expect. Really, it was pretty crowded, though the ceiling was about thirty feet high, which kept it from becoming claustrophobic.

The bridge was shaped like a trapezoid, with the wide side on the far wall, which was mostly taken up by either a huge, rectangular porthole or viewscreen.

Positioned just in front of the view of space, and all of them facing that direction, were a series of about a dozen workstations. Each with its own touchscreen displays above a series of mechanical controls.

Men and women — all still human, so far as I'd seen, and I admit I was looking for aliens — worked those stations, focused on the touchscreens.

They wore uniforms of a blue that might have become cobalt, if the material were shiny enough (which it wasn't). Long-sleeved shirts and pants for men and women alike, though fairly-form-fitting. They all wore caps with short bills, and those with long hair had their hair tied back in ponytails.

They wore rank insignia on the caps and on their shoulders. The insignias followed a clockface design described by eight small circles. Rank was indicated — as far as I could tell in a quick assessment — by which circles were filled, and with which colors: black, silver or gold.

Another row of workstations stood behind the first one, and I thought this row looked like officers. Or at least, they had silver circles instead of black, and one had gold circles.

The bridge was a busy place when we came in, a buzz of reports, orders and questions going back and forth among the working crew.

We entered from the back — the short side of the trapezoid — under some kind of raised platform with stairs to either side. The area around us was like a break station, with a handful of simple chairs, and pots of what smelled suspiciously like coffee and tea, along with a display of some odd kinds of fruits and breads.

"This way, sire," the lead soldier said. "Unless you need something?"

She gestured to the food and drink assortment. I shook my head. She nodded, and led Tiksdottir and me to the left-hand staircase and up, while one of the other soldiers fell in behind us, and the other two took up guard positions at the door.

From the platform I could see a catwalk that led from the platform all the way around the bridge.

Only one station up here on the platform, though. The captain's. With a dozen screens, and a padded armchair I immediately wanted to sit in.

Not because I was tired. Because it was the captain's chair on a spaceship.

I had to fight to swallow that urge. After all, this was an actual, working military vessel, not an "experience" at some kind of amusement park.

Didn't help that I still felt more like a tourist than a royal prince. I even noted the captain's rank insignia before I noted the man himself. Four circles filled with gold, from the one o'clock to the six o'clock position.

On the wall behind the captain's chair was the seal of whatever nation or service this ship flew for. Which, I supposed, could have been Vol-Halá. The symbol was a wolf, rampant, in the center of a white star, on a gold background.

Captain Foardanna himself had a Latinx look to him, along with gray at the temples of his black hair and tips of his drooping mustachios. But he looked as fit and strong as a man half his age as he stood and bowed to me.

"Welcome aboard the King's Fury, Prince Volner," he said, still holding his bow. "In the name of High King Ulfgar, I, my crew, and my vessel are yours to command."

"Thank you, Captain Foardanna," I said, mustering as much dignity as I could manage. "And please rise. I apologize for interrupting your mission. This royal messenger, Ulna Tiksdottir, will explain what we need."

"Thank you, sire," Tiksdottir said, picking up the thread as smoothly as though we'd rehearsed it. "And thank you for your welcome and your service, captain. The prince is newly awakened to his power, and has need to travel to the royal castle at Vol-Halá in speed and safety. We need you to get us to the closest Journey point."

"That will be in orbit around Aarwol itself," he said. "Just over a day from here, at top speed. We'll get underway at once."

He turned to begin giving orders.

"And, captain," Tiksdottir interrupted him, not speaking until he turned back. "There will be another important matter as well, once we are underway. Your ears only."

"Of course," he said, and began issuing orders to his crew to see about finishing up what they were doing — some kind of survey mission, from the sound of things — and then getting us where we needed to go. As soon as he finished, he turned back to us.

"The royal cabin, of course, is yours, Prince Volner. And I presume you'd like this messenger berthed nearby?"

"I would. Thank you, captain."

"My yeoman to take you there at once."

Those words were barely out of his mouth when a yeoman seemed to materialize behind Tiksdottir. Or at least he'd approached pretty darn quietly.

Well, Tiksdottir didn't seem as surprised by his appearance as I was.

The yeoman turned out to be a guy younger than I was. Human-looking, apart from a greenish tint to his skin that I had to check myself not to stare at. He had yellow eyes and dark blue hair, cut short under his cap. His rank was a full black dot, right around the one o'clock position.

He bowed to me.

"Sire, I am Yeoman Seisehn," he said. "If you would please follow me, I'll lead you to your cabin."

We were almost to the stairs down when a woman from the front rank of work stations called out, "Captain! Unidentified ship, three hundred marks sunwise. Appears to be closing."

"Captain," Tiksdottir said quickly. "We were chased here by assassins wearing the livery of the empire of Nulac O-Shantí. I can't believe this is coincidence."

"Noted," Captain Foardanna said, then called up a display of the approaching ship. It had an oblong, segmented shape, but roughed over with angles and small boxy protrusions.

His readout described it as a cruiser class ship from the Drol'zaxxan.

"Sire," the yeoman said, gesturing to the stairs, but I stayed him with a raised hand while I watched the captain.

"They could give us a fight," he muttered. Louder, he added. "Comms, contact the base at Teras Kasi and tell them we have a royal VIP arriving under threat. Tell them about the cruiser and request assistance. Combat stations, raise screens wond heat weapons. Navigation, you already have your orders. Get us out of here."

While the crewmen acknowledged their orders with cries of "At once, sir," the captain flipped a switch.

An alert horn sounded, followed by that affectless voice again, saying, "All hands, battle stations. All hands, battle stations."

The captain started doing something else, then seemed to realize we were still here.

"Prince Volner," the captain said in as respectful a tone as he could manage, given the impatience in his voice, "the bridge is always a target in a space battle, and my first responsibility is your safety. Please do me the great favor of letting my yeoman escort you to your quarters and safety, while I do my job of keeping you alive and getting you to Aarwol."

"Of course, captain," I said, chagrined. "My apologies."

I swear, he drew breath and I could tell he was about to say, "I don't need your apologies, I need your absence."

I didn't give him a chance, though. I turned to the yeoman and gestured for him to lead the way.

He did, looking grateful to leave the bridge himself.

As soon as we were in the elevator the yeoman said, "royal cabin," while the doors were still closing.

"Authorization," the affectless voice said.

"Yeoman Seisehn, official authorization code *zer ta'hala*."

I laughed, because I recognized those last words as Kindasi, and they meant "something important." Verbatim.

"Acknowledged," the voice said, and the elevator began to move.

"Let me guess," I said. "They told you to pick something important for your authorization code?"

His ears browned slightly with what I suspected was like a blush. "Yes, sire."

"Who all has authorization to reach the quarters?" I asked.

"While they're unoccupied," the yeoman said, "any member of command staff, any member of security or technical, anyone assigned to janitorial duties or any yeoman. Once you take residence, only command staff, security, or the captain's yeoman, me. And yourself, of course, sire."

I pointed to Tiksdottir. "She'll need access as well."

"Just tell the computer, once you're there, sire."

I nodded.

I wasn't sure exactly where the elevator took us. It felt as though we'd moved maybe a dozen or so floors decks — or what I thought of as aft, I didn't know what they called it here — and maybe thirty or so decks, well, down.

Yeah, I know. There's not really any up or down in space. But all I could think at the moment was "down." It'd been a rough couple of days, all right?

Sheesh.

Anyway.

The elevator doors opened, followed by a second set of doors opening just a hair later.

The twin sets were right next to each other. That seemed odd to me, but maybe it was important for me to be able to lock one set of doors, even against people who otherwise had access?

Then I saw the royal cabin and forgot all about doors.

After the relatively cramped conditions on the bridge, I'd figured this ship was like naval ships in the world where I'd grown up. Space always at a premium, efficiency, efficiency, efficiency.

Well, if so, that went out the porthole for the royal cabin.

The main room was round, and had to be at least forty feet across. Not to mention twenty feet tall. And from the look of it, it had to have sat right on top of the ship.

I mean, the lightbars were there, kicking out plenty of illumination. But space outside was visible through broad rings set into the ceiling. Along the surrounding walls, more large, rectangular portholes with broad views of space broken up only by three sets of doors, between them.

I had to shake my head for that to make sense. Obviously, then, those were viewscreens of some kind, and not portholes. It wasn't as though they'd given me doors that led out onto the hull in unprotected space.

In here, the deck was covered with a thick rug that seemed to be some kind of soft, white fur. Gods, what a nightmare it must've been to keep clean.

In the center sat three, curved couches. Cream-colored and well padded, from the look of them, with comfortable walking space between them, and in the middle a round, three-layer coffee table made from some dark hardwood.

Farther back to my left was a round dining table, with enough chairs for eight. Both the table and chairs looked to have been made from the same dark hardwood as the coffee table.

Farther back to my right was what I took to be a small, reading area. A pair of leather armchairs that looked as though they might recline, with another dark hardwood table between them.

Farther back and straight ahead of me, two smaller armchairs faced each other across a sleek, black table that didn't look like any kind of wood at all. Some kind of plastic or metal, maybe.

Closest to me, maybe ten feet to my right and along the wall, was what looked like a wet bar.

"You come without retinue, sire," the yeoman said. "Would you like one provided for you, for the duration of your stay?"

"That won't be necessary," I said. "What's going on with the battle?"

"I think the captain is hoping to avoid one," the yeoman said, "but your screens can show you what is happening. I'll cover that in a moment, if you please, sire."

I nodded.

"All right," the yeoman said. "Without a retinue, you won't need the rooms down there." He pointed to the leftmost door. "The other two rooms are bunks, er, bedrooms. As you are the only royal in residence, you have your choice."

I thought about asking if Tiksdottir could take the other, but she must've read the question in my drawn brow, because she subtly shook her head.

Protocols. I reminded myself that I couldn't start breaking rules before I was even had a chance to learn them.

"Where will Tiksdottir be berthed?" I asked. "And bear in mind that she is a royal messenger, and she has saved my life."

"Of course, sire," the yeoman said with a bow. "Her quarters will be right below yours, once deck down."

"Show her to her quarters, then," I said, "and Tiksdottir, return at your leisure."

"Thank you, sire," she said, and I swear there was amusement in her eyes at the way I was conducting myself. Not that I could blame her.

"Sire," the yeoman said. "before I do that, may I first tell you how to properly install yourself here?"

Well, that sounded potentially painful, but I nodded.

"Identify yourself aloud to the computer, and then claim residence. It answers to REP."

"REP, I am Prince Volner Ulfson, and I claim residence."

The last part of that came out more uncertain-sounding than I'd like to admit, but I promised to be honest about all this.

I felt the wolf tattoo on my chest itch for a moment, but the sensation passed quickly.

"Acknowledged," REP said in that affectless voice. "Welcome aboard the King's Fury, Prince Volner Ulfson."

"Anything else you need," the yeoman said, "either ask the REP, or use the tablet in either bedroom."

"Thank you, Yeoman Seisehn."

He bowed himself out then, followed by Tiksdottir, who gave me a half-bow herself, for good measure.

Then, I was alone for the first time in what felt like forever.

CURIOSITY TOOK ME BEHIND THE WET BAR. I FOUND A FEW BOTTLES OF liquids of various colors. Apart from the browns and ambers I expected, I also found a red, a pale blue, and a dark, dark green.

Cabinets below looked to hold snacks, and perhaps other options, but I wasn't hungry.

I tried to sit on one of the big, comfy-looking cream couches, but couldn't sit still.

Assassins. Possibly hostile ships.

I felt like things were happening, and there was nothing for me to do.

I jumped to my feet.

"REP," I said, "show me the battle."

"What battle would you like to see?"

I frowned. "The one the King's Fury is engaged in currently?"

"The King's Fury is not currently engaged in battle."

"Then show me that other ship in the area. That other cruiser."

"Acknowledged."

The closest viewscreen along the wall shifted its view to show me the pursuing ship. Ugly, awkward looking thing. I hoped the ship I was on looked better.

I know it was silly, but I liked the idea of spaceships being aesthetically pleasing, as well as functional.

"REP, what is the distance between us and that ship?"

"Two hundred eighty marks."

"They're closing," I said, "but not too fast." Then another thought occurred to me. "REP, can you show me this ship, from the outside?"

"Not in real time," REP said, "but I can show you a schematic."

"Do so."

Well, it certainly looked better than the ship chasing us.

It was built like a cylinder about a thousand yards long by about two hundred yards across. It had projections to both sides, in three places, symmetrically distributed.

The weirdest part was realizing that the direction my head was pointing was the direction the ship was flying. The decks were segments of the cylinder.

And my quarters were in the very heart of the ship.

All right. That made sense. It was the most defensible part. The bridge, though, was a raised portion along one side of the cylinder.

Which meant that the elevator shifted orientation without my even being able to tell.

Weird.

I was still studying the layout of our ship and keeping tabs on that approaching cruiser, when there was a knock at the door.

"Who is it, REP?"

"Royal messenger Ulna Tiksdottir."

"Admit her."

The doors opened and in she came. "Sorry for the delay, sire," she said, "I couldn't resist a shower."

"Good thought," I said, still studying the schematics. "REP, can you show me schematics for that other cruiser?"

"Schematics unavailable."

"Sire," Tiksdottir said, "there's no need for you to trouble yourself with that ship. Leave it to Captain Foardanna and his crew."

"And if that ship is pursuing us because of me?"

"Sire," she said, with a clear effort at patience, "this is the flagship of the Aarwol fleet. Her captain and crew are the best their navy has to offer, and they've already sent for reinforcements. They can handle whatever that ship offers."

A stream of something flowed out of the pursuing ship.

"Fighters," I said, immediately. "REP focus in on the fighters."

Tiksdottir sighed, but came to stand beside me.

The incoming fighters were wedge-shaped and fell into similar wedge formations as they closed with the King's Fury.

The King's Fury launched her own fighters. These reminded me of the rattle of a rattlesnake, and they assumed a convex formation. Flashes of energy began to beam between the fighters, which broke formation and fell into dogfights.

"There has to be something I can do," I said, punching one palm.

"Sire, don't you think you can best assist the crew by staying out of their way?"

I shot her a look that got me a bow of apology.

"I'm not talking about flying one of those fighters," I said, "or manning some shield or gunnery station." I slapped my chest, where the tattoo lay. "I'm supposed to be a prince with all this magic. There has to be some way I can use it to help these people who are fighting for my life."

Yes. I know they were fighting for their own lives as well, and likely other considerations. I also knew that there was a chance — slim, in my opinion, but nonzero — that this fight had nothing to do with me.

Far as I was concerned, the point stood.

Tiksdottir huffed out an impatient breath.

"Sire," she said, sounding as though she were trying to reason with a madman, and maybe she was, "you've only just met the Wolf. You haven't even been to court yet, much less learned to wield the power of Journeying. Perhaps you should—"

"Lessons are everywhere," I said, "and if there's a way I can learn to use my power and help this ship at the same time, I want to do it."

As though to emphasize my point, one of the rattleships — as I'd started calling our fighters in my mind — flared, then began drifting apart.

"You know what I need to do," I said to Tiksdottir. "If I'm a prince, it's time for me to do more than act the part."

She bowed to me. "Very well, sire. This way."

Tiksdottir led me from the royal cabin back into the elevator, and said to REP, "The royal battle station."

"Speaker not authorized for that destination. Only members of the royal family—"

"The royal battle station, please, REP," I said.

"Acknowledged."

The elevator swiftly carried us about a hundred decks towards the very front of the ship, and then toward the outer edge.

The doors opened, and the room before me was almost disappointingly small. About the size of the bedroom I shared with...

...used to share with Diane. Gods. I'd been so busy I hadn't even thought about her all day. What would she think if she could see all this?

I slapped myself across the cheek. I had to focus. Lives hung in the balance.

The royal battle station was a cobalt blue room, round, with the royal seal on the floor. The wolf's head within the circle, all done in gold. The walls were covered in screens that showed not the battle outside, but different stations aboard the ship. Shields, damage control, gunnery, the bridge, engineering, starfighter control...

Oh, hey. Looking at that one I could see how the fighters were doing as well. Good. I didn't want the fighters to be left out.

From here, I didn't survey the battle so much as those who were fighting it.

And then I understood at least part of what I needed to know. I would not help by fighting. I would help, by helping my crew fight *better*.

I strode into the center of the sigil, certain somehow that I had to do my work from there.

"All right," I said to Tiksdottir. "I get that I'm supposed to help our side, not hinder our enemies. But how do I do it?"

She shrugged helplessly. "I am not of the blood, sire. I knew of the existence of the royal battle station, but I have never been inside one. And I don't know how to best direct your magic."

She hung her head. "I'm sorry, sire."

"You have no reason to apologize," I said quickly, waving away her words with one hand. "Well, the Wolf is within me. It is from the Wolf within me that all my magic flows. I think. No. I'm pretty sure that's right."

I nodded, feeling more certain now.

"And if I am right," I said, "then I think I have an idea of what I need to do."

I needed to howl.

All right. I could do that. I'd done it before, so I could do it again.

I shook out my shoulders and arms and hands. My legs and feet. I rolled my neck around. I spread my feet to lower my center of gravity. Bent my knees and elbows. Drew a deep breath.

I threw back my head and...

Well, the sound I made was pretty much the sound any guy my age would make if he were trying to imitate a wolf howl.

But there was no power in it. No magic. Not even a drop.

"Damn it," I muttered, shaking out my limbs again as though the problem were that I wasn't limber enough.

"Sire," Tiksdottir said softly, "from growing up around the royal family, I have been able to gather this much. The howl isn't the effort. The howl is part of the result of calling your magic."

I nodded to acknowledge her words, then turned away. Watched the screens.

All right. I'd howled before. Twice during that fight against the assassins alone.

How had I done it then?

The first time, while I'd been jumping down at that assassin, I hadn't been thinking. I'd been acting.

The second time, while recovering from that blow with the sword pommel.

Need, maybe? I'd called the magic through need?

I looked at those various screens. Most of the action was still between the fighters, but the cruiser looked to be closing to combat range. I could hear our ship's gunnery officers discussing range and bearing and preparing to fire.

I focused on the fighter control screen. I could tell the friendlies from the enemies because the friendlies were blue discs and the enemies were red.

All right. Every one of those blue discs was a person fighting to protect me. A person sworn into my service. I was the prince, here. The ranking representative of everything these people had sworn an oath to fight and die for.

That meant these were my people out there. Fighting. Killing. Dying. All in my name (yes, I know, it wasn't in my name but the high king's, but this was my line of thought, all right?).

Fighting. Dying. Killing.

All for me.

And I would not let them fight alone.

"The Wolf is mightier with his pack," I shouted, "and the alpha is here!"

The howl swelled within me and came out so loud and true I half expected to shatter the viewscreens.

Fortunately, I didn't.

What I did do, though, was call up power that felt like liquid gold as it rushed out of me, through the starfighter control station, and into every starfighter we had out there.

No. Not we.

Every starfighter *I* had out there. They were mine. And I could feel them now.

Frustration welled within me. There was more I could do. I knew it. I *knew* it. But I didn't know how.

I tamped that down like nerves at the start of a tournament bout — three quick breaths, two shallow, one deep.

I felt connected to those ships, those pilots. And through me, they were connected to each other.

All right then. Where one wolf was weak, the pack was strong. Through me, these ships would be a pack. And they would fight as a pack. And they would win as a pack.

I didn't need to watch the viewscreen now. I could feel them. The pilots. They stopped being individuals, and began moving and fighting as a unit. As though a pack were actually one wolf with many claws and fangs.

The enemy fighters didn't last long then.

When the last of the enemy fighters died in a quick flare, I lost my connection.

I dropped to my knees there in the golden sigil. Sweating through my clothes and panting for breath. My pulse was racing as though I'd sprinted five miles without any stretching or warmup. My skin was almost hot everywhere my clothes touched me, which could only have been from the *tlikswul* drying itself of more sweat.

"Sire," Tiksdottir was beside me in an instant.

"I'm ... fine," I said, and swallowed. "I think ... I helped..."

"Sire, after you howled we didn't lose another fighter. The enemy lost all their fighters. And three of our ships struck vital blows to the main cruiser as well."

"So ... good then?"

"More than thirty enemy ships down, while we lost only three of our own. And those before you offered aid." She snorted. "So, yes, sire, I believe you helped."

"REP," I said. "Status ... of the battle..."

"The enemy cruiser is breaking away and retreating. The captain is recalling fighters, and has not given an order to pursue."

"Good," I said, looking up at Tiksdottir. "I think I'd like to go rest."

Tiksdottir gave me a smile that lit up her whole aspect.

"Yes, sire."

6

———————

I HAVE TO SAY, ONCE THE WORRY OF BATTLE WAS BEHIND ME, THE ROYAL cabin aboard the King's Fury was a downright comfortable place to rest.

That bed. Back home — where I grew up, I mean — there are beds they call "king size." I've since come to think of those as moderate, when it comes to accommodations.

To be fair, though, the bottom end of my "accommodations" scale has gotten pretty far down there too, compared to what I knew, growing up. But I'll get to all that.

Point is, it was the bed aboard the King's Fury that began to shift my views about what luxury accommodations really meant. Oh, so soft, that bed, but firm enough for back support. More than big enough to stretch out in, in any direction.

More space than even a tall guy like me needed. And I suspected that the bed was designed so roomy in case there were, shall we say, royal guests.

Not that I tested that aspect.

The sheets, softer than silk, but without that slippery I-might-slide-out-of-bed-any-moment feeling.

And those pillows. Man, I could get sleepy just thinking about those pillows.

Anyway, I did a lot of resting over the remainder of the day-long trip to Aarwol. Whatever exactly I'd been doing during that starfighter battle, it really drained me.

But I ate well of what the ship's galley provided. Apparently they kept a special pantry for royal guests, so I dined on things like thick steaks and fresh, orange vegetables that reminded me of a cross between broccoli and asparagus.

They offered wine, but I stuck to water. And I made sure that Tiksdottir ate the same quality of food that I did by inviting her to dine with me.

I felt downright refreshed by the time we reached just the right kind of orbit around the planet Aarwol. It was a lovely looking planet, from what REP could show me on the viewscreens. Probably about three-quarters' water, with five continents of rich-looking land.

I was freshly showered and shaved, and I'd donned clean clothes from my locker. A pale blue silk shirt. Black pants that felt tight, but stretched and moved well. Black, calf-high boots made of a very soft leather, but with good, hard soles.

On Tiksdottir's advice, I traded the longsword for a rapier, though I kept the main gauche. Apparently rapiers were more fashionable around court, and I was confident that I knew how to use one.

Oh. I should point out that I noticed something when I went into my locker again. The dirty clothes I'd thrown in there before? Back in the cabin? Well, they were still dirty, but they were now in a small box labeled "dirty clothes" in English.

Tiksdottir was dressed the same way she'd been dressed for the whole trip. The faded red shirt. The leather vest, pants and boots. Her clothes looked cleaned and pressed, though.

Captain Foardanna himself, along with his yeoman, escorted us from the royal cabin back to the room where we'd arrived aboard his ship.

That room, it turned out, was the Journey Room, built into all ships in our navy, for VIPs to use for arrivals and departures.

In other words, I was clearly not the first member of the family to use one our the Aarwol ships as a waystation on a Journey. But the captain didn't seem to mind.

In fact, assuming I could judge by his behavior in my presence, he seemed somewhat honored.

From that I could only conclude that members of the royal house interfering with his regular mission didn't happen very often.

"Is there anything more you would have of us before departing, Prince Volner?" the captain asked, and there was a formality to those words that I could only hope to match in my response.

"Nothing, Captain Foardanna. You and your ship have given me exactly what I needed when I needed it most, and for that you have my gratitude."

He and his yeoman bowed.

"Then we wish you well in your travels, sire, and stand ready to aid you again, should the need arise."

"Thank you, captain."

They left the room then, and as the door hushed closed behind them, I turned to Tiksdottir.

"Are you recovered enough for this?"

"More than, sire," she said. "Especially after your assistance with that last Journey."

"Then lead on."

She wasn't lying. She called forth her power and controlled it so smoothly she made the whole opening of the way look graceful. The coruscating flow of red and amber power around the pair of doors even looked brighter and more active.

Together we stepped up to those doors. They parted for us, and we stepped through the sheen of Tiksdottir's power.

We arrived on a platform that looked to be made of marble the color of dark amber, shot through with streaks of gold.

The noontime sky up above us was a deep, royal blue, and the sun shining down from it was the kind of bright yellow ball of fire I'd known so well from earth.

The platform we stood on was raised above a courtyard. The

courtyard was tiled in a mosaic pattern of dark reds and deep browns. Two rows of trees lined it, all of them leafy and kind of bushy, but each had leaves of a different color and shape.

The trees were fragrant. Each bore a kind of fruity smell on the breeze. Each smell slightly different, though they worked well together, so the character of the breeze changed a bit as it shifted, but was always slightly mouthwatering.

In the center of the courtyard stood a fountain, graven from more some kind of dark amber rock. It depicted a wolf, howling, with water shooting out of his mouth.

The courtyard was practically frothing with people. Hundreds of them. Some of them moving swiftly about their business. Others gathering in packs, talking loudly about one thing or another.

The sound of all those conversations clashed, but still made me smile. Life. Vibrancy. And no one trying to kill me. At least, not so far.

Past the courtyard I could see a vast city, sweeping away down the hillside and continuing on from there. The city formed a three-quarter circle around a bay — docks all along that three-quarter circle — strewn with ships of different sizes, from dinghies to massive behemoths with at least a dozen sails.

The buildings. The ships. The sails. So many colors and shapes. It would take me weeks, or maybe months, just to walk all the streets and see all there was to see.

And I admit, part of me wanted to do just that.

"Sire," Tiksdottir said gently, "the castle awaits."

I turned and my first sight of the royal castle at Vol-Halá dropped my jaw.

The royal castle took up the entire top of this hill. Gleaming amber stone, shining bright in the sun.

The main keep itself must have stood a dozen stories tall, with walls and crenelations, but even a quick count told me that more than thirty towers shot up high into the sky beyond. Some of those towers even had arching bridges to other towers.

I was still staring, slack-jawed, trying to take it all in, when Tiks-dottir spoke again, her eyes smiling at my reaction.

"Please excuse me, sire, but I meant that you are awaited *within* the castle."

I DREW AT LEAST A HANDFUL OF CURIOUS OR SPECULATIVE LOOKS FROM well-dressed strangers as I followed Tiksdottir across the courtyard and to the doors of the castle.

The double-doors filled a single peaked arch some thirty of forty feet tall, by about sixty feet wide. The doors themselves looked as though they'd been hewn from a single, massive tree. I could even see the way the grains from one matched well into the grains of the other.

Of course, I could see these things because they were closed.

Standing in front of those closed double doors, a row of a dozen men-at-arms in better plate armor than I'd ever seen at a class, a tournament, hell, even in a museum.

The joins. The rivet work. The fit. All exemplary.

Their armor looked to be even better than the set Uncle Karl got for me. But then, I suppose, the set Uncle Karl got me was intended for tournament use in a world where no one tried to kill each other with swords anymore.

Or at least, only very rarely.

The armor those men-at-arms wore was all a dark gray color, polished to a sheen that showed off the royal sigil done large on their breastplates. They wore full helms, with the visors down. Each had a sword or a mace hanging from his or her belt, but each carried a halberd in a ready position.

"The royal guard has the door closed," Tiksdottir said, frowning, as we approached. Louder, to them, she said, "Is the council in session?"

"No, my lady," came the answer. The speaker was a guardsman in the center, who took one step forward to address us in a deep, rough voice. "The council was dismissed yesterday. The castle is closed today by order of your father. We weren't told why."

I leaned closer to Tiksdottir, and spoke softly.

"Does that mean the castle is closed to us as well? Or just the public?"

"Not to us, sire," she said just as softly. "Or at least, certainly not to you. But it would be a mistake to make the guards open these doors without first knowing why they're closed."

Louder, to the guard, she said, "Thank you."

The guard clapped one fist to his chest in salute, then stepped back into line.

Tiksdottir led me around toward the left-hand side of the castle. Once we left the courtyard, we were walking on thick green grass. We left the fruity smells of the trees behind, but the warm air of the day was still scented by the grass beneath us.

As we continued on, the sounds of conversation from the courtyard grew fainter, and I could hear the cries of gulls, and the sweet tones of some kind of songbird, as well as faint, periodic shouts or exclamations from the city beyond.

I let my fingers trail along the castle wall while we walked, but the amber color of the stone didn't feel like paint. That was strange to me. The only amber I knew of, back in the world where I grew up, was a kind of fossilized sap.

Away from the courtyard, now, I noticed that the castle and courtyard were surrounded by a high wall only a few hundred feet away. A high wall patrolled by more guards. Those guards wore chain armor, not plate, including coifs, and they carried longbows and swords.

They paid us little mind, more concerned about the courtyard and what went on outside the walls.

I realized then that the platform where Tiksdottir and I had arrived was, in fact, raised just inside the edge of that high wall.

We stopped beside what seemed to be a random section of castle wall. Tiksdottir glanced about, so I followed her lead. I didn't see anyone watching us. Even the red squirrel on the grass was more occupied by something it picked at.

"Sire," Tiksdottir said softly, "touch the wall here" — she tapped a particular stone — "and say your name, including title."

I put my left hand on the wall where she indicated, and said, "Prince Volner Ulfson."

I felt my tattoo itch for a moment, and that itch carried all the way down my arm to my hand, followed by a light static shock against the stone.

A deep grinding sound came from somewhere within the stone of the castle wall. A seam formed between the stones before me. They pulled in and slid back, revealing a tight corridor, lit by small torches. Red carpeting and mahogany wood panels. I smelled the rich, old wood of the paneling.

A hidden sally port?

"Quickly, sire," Tiksdottir said, and the two of us hustled into the corridor, which was tight enough that we couldn't stand side-by-side.

I led the way, for once.

Tiksdottir was barely inside before the grinding sound came again and the wall sealed itself behind us.

I frowned the moment the wall was closed. I stood right next to a torch, but I didn't smell burning wood or pitch. Didn't feel any heat.

I reached up toward the flame, then into the flame, without getting burnt.

The wood of the torch itself looked to be blackened by fire, but this fire was nothing more than light without heat.

"Cool," I said, smiling despite myself.

Weird as this may sound, even though I'd traveled across worlds over the last couple of days, and even used magic myself, these torches, they were like the locker.

These things, these were *magic*. And that was just too cool for words.

"Sire," Tiksdottir said, then shook her head and gave me a moment to play with the illusory fire.

Around the time a fleeting wish to show Diane one of these torches saddened me, Tiksdottir said, "We really should continue on, sire."

I nodded, and moved aside so she could lead. Since she was the one who knew where she was going.

The corridor stayed narrow, but only continued another hundred feet or so before it ended in a door. From there, we seemed to double-back toward the outer wall, following more tight passages and mounting narrow staircases.

"Huge freaking castle," I grumbled, "and they couldn't make corridors wide enough for comfort?"

"We entered through the hidden ways, sire," Tiksdottir said. "We're moving behind and between rooms right now."

No sooner did she say that than we passed a small door, and then what looked like a sliding panel for spying.

We passed a few more of those as we moved along more tight corridors, and ascended more tight stairwells.

We were about six floors up, by my estimate, when we reached a landing where someone was already standing.

He was about my age, with short blonde hair, rakishly disheveled, but a neat blonde Van Dyke. His shirt was pale blue, and his sleeves blousy, but his black pants were as tight as mine. Though his boots were taller, reaching his knee.

I noted that he also wore a rapier at his belt.

"Ulna Tiksdottir, isn't it?" he said, with the kind of high, clear voice that probably meant he had a good, tenor singing voice.

"Yes, sire," she said with a bow.

"And who is this with you?" he asked, with an eyebrow raised imperiously high. "He has the family look about him."

"Prince Cassiel," she said formally, moving as much to one side as she could for the introduction, "may I present your cousin Prince Volner."

To me, she then said, "Prince Volner, may I present your cousin, Prince Cassiel."

I didn't remember the name "Cassiel," but there were a *lot* of names on that family tree.

"Ah," Cassiel said, giving me a smile I wasn't sure I trusted. "Uncle Alvin's son, come home to us at last. Welcome, Volner."

He extended his hand, and I hoped to whatever gods might be listening that I was supposed to shake it.

I did. No one acted surprised.

"Thank you, cousin Cassiel," I said, then struggled to figure out something neutral, but true to add. I settled on saying, "It is good to finally see Vol-Halá."

"Of course," he said, and his wolfish smile told me I hadn't fooled him in the slightest. That he knew I didn't trust him, and he seemed to approve. "You were close with Uncle Karl, I believe."

Crap. How much did these people know about me?

"Somewhat," I said, trying for dismissive. I wasn't sure I fooled him then, either.

"I imagine you need to formally present yourself to the high king," he said, and glanced at Tiksdottir.

"That is the very reason I have brought him, sire," she said.

"Well," he said, looking me up and down, "that will be rather difficult as the high king has vanished."

"Vanished?" Tiksdottir said, showing even more shock than I would have expected. Her hand flew to her hilt as though convinced enemies were storming the castle.

"Well," Cassiel said, "that was the word the high queen used. And your father claims not to know where he is." He shrugged, a slight movement, before adding, for my benefit. "He goes walkabout from time to time, but usually he at least announces that he's going."

"But if the high king has vanished—" Tiksdottir started, but Cassiel interrupted her.

"Then your father probably needs you." He gave a dismissive wave of his hand. "Go to him. I'll see my cousin safely to the high queen for formal presentation." To me, he added, "It really should be our greatest grandfather, of course. But the high queen'll do in a pinch."

"No," Tiksdottir said, then quickly added, "sire. My orders were to bring Prince Volner myself."

"As you like," he said, with another slight shrug. Then gave me a lopsided smile and a clap on the shoulder. "Volner, it is an absolute pleasure to meet you. But you're going to have to become a much,

much better liar. Not everyone in our family is as ... *easygoing* as I am."

Cassiel waved away my own attempt to say something nice, and wandered off down the stairs.

And as he left, I wondered, just what had *he* been doing back here among the secret doors and spy windows?

TIKSDOTTIR KEPT ME IN THE TIGHT, HIDDEN CORRIDORS, AS WE MOVED about the royal castle. And tight as the confines were, even here I could tell this was a royal castle. The soft, red carpeting underfoot. The dark, mahogany paneling of the walls, with its rich, oiled wood smell.

And, of course, the torches that shed light but not fire, even while they seemed to burn through their tips.

Tiksdottir did, at one point, have me wait in the corridor while she slipped out through a concealed door and spoke to a servant.

She looked worried when she returned.

"It may be worse than I thought," she said. "Different groups of family members have retreated into conference. And since the council was dismissed yesterday, there's no formal court in session."

"I take it there should be?"

"An empire this size?" She nodded. "There are issues to discuss every single day. But no petitioners are being admitted."

"What does this mean?' I wanted to add, "for me," but that just sounded way too self-involved, considering how big a deal this seemed to be.

"It means that at least some of the family members are speculating that something has happened to High King Ulfgar."

"I take it you mean something fatal?"

"Or near enough." She drew a deep breath, let it out in a quick puff. "Well. I'm supposed to present you to court. But if court's not in session, I can present you to the high queen and to the royal constable. Hopefully at the same time."

She gave me an apologetic look. "That won't be the formal home-coming you deserve, Prince Volner, but—"

"I won't know most of these people by name, anyway," I said. "And once we get that over with—"

"Then you'll be free of me, and may go your own way. Of course, sire."

"That's not what I was going to say at all," I said, stopping her as she started to turn away. "Ulna Tiksdottir, make no mistake. You may have been acting on the high king's orders, but I am past grateful for all you've done for me. You are *hardly* a burden to be shed."

She smiled faintly, and with a small bow, said, "Thank you, sire. Now let us see you to the high queen."

That turned out to require only another two flights of narrow stairs and three long hallways, before we reached a door that looked to slide, instead of opening normally. And something looked odd about its mechanism, but I wasn't sure what yet.

She knocked on the door. A complicated pattern that took about fifteen knocks, and none of them very loud.

The door slid open, and the oddity of its look fell into place.

It didn't slide along the corridor wall, either, but looked to follow a curved track away from the wall, though I couldn't tell where it went.

The man standing in the doorway had to be her father, Tik Garrison. He had the same tanned skin, the same bright brown eyes, and set his mouth the same way. Though his mouth, like his jaw, looked distinctly more masculine than hers did.

And, personally, I thought her eyes were prettier.

He stood almost as tall as I did, and his black hair was sprinkled liberally with gray. He dressed finely as a courtier, with a soft gray shirt and tight, dark brown pants tucked into his high, brown boots.

The keys of his office he wore on the opposite side of his belt from his rapier.

"This must be Prince Volner," he said, seeming to ignore his daughter. He had a strong voice, clearly used to giving orders himself.

He gave me a deep bow. "It is my very great pleasure to meet you at last, my prince."

"Thank you, Constable Garrison," I said, hoping I was doing this right. "It is my pleasure, as well, to meet the father of the woman who has saved my life more than once in the last few days."

"I did no more than my duty," Tiksdottir said, giving me and the constable bows, in that order.

"I've no doubt," Garrison said, not even glancing at his daughter, which was starting to piss me off. "Come, Prince Volner, and be presented to High Queen Delfina."

After the tight corridors and stairwells, the room I entered then felt decadently big. Truth was, though, for the royal castle, that room — the small council room, as I'd learn later — was modest. No more than thirty feet across at the widest point, and fifty feet long.

The room was shaped like two bubbles coming together. One with a radius of about twenty feet, and the other with a radius of about thirty.

The larger of the two rooms had chairs along the walls, positioned in sets of three, beneath a series of twelve tapestries, each bearing a different royal crest and a scene I presumed was important to the history of that royal family.

We came in from a small space between tapestries.

In the center of that part of the room stood a small dais, one step up, with a lectern that faced the small room.

The small room had only one tapestry, that of the royal family of Ulfson. It featured not only the royal sigil, but a scene of High King Ulfric deposing the tyrant, Emperor Emerlaine.

The top half of the smaller room was a spiderweb of stained glass, featuring the royal sigil done in amber, surrounded by reds and blues and greens.

Only two seats in that room. Simple thrones of dark amber, on a dais *two* steps up.

The one throne was empty.

On the other sat a woman who was far too young to be High

Queen Delfina. I mean, she wasn't a child, but this woman looked even younger than Dad. I figured her for early thirties at the oldest.

Her smooth, pale skin had yet to show any sign of wrinkling. Her long, curly golden tresses were without even a starter set of gray hairs.

She wore a gown of midnight blue that matched her eyes, and tapered around a body that even the least charitable observer would have trouble finding fault with.

In her hands, she held the royal scepter, but from her expression she wasn't happy about it.

"My queen," Garrison said with a small bow.

My eyebrows shot up. This woman was High Queen Delfina? Mother to eighteen children over the course of … what … millennia?

She could have been a grad student.

But Garrison was still talking.

"The message from Aarwol was true. May I present your thrice great grandson, Prince Volner."

Garrison bowed even lower then, as did Tiksdottir.

For lack of anything better to do, I bowed too.

"Rise, my child," High Queen Delfina said in a voice so sharp I had no doubt could slice cheese at fifteen paces. "I see the Wolf in you, and the Wolf bows to no one."

I straightened up. The other two held their bows.

"So," she said with a sigh, "I take it by his absence that Alvin continues to deny himself his family?"

I fought with how to defend my dad while still being honest. But, hell, does a wolf mince words?

"He does," I said with a nod. "I knew nothing of my bloodline, except stories told as fantasy by Uncle Karl, until Tiksdottir arrived with my legacy."

"I feared as much," she said with another sigh. Some of the edge came off her voice as she continued. "You come at a dark time. My husband is missing. The family has begun nipping at each other's haunches. And I cannot spare any of the three I would send you to for training."

"My queen," Garrison said, while still holding his bow. "An untrained prince is dangerous to himself and others."

"No one taught my husband to use his power," she said. "And yet I'd say he did quite well. In fact…" She tapped her jaw. "Yes. Tiksdottir, rise."

Tiksdottir straightened and said, "At your service as ever, my queen."

"Go to the library and fetch *Trails of the Wolf*."

"At once," Tiksdottir said, then turned and left swiftly through the main door in the larger room.

"That book," High Queen Delfina said to me, "was written by Ulfgar in his youth. The techniques have been refined a good deal since then, of course, and modern methods of Journeying are much faster than the old ways. But it should serve you well in teaching you at least the rudiments of your magic."

She smiled then, almost as though sharing a secret with me.

"Besides. Not all of your kin have bothered to learn the old techniques. You may find that they open ways for you that others would not see."

"Thank you, my queen," I said.

"No," she answered quickly. "You are to call me grandmother, grandmama, or Grandma Delfina. Just as you are to call my husband grandfather, grandpapa, or Grandpa Ulfgar. That is clear?"

"Yes, grandmother."

"Very good, Volner," she said, giving me a broad smile then that I'd like to think was sincere. "Now come give your grandmother a kiss."

I approached the throne, and we kissed each other on the cheek. She smelled of lavender and rose petals.

"Do yourself a favor," she whispered to me while we were close. "Take the book and go off to other worlds to study and practice. Get yourself some seasoning where you'll be safe from the machinations of the family."

I nodded as I stood away.

That was the moment when Tiksdottir came back into the room, carrying a heavy tome, wrapped in a soft, white cloth.

"Oh," High Queen Delfina said, with what I was sure was only the pretense of having a sudden thought. "You'll need someone to show you around. Tiksdottir, I hereby task you to Prince Volner as guide and attaché for a period of..."

She tilted her head back and forth as she pretended to consider.

"...no less than six months. See to his health, his safety, and to the best extent that you can, his learning about what it means to be a prince of the blood."

"Yes, my queen," Tiksdottir said, frowning in confusion.

"There," the high queen said, looking me up and down. "I think that shall do for now." She flicked her hand in a go-away gesture. "You're dismissed. Go on."

I think I was as confused as Tiksdottir when we left.

***

As Tiksdottir and I left the high queen's presence, the hallway outside was much more what I'd expected from a castle the size of the royal castle of Vol-Halá.

It was wide enough that five people could walk abreast, without feeling crowded. And none of them would even be in danger of stepping off the red carpet that ran down the middle of the hall.

The amber stonework was more visible in here, covered only by tapestries and paintings that were an odd mix of peaceful landscapes and seascapes with scenes of battles and executions.

I looked for more of those heatless torches, but I didn't even see sconces for them. In fact, I couldn't tell where the light in here came from at all. Though the hallway was certainly bright enough. I could see a hundred feet in either direction, including a handful of doors.

"Well, sire," Tiksdottir said, frowning, "I suppose the best place to start would be your rooms..."

"No," I said. Then quieter added, "I'll explain later."

"Then where?" she asked, not keeping her voice down.

"First, the book, if you would."

She handed it to me without a second's thought. I opened my locker and stored the volume on top of a set of other books that were already waiting, unread, in a box in the near left-hand corner.

As I put the locker away, I muttered, "Where did those books come from, anyway? And the weapons and such?"

"The royal wizard was in charge of selecting books for your locker, as she has for every locker built during her tenure."

I frowned at Tiksdottir. "This family has magic out the wazoo, and they employ a royal wizard?"

"The wah-zoo?"

"Doesn't matter," I said. "Just an expression."

"All right," she said, brows down as though certain she was missing something. "But yes, the role of royal wizard has existed for time out of time. Ours is Ganna, and she has been High King Ulfric's royal wizard since the time of Emerlaine. She's the one who really should be teaching you to use your magic."

"Well," I said, "never mind her now. I suspect she's got more on her plate than she needs at the moment anyway. But I'm hungry. Let's go into town and find something to eat."

"But the castle kitchens will be more than happy—"

"I'm sure they would," I said, trying to give Tiksdottir a significant enough look that she might understand what I didn't want to say aloud. "But I want to see something of the city."

"Of course, sire," she said, and from the way her eyes narrowed, she clearly knew I was trying to tell her something, even if she wasn't sure what.

Tiksdottir started down the hall, but I cleared my throat.

"Perhaps the way we came in..."

She nodded, and soon we were slipping through tight corridors and down narrow stairways.

As we did, I thought about what the high queen had said, and what she'd implied.

I had a whole new family. But instead of being one big pack, the moment something even *seemed* to happen to the alpha — the high king — it splintered into smaller packs, each presumably with its own alpha, trying to figure out how to make theirs the top wolf.

I wasn't sure the analogy held up, but it was all I had to work with.

If I understood the high queen correctly, as the newcomer, I would be nothing to them right now except a pawn to be used, and sacrificed if necessary.

In fact, sacrifice might be a desirable endgame, as far as some of them were concerned. Since I was second in line for the throne, according to one way of reckoning things.

Some great homecoming.

Yeah, getting out of town sounded really good.

Only one problem, there. Tiksdottir brought us here by Journeying only a few hours ago. I couldn't ask her to attempt another Journey so soon. But I didn't know how to do it myself, yet, either.

I needed time. Either time for her to recover her power, or, better, time to figure out how to wield my own power.

And I would not find that time here in the castle.

The trip back down through the castle to the the hidden door we'd entered seemed to go faster than the trip up had gone. Or maybe I was just that lost in thought. I know I'd started thinking about Diane, and Uncle Karl, when all of a sudden Tiksdottir said, "We're here."

Here, of course, was not some restaurant in town, but the concealed, sally port door we'd come in through.

"You'll have to open it the same way you did before, sire," Tiksdottir said.

I placed my hand on the wall and said in a clear voice, "Prince Volner."

The grinding sound came again, and the way opened up for us into the bright, sunny afternoon.

Where Cassiel was waiting for us.

7

———————

Thick green grass, rich blue skies, joyously singing birds. My exit with Tiksdottir through the hidden sally port should've felt like stepping out into one of the peaceful landscape paintings I'd seen during my brief look inside the royal castle proper.

One problem with that, of course, was that most peaceful landscapes wouldn't include soldiers with longbows on the wall only a few hundred feet away.

And I was pretty sure there was nothing peaceful about finding Cassiel waiting for us outside that sally port door.

He smiled, as the door opened.

"Volner," he said, hands out wide as though presenting me. "What a happy coincidence. I was just thinking about you."

I frowned. "No. You weren't. I'm guessing you finished whatever business you had in the royal castle's hidden ways, and probably only came through the door just ahead of us."

"The Heart," Cassiel said, as though correcting me.

Before I could ask what that meant, Tiksdottir stepped up to whisper the answer to me. Cassiel didn't wait for her.

"The Heart," Cassiel said, "is what we, of the blood, call the royal castle. It is, after all, the heart of the empire, the heart of the city, and the heart of the family itself, in some ways."

"All right," I said, but before I could get back to the rest of my point, Cassiel started talking again.

"This is why I'm glad I ran into you," he said. "There's still so much you don't know about us and how we live. You really should have a proper guide." He smiled. "Happily, I'm at loose ends at the moment."

"I'm not, though," I said. "We were about to—"

"Get something to eat?" Cassiel said, cutting right across the lie I'd been preparing about some kind of mission for the crown. "I should say so. After all, you came in from Aarwol. And I don't have to tell you, the food they keep for us aboard those ships is..." — he wiggled a hand — "passable fare, but hardly worthy of the likes of us."

"I thought the steaks were—"

"Just what I'm talking about," Cassiel said, slipping an arm about my shoulder and starting to steer me across the grass. But not toward the courtyard — toward the wall. "Their steaks are thick enough, I suppose, but they don't season them properly. And the quality of the meat, well, I don't have to tell you—"

He must have seen my frown.

"Or perhaps I do," he continued. "Volner, Volner, Volner. How you must've suffered, growing up on whatever deserted island of a world Uncle Alvin chose for his ascetic self-punishment."

"Self-punishment?" What the hell did Dad have to punish himself for?

That wasn't the part of his sentence that interested Cassiel, however.

"I can only imagine the terrible conditions and even worse food." He shuddered. "But I shall now introduce you to Daeron's. Finest seafood in Vol-Halá, which is saying something."

Cassiel was telling me about the amazing varieties of fish and shellfish and more available at Daeron's as we reached a door in the outer wall that hadn't been there a moment before. I'm sure of it.

Of course, even if it had, it would've been difficult to spot, as it blended in perfectly with the amber of the wall's stone.

The door led us through a tight tunnel, where two guards checked us before letting us through.

We came out through another door, to find a coach waiting for us. Gleaming black woods for the simple, yet elegant design, along with golden trim. The royal sigil blazoned on the doors, and on pennants flying at each corner.

The only thing missing was a driver and horses.

That didn't trouble Cassiel, though, as he herded me into the coach before following me inside. He was about to close the door behind him, when I said, "Wait. Tiksdottir is coming with us."

"I shouldn't think so," Cassiel said with a frown. "I agree she's pretty, in a common sort of way, but she's a Tiksdottir. She has duties of her own to see to."

"And I am one of those duties."

"Really?" Cassiel said, and the way he said it made Tiksdottir blush.

"Nothing like that," I said quickly, feeling a little too warm myself. "She is to serve as my guide and attaché while I learn the ways of the family."

"A Tiksdottir for that?" Cassiel frowned. Shook his head. "Whatever is greatest grandmother thinking?"

"I have every confidence in her."

"I'm sure you do," Cassiel said, but this time his tone was off-handed, rather than insinuating. "And it's not Tiksdottir's competence I question, it's her appropriateness."

He turned to me suddenly. "You *do* know how to use that rapier, don't you? You certainly move as though you do."

I nodded.

Cassiel tugged at his Van Dyke. His eyes widened. "Just how sheltered did dear old Uncle Alvin keep you?"

"What do you mean?"

"Have you ever even killed, before? Not an animal, I mean. A person."

"I killed a Nulac assassin not three days past."

"A *Nulac* assassin?" Cassiel smiled. He turned to Tiksdottir, still standing on the smooth bricks of the roadway. "And you killed one or two yourself, didn't you? In saving my dear cousin here."

"Yes, sire," Tiksdottir said, her tone more formal than she used with me. "Two."

"Ah," Cassiel said. "It all comes together then. Who better for you to trust than someone you've already fought and killed alongside?" He smiled. "Well, apart from me, of course."

"Point is," I said, "she's coming with us."

"Of course, of course," Cassiel said, smiling indulgently. He turned to Tiksdottir. "Climb aboard."

I expected her to enter the coach then, but she didn't. Instead, she climbed up to the empty driver's seat, on the outside of the coach.

I started to object, but Cassiel raised a hand to ask for the chance to speak first. I nodded.

"You like her. I understand. Comrades in arms and all that. But this" — he gestured vaguely to the city — "is the capitol. In the hinterlands, you may do as you like without question. Here, there are formalities we *must* follow."

He paused a moment, watching me to make sure I was listening instead of awaiting my turn to talk. But I admit, I was listening. This was the most serious I'd heard Cassiel sound yet, and I needed to know where he was going.

"She is a Tiksdottir. She is castle staff. A royal messenger. *Important*, as such roles go, I grant you. But she is still castle staff Not royalty. Not even, strictly speaking. nobility. But you and I are princes of the blood. Children of the Great Wolf. She does not ride with us. She does not dine with us. Not here in the capitol."

"I don't like it."

"You don't have to like it," he said. "But you have to realize that we have many, many enemies. And that includes some of our current friends, like those ridiculous Hybrasi. They watch us always, and if you flout so simple a convention, they will target you for manipulation in ways you will not see coming."

"How?" I asked.

"By throwing something in your path that you *can* see coming, then making their real move while you congratulate yourself on what you avoided."

"But how?"

"You'll find out all too soon," he continued, half-ignoring my question, far as I was concerned. He kept talking, though. "Worse, the family will take it badly. Our internal factions are gathering allies about them. They'll see you as fresh meat, to be manipulated or eliminated. Especially if you don't even know how to behave, to suit your rank."

"And how do I know *you* don't want to manipulate or eliminate me, cousin?"

"You don't," he said with a smile and a shrug. "And thus, does your education begin."

THE RIDE THROUGH THE CITY DOWN ALMOST TO THE DOCKS WENT MUCH faster than I expected. In fact, I suspected that other traffic — horses and other coaches, as well as foot traffic — moved aside for us.

Along the way, Cassiel made sure to point out locations of interest. Queensgrove Park, lined with its grapefruit trees. Apparently the grapefruit wasn't native to Vol-Halá, and when the high king married then-Princess Delfina, he had a hundred grapefruit trees planted a short walk from the Heart, so she would always have fresh grapefruit available.

The fruits of those trees looked more reddish than I remembered grapefruits being, but before I could ask about that, Cassiel had moved on to explaining how Queensgrove Park was a favored place for dueling.

Duels, apparently, were perfectly legal in Vol-Halá, so long as they followed the rules.

Of course, this subject immediately distracted Cassiel from whatever other tour guide duties he might have had in mind. Instead he started recounting the proper way to challenge and answer a duel here in the capitol, along with a story of how he won his favorite horse, Thunderhead, in a rapier duel that lasted six hours.

We arrived at Daeron's while Cassiel was demonstrating the wristwork he credited with his winning parry-riposte. And I have to admit, his wristwork was impressive. Better than my own, certainly.

Mind you, he never did mention *whom* he'd been dueling, or what insult or wrong had led tot he duel in the first place.

Apparently these things weren't nearly as important as explaining how he'd won, and that Thunderhead was a brilliant coal-black stallion, smarter than most people, and strong enough to ride all day and night without tiring.

He did, finally, pause long enough for us to leave the coach and give me a good view of Daeron's.

Daeron's was an odd mishmash of styles. It looked as though it started life as a warehouse built of the detritus of a hundred shipwrecks.

But over time, refinements had been added. Rough wood smoothed and re-lacquered in places. Some portholes had been sealed with what looked like pitch. Others had been replaced with windows of fine glass.

But the casements of those windows were of metal, and gleamed like sea green aluminum.

"Look there and there," Cassiel said, pointing to a couple of spots near the foundation, "That's good gava they've used to reseal and strengthen the wood." He smiled. "They've done it all throughout, of course, but it's most obvious there."

If it was, I couldn't tell. I was about to ask *how* I could tell, when Cassiel called to a rough-looking sailor who stood by Daeron's front door.

"Two princely patrons for your master, Cull. The royal table, if it's available."

"It is, sire," Cull said, with a voice so smooth I did a double-take. The man's rough clothing was stiff with saltwater. His long, reddish beard had been hacked into a rough shape, rather than trimmed, much like the hair sticking out under his watch cap. And he was built as though he should've been hauling anchors out of the sea hand-over-hand, rather than watching the door of a reputedly fancy restaurant.

And yet, his voice sounded as smooth and cultured as Garrison's.

And even weirder still, as he opened the door to admit us, Cull said, "Welcome to Daeron's, Princes Cassiel and Volner."

This guy knew who I was?

This guy?

I managed not to stare in slack-jawed wonder at that, but Cassiel shot me a smile that might as well have said, "I told you. We are watched everywhere, here."

Tiksdottir followed us in, receiving her own, less formal greeting from Cull.

No sooner were Cassiel and I through the door than we were met by a pretty young hostess. With her golden curls falling to her waist and her simple sea-green dress, she looked as though she could have been the figurehead of a cargo ship.

She bowed as she greeted us, again both by name, and escorted us around the edges of the candlelit main dining room, where scores of diners were already enjoying a late lunch or an early dinner.

Despite the windows, light didn't seem to come in from the world outside. The only lighting came from the candles at each small table. So the room seemed comfortably dim.

The hostess led us behind the large, well-stocked bar and up a staircase, then out onto a deck.

Oh, but it was beautiful here. Open to the sky, with a view of the whole of the harbor.

Two big men were positioning a table-for-two, while four others were carting away another half-dozen tables.

Soon, Cassiel and I were seated at the only table here on the second-floor deck, right up near the railing. Our table had been covered in cloth-of-gold and provided with a small vase with two large, fragrant white roses.

How fragrant? Well, we were right down near the port. And yet, sitting there, I smelled the roses, but not the port. Not the sea, nor the smell of decay.

Only the roses. And yet, the smell wasn't overpowering. It was more of a background scent.

Quite a trick, that.

Cassiel ordered for us, the specialty of the house. Pula fish, with fried clams and a salad of mixed greens and tangy citrus fruits I didn't recognize.

The pula fish, for that matter, was new to me. It reminded me of salmon, in texture, but had a richer, hearty flavor that managed to grow smoother and lighter through the meal, so that by the end, I felt full, but not overfull.

Might have helped that Cassiel had paired the fish with a crisp white wine that was downright tasty.

And as we ate, of course. We talked. Or rather, he talked. Conversation with Cassiel was ... difficult. He controlled it like a fine symphony conductor, knowing just when to hit me with a question so that I had to struggle not to talk about my mother, or where, exactly, I'd grown up, or how I'd spent my years before coming to the capitol.

I didn't know why, but I suspected those details would have told him far more than they told me.

Most of the conversation, though, wasn't about me. It was about the family. There were about sixteen factions within the family, and Cassiel knew all of them.

He spent most of that meal trying to explain them to me. But there was so much information, by the time we were done I wasn't sure I'd really heard any of it. Or understood any of it, at least.

I know that a few points, though, were clear to me.

One, Cassiel didn't admit to being part of any of those factions, calling himself one of the few nonpartisans of the family.

Of course, I didn't trust that at all.

Two, there were five factions jockeying for position right now, in case it turned out that High King Ulfgar were indeed dead. One of those factions was run by — or for, I wasn't sure which — Grandpa Larsek.

If Grandpa Larsek — whom I had yet to meet — took the throne, then I became crown prince, and the focus of a *whole* lot of attention.

So, naturally, Grandpa Larsek's faction would be out to ... secure my support. Or secure *me*. One way or the other.

The other four factions would either want my support — which, apparently, could help decide how the laws of succession were interpreted — or, lacking that, my death.

My death would, according to Cassiel, weaken Larsek's position and muddy the line of succession further.

I was still trying to keep it all straight in my head as we finished off the delicious raspberry sorbet the hostess had brought us personally, to end the meal. So I wasn't ready when Cassiel spoke.

"So where do you want to go hide?"

There was nothing elegant about the way I managed to choke on a bite of sorbet.

"Come now," Cassiel said, smiling and pretending not to notice the way I struggled to get my coughing under control. "You haven't even met your grandfather, have you."

He didn't make it a question. Which was just as well, because I was busy drinking water to clear my throat.

"And since you haven't," he continued, "you couldn't know whether or not to support his claim. Unless you just wanted to further your own claim. But to me, you look like you're going to say you don't want the throne."

I had to check myself from spitting out those very words. I held back and stared at him, instead.

"Good," Cassiel said with an approving nod. "Don't commit yourself. It's far too soon. You've only just entered the game. But your ... shall we say, reflexive response ... is obvious, all the same. You grew up on some backwater world, likely with no idea of the scope of your potential inheritance. It would be only natural to want to refuse the throne."

I scraped out the last of my sorbet and finished it, to make sure I had the good raspberry taste in my mouth. And as a way not to answer.

"Any way you look at it," he continued, "I am no threat to you. Even the most charitable interpretation of the inheritance laws places me no closer than eighteenth from the throne. Which, in this family, might as well be ten thousandth."

"And I'm sure there's no way you could gain power by trading me," I said, voice dripping with sarcasm.

"Good," he said, nodding approval again. "A little overt for my tastes, but still, well said."

He sighed then, and gave me a look that might've been frank, or might've been cunning.

"I take it this means I haven't won your trust with my stirring honesty?"

"This from the man who told me I needed to get better at lying?"

He chuckled. "Fair enough. Trust among the family is a rare enough commodity, and I admit I hoped you wouldn't be jaded enough yet to deny it to me."

He held up a hand before I could answer.

"No, no," he said, "don't insult us both. Now. The logical next step for you is to retreat to some other world, where you can learn in relative safety" — he chuckled at his own inadvertent joke — "what it means to be a prince of Vol-Halá. And with a Tiksdottir by your side, to aid you."

He nodded judiciously. "Greatest grandmother's plan, no doubt. Oh, don't bother confirming or denying it."

"Confirming or denying what?" I asked with fake innocence.

"I knew I'd like you," Cassiel said with a smile. He pulled a knife from his boot and set it on the table. It was a thin black stiletto, with a dark ruby on the pommel. "Take this dagger. If you've need of me, sketch the family sigil with its tip, then stab the center."

I frowned, considering. I could feel a kind of latent power to the dagger, focused on the tip and the ruby.

Cassiel leaned forward, and said softly, "There are some problems that Tiksdottir won't be able to help you with. Don't let caution or spite make you a fool. Take the dagger."

I did.

The afternoon air was warm, and salty from the ocean, when we emerged from Daeron's. The sun was only an hour or three from setting now, in the rich blue sky, and all around us the discourse of gulls and people, going about their business.

Down here the streets looked to have been shaped and molded from crushed brick, as were many of the newer buildings, though the latter had, at least, been painted. Interspersed among them, though, were plenty of older buildings. Wooden construction that reminded me of movies I'd seen set in northern Europe, in the Viking age.

The clothes down here, in general, were rougher and simpler than I'd seen in that courtyard by the castle, and the coaches down here were pulled by horses or mules, as were the carts that weren't just pulled by hand.

The odors of people working fought for dominance with the smells of the sea, and I found myself glad for the lingering taste of raspberry on my tongue.

Cassiel offered me a ride back to the Heart, but wasn't the least surprised when I turned him down.

"Understandable," he said, and I got the impression that his words were for anyone who might be listening, even though he gave those words no special volume or intonation. "It's a fine day for a walk down by the harbor. See you at dinner then."

I barely had the chance to say goodbye before he was back aboard his coach and rolling.

"A walk, sire?" Tiksdottir asked, stepping up beside me.

I tried not to startle, but I'm not sure I succeeded. "You do move quietly, don't you?"

She inclined her head to the compliment.

"Yes," I said, continuing, "I was thinking of looking over some ships for a venture I have in mind."

She walked beside me now, without my even having to ask, which I appreciated. Her eyes never stopped moving, though. Anyone watching would know her as my bodyguard, not my date.

"How soon could you safely handle a Journey again?" I asked softly.

Tiksdottir waited to answer until we passed a pair of young men pulling their mother, and a load of potatoes, in a hand cart.

"If your need is great, I could Journey right now," she said.

"I'm not sure it's that great." I waited for the rest of that sentence until we passed two, fairly well-dressed merchants, arguing about the price of flax. "But the sooner I can be away from the capitol, the better."

"Are you certain, sire?"

"Positive."

A young woman stepped in front of us then, and to say she didn't fit in with the rest of the crowd would be an understatement. For one thing, she wore a fine gown the color of muted gold, with darker vertical stripes through the body and flaring skirts. And she wore that gown like a weapon.

It was low-cut, with a sapphire dangling at the end of a silver chain, as though to make sure eyes were drawn just where the she wanted them.

Her chestnut brown hair was softly curled, and danced about her shoulders as she bowed deeply to me.

That I kept my attention on her hazel eyes as she bowed seemed to either amuse or impress her.

"Prince Volner," she said. "I bid you welcome to Vol-Halá on behalf of your cousin, Princess Richette. The princess invites you to an impromptu party to celebrate your homecoming."

"That's very kind of her," I said, glancing at Tiksdottir, who seemed to be watching everywhere at once. "When is this party to take place?"

"I could take you there straightaway, sire," the emissary said. "Her coach stands ready only just there."

She pointed. I held eye contact.

Cassiel's warning rang in my ears. This emissary, she was the obvious manipulation. Which meant the subtle one was coming. So since she wanted me to look elsewhere, I kept my attention on her and trusted Tiksdottir to watch my back.

"I couldn't possibly attend right now," I said. "Please convey both my thanks and my regrets, but I'm about important business of a time sensitive nature."

"I would be happy to accompany you until your business is complete," the emissary said, "and then conduct you to the party afterwards."

"An offer I sincerely appreciate," I lied, "but it will take some time, and I'm certain my" — I glanced at Tiksdottir — "cousin?"

She nodded.

"Cousin," I continued, "has more important duties for you than to wait around on me."

"I assure you, sire—"

"And I assure *you*," I interrupted the emissary while thinking quickly. "My negotiations will be difficult enough, without having someone watching over my shoulder. Please do convey both my thanks and my regrets."

She drew a deep breath slowly, as though putting on a show. "Are you certain this business is so pressing, sire? Certainly Tiksdottir here could convey your desire for a delay until tomorrow. As a prince of the blood, any would-be business partners would be fools to deny you."

I raised an eyebrow, hoping I looked imperious, rather than like a poser.

"Do not presume to tell me my business, emissary," I said.

"My name is—"

"I didn't ask. You have completed your task for my cousin. I have received her invitation. I am now giving you your next task. Return to Princess Richette. Convey to her my thanks for the party and the invitation, and my regrets that I am unable to attend."

"But, sire—"

"You are dismissed."

Heart pounding, I stepped around her and continued down the street. Tiksdottir stayed a step behind me until we reached the end of the block, where I turned into a fishmonger's that smelled about the way I'd originally expected Daeron's to smell.

"The princess Richette will take your refusal as an insult," Tiksdottir said.

"Please," I said. "It was an *impromptu* party, and she sent a pretty darned overt emissary. As though she thought a pretty face and impressive cleavage would somehow beguile me. *I'm* the insulted party here."

"I do believe you're learning, sire," she said. She started to say something else, but the fishmonger spoke then.

The fishmonger was a beefy man, with a ready smile, who was as hairy as it was possible for a bald man to be.

"Good day to you, my prince," he said, bowing and touching his forehead. "How may I serve you?"

"A moment," I said to him. Softer, to Tiksdottir, I said, "Will this doorway do?"

"Not well, but from here I can at least get us away from the capitol."

"Do it," I said, and turned back to the fishmonger. "Your fare is impressive, good fishmonger, but today I only have need of your doorway."

"Of course, sire," he said, bowing again and touching his forehead.

I tossed him a silver coin all the same, for his trouble. He fawned as though I'd just bought half his stock.

As I did that, Tiksdottir called up her power, gathered it together, and hit the doorway with it.

Just as we stepped through, I swear I heard a man's voice call, "Prince Volner! Wait!"

TIKSDOTTIR AND I STEPPED THROUGH HER POWER AND INTO A RAVINE. The world around us reminded me of parts of Arizona and New

Mexico, the way I remembered them from a few camping trips with Mom and Dad.

The ground was dry and hard, a sandy, almost pink coloring. The jagged cliff walls around us mostly looked like sandstone, in shades of reds and yellows.

Rushing past us with a roar, a wide, fast river came right out of the split in the cliff face where the ravine began, in a low waterfall.

The sun looked to be about the same place in the sky as it had been in Vol-Halá. Assuming it was west I was facing, and not east.

Scrub bushes and cacti were scattered along the ravine.

The smell of the river was sweet, and it misted the air, keeping the hot sun from being oppressive. Probably also helped that the ravine formed a bit of a wind tunnel, and a constant breeze whipped our hair and clothing.

Funny thing about the breeze. It changed direction slightly on an irregular basis, so that sometimes it was drier and sometimes wetter.

In the distance, I heard the long, yipping song of what I hoped was a coyote.

Well, I suppose that if I didn't encounter the creature, it could be anything it liked. But coyotes were at least a familiar idea. And I was finding that each time I Journeyed someplace new, I cast about for anything familiar I could tie my new experience to, to help me understand it.

I turned to ask Tiksdottir a question. She'd staggered against the cliff wall, her nose bleeding profusely.

"Ulna!" I said without thinking. I snatched a handkerchief out of a shirt pocket, which she gratefully accepted and used to staunch the bleeding.

Leaning her back against the cliff wall, she eased herself down to a crouching position and tilted her head back.

She looked too pale. And too sweaty. And shaky.

"What can I do?" I asked.

"Call me ... Tiksdottir ... sire."

"Seriously?" I said. "You're worried about that now?"

"Habits ... matter. Don't ... want ... wrong people..."

"To overhear, fine," I said, exasperation puffing out my breath. "Well, *Tiksdottir*, what can I do?"

She dropped the knapsack of food off of one shoulder.

Wait. I hadn't noticed her carrying that before. Not in the Heart, not in the restaurant, not on the street, and not in the fishmonger's.

But she had it now?

I opened the pack, and started to hand her a ripe, green apple.

She shook her head. "Meat. Sire."

I dug a little deeper, and found slices of what I thought might be roast beef. Though the texture didn't feel quite right in my hand.

I handed her slices while she chewed them slowly. Deliberately.

"Water?" I asked, pulling a canteen out of the pack.

She shook her head.

"I'm surprised you can eat at all," I said, hoping that talking would get my own nerves to quiet down. "After that meal at Daeron's."

I frowned at her. "At least, I'm presuming you did eat at Daeron's?"

She nodded. Gave me a faint smile. "Always do. When ... I'm in town."

I realized then that Tiksdottir was down and recovering, and I had my back to the world. A chill up my neck swore to me that something bad was about to happen.

I whirled as I jumped to my feet, whipping out my rapier and dagger.

Nothing but the wind. The rush of the river.

"Safe here," Tiksdottir said, taking one more slice of roast maybe-beef.

"Unless we're followed," I said, not willing to drop my guard yet.

She didn't say anything, but from the corner of my eye I saw her nod.

"You didn't seem in this bad shape before we left," I said. "You called up your power easily enough."

She didn't answer. Just kept gnawing on a slice of meat. But then I hadn't asked a question yet.

"Which means you did have the power for a short Journey,

without doing" — I gestured to her current state — "that to yourself. I mean, you're worse off now than after that double-Journey a few days back. What gives?"

She swallowed. Panted for a few breaths.

Before she could answer, an armored figure came out of nowhere, rushing at me and roaring a challenge.

He wore armor of thick brown leather, with rings of metal sewn into it all over the torso, along with a steel half-helm with a nose guard. He was armed with a spiked mace and a small, buckler shield.

Weird, the way time can seem to slow down at moments like that. I swear, I seemed to have all the time in the world to wonder where he came from. Why he had that bushy brown mustache. Why I was still armed with a rapier and main gauche, when clearly this was a sword-and-board fight.

"No," Tiksdottir tried to cry out, but her voice was just too weak. Just trying to listen to her talk over the rushing of the waterfall and the river had been hard enough when someone wasn't trying to kill me.

Now with my focus on the onrushing warrior, I didn't have time to listen to her tell me how she should be the one fighting.

I let him get close before darting to his shield side.

He led with his mace. Initial swing went wide as he passed.

He skidded to a stop as I closed with him.

He pivoted well, attacking mid-line with his mace.

I turned into his strike. Slashed his wrist with my main gauche and his arm with my rapier.

His armor stopped my main gauche's cut. My sword slashed right through the leather, drawing a dripping red line on his bicep.

His mace went tumbling.

Then I fell victim to an attack I'd used scores of times myself.

He punched me with his shield.

The blow slammed into my shoulder. Knocked me sideways. Didn't hurt much, though. Bruise maybe. Nothing worse than I'd had in tournaments back home.

I gathered my feet and spun. Weapons up to guard.

He'd pulled a long-bladed dagger, but he dropped it to the ravine floor. His weapon arm was bleeding faster now, dangling limp and useless.

He shifted his stance to lead with the buckler.

"Stop," Tiksdottir called out, voice a little stronger now, though she still sounded too breathy to be feeling fit.

Neither of us paid her any mind.

Getting past that shield would be difficult. But if I could time his strike, I could cut his leg. Maybe his torso.

He rushed me, shield up like a ram. I jumped wide, out past his elbow.

He was ready. Swung for me. Couldn't connect.

I turned to slash whatever I could reach.

Something punched my ribcage, low on the left side.

For a crucial moment, I lost all will to attack. Pain soared all through me.

Air. I couldn't get enough air. No matter how frantically my heart beat, I couldn't make my lungs work right. The world started going red on me. Couldn't get enough air.

And why did a punch hurt so badly? I could feel the pain of that punch all the way up to my scalp and down to the soles of my feet. That wasn't right at all.

I had the feeling I should know what had happened to me. What that punch meant. But in the moment, I couldn't assemble the pieces past the pain.

And I had a more important matter right in front of me.

The warrior with the buckler turned to finish me with a blow from the edge of his shield.

I tried to raise my weapons for defense, but all the strength seemed to have left my arms.

No. I would not go out like this.

I gritted my teeth. Raised my weapons.

Something was sticking out of my back now. I knew that much. Could feel it as I raised my guard. Crouched to fight.

So there was someone behind me. But I couldn't worry about them. Not with an enemy in front and closing.

I had enough left for one more attack. And that buckler man was going down.

Tiksdottir started yelling something.

Good for her. She must've been recovering well, to have that much voice. Too bad I couldn't understand her words past the roaring of blood past my ears.

Or was that the waterfall?

No. Definitely the blood.

The warrior came on with his buckler.

That jerk behind me punched me again. This time the right side of my rib cage. Up high. Pain spiked high.

Too high.

The world went black.

The last thing I heard before I lost consciousness was Tiksdottir's shouting. And some of the words finally resolved into clarity.

"Stand down in the name of Tik Garrison!"

8

I DID WAKE UP.

Obviously. I mean, I'm here to tell you the story. I suppose, in theory, I could be telling this story from the afterlife, but let's be honest here.

After all the weird shit I've seen over the course of my life — and I've seen more than most, even among *my* family — I've never seen anything that tipped the scales for me one way or the other on the whole "afterlife" thing.

Yeah, I've fought the undead from time to time, when I was in worlds that allowed for them to exist, one way or another.

But the undead always struck me as less of an "afterlife" kind of thing, and more as an "unholy abomination" kind of thing.

And sure. I've seen people contact the dead. But the way I see it, that doesn't have anything to say about an afterlife one way or another.

I mean, what are you really contacting, when you contact the dead?

You get something like a spirit that resembles the person you're expecting. And maybe they can even answer a question or two that only Aunt Martha or whoever could answer.

Well, the problem there is that it's never safe to assume that *anything* is private, exclusive knowledge. No matter how few people might be present when an event happens, those are only the people you *notice*.

Plus, you never really know what other people tell their friends and family, even if they don't admit it to *you*.

So, maybe that's knowledge exclusive to Aunt Martha, and maybe it's not. Still. Let's say for the sake of argument that it is.

So. When the apparent shade of dearly departed Aunt Martha answers your test question correctly, what does that mean?

Does it mean that Aunt Martha has come back down from heaven or wherever just to answer your test question?

Does it mean that poor Aunt Martha is stuck here, floating around in some netherworld? Not really here in this world, but not off in some heaven either? Just so she can be available to answer your stupid test question?

Or maybe, just maybe, does it mean that you've contacted some kind of *spiritual echo* of Aunt Martha?

Lots of those contact-the-dead types seem to think that the longer someone's been dead, the harder it is to contact their spirit. Or that maybe information from this world gets hazy from "the other side." Or some other kind of excuse that always sounds to me as though they've reached not an actual person, but some kind of spiritual remnant. Maybe the psychic imprint they've left on the cosmos, when they died.

Now, I don't know about you, but I personally like that last idea best. I mean, look at it this way.

If Aunt Martha is dead, and her spirit is stuck just hanging around, waiting for someone to call her up for a conversation, that's just sad. If that's an option for the afterlife, I'll take what's behind curtain number two, thanks.

If Aunt Martha has moved on to an afterlife, heaven, reincarnation, or what have you, then what? Her spirit has to take a time out from her reward (or suffering, if Aunt Martha wasn't what we'd like to call a "good egg") to come tell you she didn't hide any money in the walls, no matter what Uncle Henry insists?

Sheesh.

If there's an afterlife, whether I get a good one or a bad one, just leave me there, all right? Don't go calling me up to chat. I've either earned my fun or I deserve what's coming to me, but I don't want it interrupted by people who can't find their own answers in this great, vast collection of universes we have to play with.

Got a little intense there. Sorry.

Point is, far as I'm concerned, if you contact the dead, you're just getting the spiritual equivalent of whatever was left on someone's hard drive when they died. Porn and all.

Now where was I?

Oh, yeah.

I'd just been punched twice in the back, while fighting that one warrior in the ravine. Right after Tiksdottir had told me that she'd taken us someplace safe.

I lost consciousness. But I did wake up.

Consciousness didn't so much sweep over me as seep in like a gentle fog.

First, I became aware of two dull aches in my back. Even though I was lying on my back.

I was lying on something soft, though. I wasn't even really thinking yet, but some connection made at about the spinal level of my neurological system suggested I was lying on a bed, and no part of me disbelieved it. I was also pretty darned sure I was naked, except for a tightness around the two dull aches in my torso.

I was either too hot or too cold or both, depending, and the answer seemed to shift in an irregular pattern.

The dryness of my mouth came next, along with a foul, bitter taste. Then, slowly, the recognition that I wasn't alone.

I couldn't hear or see anyone, per se. I mean, I'm pretty sure my eyes and ears were working, but I wasn't conscious enough yet to see or hear.

Still, I had this indefinable sense that someone was nearby. A guard, maybe, keeping an eye on me. In case I did something crazy like get up and try to run.

Eventually, though, I could open my eyes. The world was white and red and yellow blurs, until I managed to blink some sense to it.

I was lying on a white bed. A single, which felt insulting. After all, I hadn't slept in a single bed since I was a kid.

The walls were reds and yellows, the same muted colors as the ravine had been.

Hey. Sandstone. That was what I was looking at.

Nah. Too smooth and solid-looking for sandstone. Even shale would be better a better guess than that.

It probably wasn't shale either, but I decided it was shale until I learned otherwise.

I could hear muffled conversation, as though from a room or two away. Maybe just on the other side of a closed door.

Blues and whites. Rectangular...

A window? Yes. There it was. Just past where Tiksdottir was sitting in on a wooden stool.

Tiksdottir!

I cleared my throat.

"Sire!" she said, leaning closer.

Before she could say anything else I said, "Are we prisoners?"

My voice sounded as though I'd been gargling broken glass and caltrops.

"No, sire," she said quickly, fetching me a brown ceramic cup of ice chips and feeding me one with a small pair of wooden tongs.

I didn't want the ice chip until it got to my lips. Then, it was bliss itself, and my tongue melted and sucked it away before most of my dry, foul-tasting mouth could get any of the moisture.

She spoke as she fed me a few more.

"I am grievously sorry for what happened, sire," she said. "You should never have been attacked here. To hear the guard tell it" — she took on a tone that suggested she didn't particularly believe the guard — "he saw me down and bleeding, and you standing over me, weapons out and looking for trouble."

"Where?" I managed, but she fed me more ice.

"Out by the waterfall." She rolled her eyes at herself as she realized what I meant. "This place is … something of a vacation home for my family. It was the absolute upper limit of a Journey that I could reasonably handle, in terms of distances, and only then because I've been here so many times."

"Vacation…"

"Yes," she said, giving me a small smile. "I'm sure it doesn't feel like one to you right now. And I am sorry about that, sire. When the crossbowman saw you fighting with the guard, he assumed you were an enemy and put two bolts in you before I could stop him."

Oh. So that was what had punched me in the back. Bolts.

Two of them. But I was still alive…

"We keep an excellent healer here, sire. And though you're yet growing in your power, the Wolf in you is still strong enough that your life wasn't in danger, so long as I got you aid. A year from now, you could have fought on, even with those two bolts in your chest."

"Still rather avoid them."

She chuckled, then tried to pretend she hadn't.

"You have the right to ask for their lives," Tiksdottir said. "You're of the royal house, and they attacked you without reason. Even if they thought they had one."

"No," I said. "They were guards acting like guards. I would've preferred if the first one had *asked* what was going on before attacking me, but I imagine they don't see a lot of action?"

"They don't, sire."

"As I thought. And with you down and bleeding, it was an understandable mistake. I'll live through it, and so should they."

"Thank you, sire. I'll tell the castellan."

"This is a castle?"

"Carved into the cliff beside the ravine, sire, with the entrance behind the waterfall. Yes."

"Sounds like a good place to hide. Good choice."

"Thank you, sire."

My stomach rumbled loud enough to wake the dead, or at least their spiritual remnants.

"Shall I see about your lunch, sire?"

"Please."

As she did, I checked myself over. The shield blow to my shoulder hadn't even bruised. I did have bandages wrapped around my torso, but underneath the wrappings didn't feel like the kind of creams or ointments I was used to from home.

Over the wounds felt like something thicker. Poultices, maybe?

That healer better be good as advertised, then. Because, given a choice, I could be convalescing someplace with all kinds of advanced medicine. Or even the current kind of medicine I was used to.

If I was dealing with some jackhole talking about humours, I was going to insist Tiksdottir get me out of here and to someplace sterile.

I hoped that wouldn't be necessary, though. In terms of places to hide, I could do a lot worse.

THE HEALER TURNED OUT TO BE A WIZENED LITTLE WOMAN WITH DARK skin and dark eyes, but shockingly white hair. Shocking not just in brightness, but also in the way it shot out in all directions.

She wore half-moon glasses that hung down around the tip of her long nose. And no matter how many times she came to poke and prod at me, to chant quiet little spells of healing and change my poultices, I never once saw her actually look at anything through those glasses.

Not. Once.

I'd've considered the glasses an affectation, except that she really didn't dress to impress. Or maybe she was the only one I'd met in the last couple of weeks who didn't think I was someone worth impressing.

Actually, I kind of like that take on it.

Anyway, she wore baggy clothes, clearly chosen for comfort and utility, rather than for appearances. The colors were all right, and went well enough with her complexion — bright reds and yellows that were downright sunny to look at.

Problem was, her tops all had horizontal stripes and her bottoms — whether they were pants or skirts — all had vertical stripes.

The combination was kind of painful to look at.

She knew her business, though, and I was back on my feet within just over a week, feeling pretty darned good, if I said so myself.

During that week of recuperation, I read. Tiksdottir helped me retrieve *Trails of the Wolf* from my locker, and I resolved to read it twice. Once through quickly, to get a feel for what it had to say, and once through slowly, to try to absorb its lessons.

Which would have been fine, if the damned thing had been a textbook.

Needless to say, it wasn't.

No. It seems that thrice-great Grandpa Ulfric wrote the memoirs of his first days after encountering the Great Wolf, and figuring out how to use the magic he'd won from the encounter.

His words. That bit about "winning" the power. Not mine. I remembered well what it was like to meet the Wolf, and nothing about the experience felt like "winning" to me.

Really, the book read more like the journal of a high school student than some great treatise on magic. Three whole chapters in the middle of the book were devoted to how badly he wanted to have sex with some woman named Trista.

(Spoiler alert: he did. Sort of.)

After two full readings, and a great deal of swearing on my part, I thought I was starting to get an idea about how he discovered the power of Journeying.

And the bitch of it all was that his tryst with Trista turned out to be not just relevant, but the turning point in figuring it all out.

He was out riding one day, and pondering when and how he could approach Trista to make her amenable to his overtures.

Mind you, far as I could tell from reading, just going ahead and talking to her instead of "sighting her across the village" would have been a huge step in the right direction.

As I said, it read like the journal of a high school student.

Anyway, he was out riding, and pondering Trista, when he came to a decision.

He was of the Wolf. The Wolf was a hunter. It sighted its prey, and it went after that prey.

Not very enlightened phrasing, I'll grant you, but he was going somewhere with this.

Literally.

Thrice-great Grandpa Ulfgar was riding his horse, and decided to pursue Trista and "make her (his) own." He rode with such focus on that goal, that he stopped paying attention to where he was riding.

When he'd left the village, he'd gone riding along a fjord on a pleasant morning, just as spring was thawing the snows.

But he found "Trista" by a waterfall, in a woods he didn't recognize.

Caught up in teenage hormones, he didn't stop to question where he was or how he'd gotten there. He saw Trista, she smiled at him, and mutually desired, consensual hijinks ensued.

It wasn't until they parted afterwards that Ulfgar realized that the sun was in the wrong position. And that the day was warmer than it should've been. And that he didn't know where these woods were, or even what trees they were. He was used to mighty evergreens, and all around him were trees more like cherry trees or acacias, if I read his journal right.

The smells, the birdsongs, all of it was strange to him.

Now, he doesn't admit this in the journal, but I'm pretty sure he panicked then. I mean, I sure would have. And I couldn't help but notice that he didn't start riding again until the sun was "much lower in the sky."

I figure that meant he'd lost some time to good old, hyperventilating panic.

And when he did start riding again, he had only one thought.

Home.

He was going to ride home, even if the ride took him the rest of his life. He didn't recognize the trees? Didn't matter, he was riding home. Didn't recognize the river, or that lake? Didn't matter, he was riding home.

Sometime during the ride, he realized he'd left those woods behind, and was riding once more along the fjord, passing snowmelt and sighting the smoke of his village.

He'd found his way home.

Trista "pretended" not to have met him at the waterfall, nor to even have known what he was talking about. At first, Ulfgar attributed that to "maidenly modesty."

Before long, though, he came to realize that she honestly didn't have any idea what he was talking about. Because the woman he'd met at the waterfall had been a different "Trista" entirely.

Same hair. Same eyes. Same everything. She even answered to Trista. But she was not the woman he knew from his village.

From there, he could only conclude the truth that started him on the path to Journeying.

He, Ulfgar Ulfson, had found a way to walk the trails of the Wolf. Which was what he called Journeying for a long, long time. Walking the Wolf's trail.

And it seemed that he'd stumbled on the most basic way to do it. Focusing on a goal so completely that all concerns about the world around him faded away. Only the goal mattered.

I knew I had to try it.

ONCE I FIGURED OUT THE SECRET OF *TRAILS OF THE WOLF*, I READ IT A few more times. Part of that was, of course, my devotion to figuring out how to use my newfound powers.

I have to admit, though, that there wasn't much else to do while convalescing. The healer — whose name turned out to be Jakoby — had good spells and poultices, but healing still took a lot out of me.

Soon as I was able to walk, though, I started pushing myself. I didn't just cross the room to use the bathroom instead of relying on the bedpan. I walked the hallway stairwell to stairwell, stopping along the way to look at photographs along the wall that seemed to tell the story of about a hundred generations of this family.

Enough that they really should have had a surname beyond the name of their parent. At least, in my opinion. When I raised the subject to Tiksdottir, she simply shrugged and said that names like those belonged to noble houses. Which hers was not.

"Wait," I said to her, after I'd brought the question up for the third time, while she watched me eat a dinner of fried liver with steamed broccoli and cauliflower. "Your family has the power to Journey, even if it's a lesser version of what my family has. You also have plenty of experience, among you, in politics and the various skills required to rule. Surely you guys could have a noble house of your own by now."

She started to say about three different things, but stopped herself each time. Finally, she blew out a breath, and threw her hair back over a shoulder.

"Sire," she said then, "do you know what my life would be like, if I were a princess?"

I suspected I knew, but she sounded like she was going some-where, but I just frowned and savored a bite of liver. Honestly, the way it was spiced here made it downright tasty.

"Do you think I could wear clothes like these?"

She stood and turned around. She was wearing her favored, weathered brown leather pants and boots, along with a faded black shirt, buttoned casually with her sleeves rolled back halfway to her elbows. Her rapier and long knife hung from her belt.

"Well, I would imagine you'd still have some flexibility in that regard."

"I would not," she said. "Or at least, I would not most of the time. The role of a princess among the great kingdoms is politics. I would be sent out to other kingdoms as a diplomat. I might be allowed to handle certain business dealings. My inevitable marriage would be more about alliances and power blocs than anything else."

"There are no princesses allowed to lead in war?" I said. "I find that hard to believe."

"A few," she said. "A very few. And not the oldest daughters, which

I am. Oldest daughters, like oldest sons, have to worry about inheritance and politics. Only the younger princes and princesses can seek the military life, or devote themselves to other pursuits."

She shook her head. "If my father sought a kingdom of his own, my life would be gowns and balls, court sessions and diplomacy."

"You *would* look good in a gown," I said, which got me a chuckle and a twirl before she sat again. "But I get your point. You're more a woman of action than words."

"Furthermore," she said, "if father made himself king someplace, my treatment would be based on his kingdom's relations with whatever other kingdom I entered. I might even be held as a hostage against his behavior."

My turn to chuckle. "Good luck to the fool who tries to take you hostage."

She smiled and bowed her head to the compliment.

"As a royal messenger for the high king himself," she said, "no kingdom dares to give me anything less than a respectful welcome and proper attention. And none would dare bar me from leaving."

"Not even after, shall we say, a mysterious death?"

She gave me a frank look. "Do you think such a death could be traced to me?"

"Traced to you? Likely not."

"Then they have no cause to hold me without risking the high king's wrath."

I nodded.

"In some ways," she said, "my family has more power than any save your own." She shrugged. "Why trade that to be lords of something lesser?"

I almost — *almost* — asked what would happen to her if something happened to my family.

But really, lying in a sick bed while her family's personal healer looked after me and she tended my every need made the answer obvious.

Part of her family's job was to make sure nothing bad happened to my family.

I have to admit. Much as Tiksdottir seemed to like me, that realization made me wonder how much of that was sincere and how much was just a manifestation of our relative roles.

Whether she liked me or not, she needed me. Especially since, according to one line of thinking, I might just be next in line for the throne. Assuming something bad had actually happened to High King Ulfgar.

I couldn't afford to like her too much. And she couldn't afford to like me too much. Our roles meant that we could never be more than friendly co-workers.

Sad, in its way, but perhaps for the best.

Have to say, though. Whether it was genuine affection or just her role, Tiksdottir did a good job taking care of me. Not just making sure I had food and the healer and such. But as I recovered, she encouraged my moving about.

And as soon as I was able to raise my weapons, she worked with me to get my muscles moving and happy again.

We began sparring twice daily in a courtyard below a false sky.

Turned out that the window in my room wasn't a window, per se. Well, it was built as a window, but on its own it would only have shown me more of the rock I decided was shale.

Instead, the window had been enchanted to show me a view of a valley a few miles south of the ravine.

And much the same way, the "courtyard" wasn't open to the sky. The ceiling had been enchanted the same way, to show the same view of the sky we'd see if we rode a few miles north along the ravine.

No two windows or "views" came from the same location. This was, I learned after asking, to help keep the location of this keep harder to find.

Finally, though, I felt fit and ready to see about taking my first steps along the trail of the Wolf.

I was just telling that to Tiksdottir, while she kept me company as I ate dinner a dinner of a fine beef steak with a mixture of good root vegetables, lightly seasoned.

(She didn't eat with me, though. Apparently she couldn't risk any of the staff seeing her dine with a member of the royal house. Her father would have ... taken it amiss.)

"And I think I'll be ready to start after dinner," I said, sitting at a low table under the window, while she sat a half-dozen feet away, on her stool. "Or at least tomorrow morning."

"You are certain, sire?" she asked. "You'd rather not wait a few more days?"

"I feel fine." I rolled my shoulders, showing her how I didn't even feel a slight urge to wince. "Or is this your way of telling me my attacks are still too slow?"

"Your attacks are very good, sire," she said, not rising to the bait. "I just want to be sure. If we are to do this, I must take us away from this world first. I might not be able to get us out of trouble, if the worst should happen."

"We couldn't leave from here?"

"Sire," she said, as though this should have been obvious, "the technique you've spoken of will leave ripples through the worlds you pass. A trail that others could follow."

"Ah," I said, as understanding blossomed, "and one end of that trail could lead someone here. Your family's secret getaway."

"As it is, I'm not sure Father will be happy that I took you here. If others find this place..."

"Say no more about it," I said. "We'll leave after breakfast. You can take us to any starting point you like, and I'll lead on from there."

I wondered, though. The nature of Journeying, if I was understanding thrice-great Grandpa Ulfgar's journal correctly, was all about focusing on a goal-destination until reaching that goal-destination.

So anyone who knew this place existed could...

Oh. I might be the only member of the royal family who knew.

Made it even more understandable that the guards would attack me. They'd probably never seen a member of the royal house before.

Yes, even though she barely let me see any of the place, Tiksdottir took a big chance in taking me here. And I didn't doubt that her father would disapprove.

Strongly.

THE NEXT MORNING, WE ROSE BEFORE DAWN. OUT THE ... WELL, IT functioned as a window, so I'll call it one ... window in my recovery room, the sky was still on the dark side of gray as I dressed.

I opted for a rich, royal blue *tlikswul* shirt today, and dark gray pants of the same material. I wore the same good leather boots I'd been wearing recently. They seemed to do well with lots of walking, and that would be important.

According to the book, thrice-great Grandpa Ulfgar had ridden a horse when he traveled the Wolf's trail, but I hadn't grown up on horseback the way he had. I didn't want the distraction.

I wore a longsword by my side again, in place of the rapier. This wasn't a court function, and I was a little more comfortable with it. I stuck with the main gauche, though, since shields were cumbersome to carry.

Speaking of cumbersome, I had found armor in my locker, when I went through it a little more thoroughly over the past few days. Fine plate armor that appeared to have been crafted specifically for me. I only tried on the greaves and vambraces, but they were quite comfortable.

I particularly liked that the armor was enameled — at least, I was pretty sure it was enameling — in shades of gray to mimic a wolf's coat, with the royal sigil in gold over the heart.

Speaking of wolves, the helmet was done in the style of a wolf's head. Very cool.

Wearing armor though, even the most comfortable and attractive armor I'd ever owned, sounded like too much work, and too much like an advertisement for trouble.

Tiksdottir was wearing that faded black shirt again when she came in, along with her leathers, and her habitual sword and long knife.

I specifically looked for her knapsack, and didn't see one.

"Tiksdottir?" I asked.

"Sire? Something before we go?"

"Should we bring any food?" Admittedly, a strange question, since we both knew that there was food in my locker. Food which didn't appear to age or spoil.

"I have it covered, sire."

"Do you have a locker of your own then?"

"Nothing so grand or useful as that," she said, then gave me a mischievous smile. "Though I wouldn't mind holding onto a *few* secrets, if my prince will allow me."

"Of course," I said, shaking my head.

She turned then, called forth her power, and sent it into the doorway leading out of my room. She did this easily, and it seemed that while I'd been healing, she'd been recovering herself as well.

We stepped through the sheen of her power…

…and onto a crossroads.

The sky above was a pale blue backdrop for racing storm clouds.

The crossroads itself was bare dirt striped by wagon ruts, and stank of horses and hay and mud. A dead or dying yew tree hung limply nearby, with the remains of a rope dangling from one branch.

A stiff wind came up, smelling of rain.

Rain that was much needed by the area around us. From what I could tell, despite the smell of mud and oncoming rain, the land had been dry for far too long. Lots of cracked dirt and crops so badly failed I couldn't tell what they should've been.

Abandoned, perhaps. The whole area felt abandoned. Despaired. Even in spots that looked muddy, the mud seemed more like a mere smear across ground that had all but forgotten what water tasted like.

"Cheery place," I said.

"Should be easy to leave then, sire," Tiksdottir remarked.

"And it came easily to mind, did it?"

"What were we saying about secrets, sire?"

"Fair enough," I said.

Now. I'd been thinking over the last few days of what I might

Journey for. I needed something I really wanted to find. And I had too many ideas on that front.

I could go home and talk to Mom and Dad. That was tempting.

I could go near to home and talk to Denise. Show her what she was missing out on. But that was a bad idea and I knew it.

Truth was, if I went back to the Bay Area that I knew, and anyone was looking for me, I'd lead them right to Dad — which would have been bad enough, given that he was doing some kind of self-imposed exile — or to Denise, which would have been worse.

Whether they were looking to eliminate or manipulate me, anyone chasing me right now didn't need the leverage that Denise could afford them.

No, we weren't together anymore, but that didn't mean I'd let something bad happen to her.

Which meant there was only one place to go. At least, one place that was obvious to me, but hopefully wouldn't be obvious to anyone else.

I'd seen the battlefield where Uncle Karl fell. Hell, I'd half-lived his death with him. I should have no trouble finding it.

Or at least, as little trouble as I'd have finding anyplace else.

I tapped the tattoo on my chest. The physical reminder of my connection to the Great Wolf, which was inside me. Part of me, as I was part of it.

Him?

No. The Great Wolf was beyond gender, per se. If the Great Wolf was a he, it was because I was a he. For my cousin Richette, the Great Wolf was likely a she. So really, "it" should be a good...

I was delaying. Procrastinating.

Stop it.

The Great Wolf is a he because I am a he, and on some level, the Great Wolf and I are one.

I. Am. The Wolf.

And I sought the field where my uncle fell.

I'd considered seeking Uncle Karl's body, but that might just lead me back to Vol-Halá. After all, they'd probably recovered the body for the funeral.

A funeral I had to miss, because of politics and factions and bullshit.

I'd never really forgive the family for that.

But I could find the battlefield where my favorite uncle died. I could visit it, maybe learn something of his death.

Maybe even find this golden knight, and have a word or two with him…

Find the battlefield first, Volner.

I shoved the distracting thoughts out of my head. This might prove more difficult than I expected.

I puffed out a breath. Shook out my hands.

"All is well, sire?" Tiksdottir asked, while scanning for threats. I doubt she saw anything more threatening that the pair of vultures I could see circling in the distance. Circling what?

That didn't matter.

I was the Wolf. I had my goal. All I had to do was walk to it.

I focused down hard on everything I remembered about the dream where Uncle Karl died. The smell of blood and mud and offal. The cold, whipping wind. The crashing of steel and the screams of the wounded and dying.

I turned to the left and began to walk.

9

———————

I felt like a wolf on the prowl. Hunched forward slightly, arms bent. Loping, more than walking.

Tiksdottir followed behind me. I could feel her. I could smell her. But she didn't matter. Only the goal mattered.

Somewhere in the distance ahead of me was the battlefield where my beloved Uncle Karl died. Everything within me told me so. All I had to do was get to it.

Step after step.

I was only vaguely aware of the world around me as I went. I knew it was no longer a dried dirt road rutted by the wheels of countless wagons, running between cracked, abandoned farmland.

But what it was, was harder to describe.

It was as though I moved through a tunnel. A shifting, swirling tunnel of various shades of amber.

Translucent, after a fashion. With vague impressions of trees or mountains or buildings on the other side of the tunnel. Skies above that might've been pale blue or purple or green, for all I could tell their color, though they shifted from dark to light to dark with no apparent rhyme or reason that I could follow.

Perhaps, though, that was because my surroundings, the tunnel, the world or worlds beyond, they didn't really matter. Not now.

Only one thing mattered. One world. One battlefield. And every step brought me closer. Through space. Perhaps even through time.

My awareness of the tunnel and what lay beyond only mattered in one respect — every so often I needed to turn. I didn't understand why, except that I was making my route more true and direct than it had been the moment before.

Small changes, but necessary ones. Sometimes just to the left, others to the right, yet always, always getting closer to my destination.

It was exhausting. I felt as though I was dragging a five-hundred-pound block of ice, while steadily pushing through curtains that weighed two hundred pounds each.

I managed to barrel through the first few such curtains by enthusiasm alone. But then effort set in, over the next two dozen or so.

By the time I was passing the thirtieth or fortieth such curtain, I was sweating profusely and starting to burn in the legs and back and arms.

Another ten, and my legs were shaking. My lungs strained to get enough air. I felt lightheaded. My heart thumped as though protesting what I was putting my body through.

But I wasn't done.

One more.

Then one more.

Then one more.

I kept doing that to myself. Saying I would go just one more, and pushing the limit further and further away.

But I could only trick my body this way so long.

I finally collapsed, an exhausted, panting mess, at the bottom of a sand dune, under a dark purple sky filled with twinkling blue stars. I smelled the sea, and heard gulls and the gentle rising of the tide.

Sand immediately clung to my sweaty skin, and my whole body felt too warm from the way the *tlikswul* rid itself of my sweat.

Tiksdottir shoved food at me. Slices of that roast meat she'd wanted after pushing herself too far.

It didn't taste quite like beef. Closer to lamb, despite the texture, and the taste of prey animal awakened a powerful hunger in me.

I ate as fast as my desperate breathing allowed me. And Tiksdottir stood there, sword in one hand, watching for danger and feeding me slices of meat.

I sat up as soon as I was able, but my body wasn't happy about it. I felt as though I'd just fought in a dozen straight tournaments without even a break between fights. As though it wasn't just that every muscle in my body was exhausted — not to mention the kind of fogginess that comes with mental fatigue, though the meat was already helping with that — I swear I felt as though I should've been covered with bruises.

"You pushed too hard, sire," Tiksdottir said, though there was no judgment in her tone.

"I needed ... to see ... how far I ... could get us."

"Testing yourself," she said, "and pushing your powers. Those things are smart. But if we'd landed someplace hostile? What could you do about it, sire?"

"Fair enough," I said. "At least that doesn't seem to be the—"

"Drop your weapons!"

"—case."

That interruption had come from a man carrying what looked like a semi-automatic crossbow. The thing had a magazine of at least a dozen bolts, ready to go as fast as he could pull the trigger.

I wasn't feeling all that eager to get hit by a single crossbow bolt again, let alone a magazine's worth.

And it might've been more than that. This guy had friends. Four of them, melting out of the shadows. And all of them similarly armed.

Similarly armored, too, They seemed to be wearing cloth brigandine armor, with long skirts covering the legs, over cloth leggings and boots. They wore small, hat-style helmets, with spikes on the top.

"Sire?" Tiksdottir asked.

"Better do as the nice man says," I said aloud. Then, softer, added, "for the moment, at least."

She dropped her sword and long knife. I drew my sword and main gauche, and dropped those as well.

"Step away from them," their leader said, gesturing with his crossbow to make clear which direction he preferred.

We did this, while one of his friends collected our weapons.

"So," I said, "are you bandits then?"

He spat. "We are soldiers of the great Graf Korga. Who are you to come armed so close to his keep?"

So close to...

Oh.

Apparently my senses had been holding back on me, while I was desperately devouring those slices of roast something. Not a thousand feet off to my right, just where the dunes met some kind of farmland, I could see a rough, blocky castle.

Wasn't much to look at, given where I'd been only a few days ago, but it looked stand two stories tall, and had a strong stone wall surrounding it. The main keep looked pretty wide, too.

It also had scorpions are every corner of those walls, and two massive catapults on the top of the keep itself.

Yeah. People didn't mount weapons like those unless they either liked to fight, or had neighbors who liked to fight.

Either way, did sound as though we were headed for a fun conversation. People who kept siege engines on their castle also tended to have dungeons. And err on the side of paranoia.

All right. I was assuming. But I didn't think it was a stretch.

"Answer," one of the other soldiers said, gesturing with his crossbow. But the leader raised one hand for patience, before stabilizing his crossbow and turning his attention to us.

It occurred to me that if he started firing that thing, the bolt-changing mechanism would probably make it difficult to control. Harder to aim.

Of course, even if I was guessing right, I was in no position to take advantage of that. Not in my current state.

"We're travelers," I said. "We have no gripe with your graf."

"Pretty far from the road for travelers," one of the soldiers said to their leader. "More likely spies. Or scouts for Graf Cullen."

"Where are you headed?" the leader asked.

There are some questions you can hesitate to answer, and get away with it. "Where are you headed" is not one of them. Problem was, I didn't have a ready answer that I could explain. And if Tiksdottir had ever been to this world, she didn't know its geography well enough to suggest a destination.

So between us, we hesitated.

"Right," the leader said. "You're under arrest. The graf will hear you out. Turns out you're innocent, you'll be back on the road by midday tomorrow. Turns out you're not, well, I'm sure we don't have to tell you what happens to spies."

I was pretty sure I knew what happened to spies. I hoped I was wrong, but asking didn't seem like a winning option.

⸻

As I was already in a state of exhaustion, I'm pretty sure I made a bad impression on the soldiers as they marched Tiksdottir and me back to the graf's keep.

I did try reminding them that while they escorted us back, they were missing out on catching any *actual* spies or scouts they might have found if they let us go and continued their patrol.

The argument didn't carry much weight.

We found the graf at his dinner. He dined alone at a small stone table that had been filigreed within an inch of its life. The table was covered with many dining options, mostly involving meats and pastries, but with a token nod toward roughage in terms of a single plate of green vegetables.

I admit. The savory fragrance of his dinner set my mouth watering and my stomach rumbling. I was feeling better from those slices of roast whatever, but they hadn't been very filling.

The hall around the graf was stone, with the floor covered with rushes, and the walls with tapestries dedicated to the military prowess of either the graf's youth or his forebears. The hall was lit by a candelabra that had to have boasted at least a hundred candles.

Now, all that light might've been too much for a man who dined alone.

Except that he didn't *exactly* dine alone.

Oh, he was the only one seated at his table, and he was certainly the only one eating.

However, a string ensemble with a drummer played stirring music, heavy in its rhythms, while fourteen scantily clad dancers did their best to entertain and titillate the graf while he ate.

And the graf was an equal opportunity lech.

Both men and women did their dancing for him, with their bodies shaved and their skins oiled to shine under candlelight. None of them wore more than strips of clothing that offered peeks at what lay beneath every time they twirled.

And they twirled a lot.

The skin tones and hair colors of the dancers varied. Their builds did not. Whether he was looking at men or women, it seemed that the graf liked them slim and supple.

A large contrast to the graf himself, with extra emphasis on the large. Even sitting he was as tall as I was, and I suspected he'd stand nearly a foot taller than me if he stood.

He'd had big muscles in his youth, and while he looked as though he'd kept most of them under his heavy, noble finery, he'd layered them over with a solid layer of fat or three.

His skin looked as though he'd been riding the sands of his lands every day of his life. Weathered and dark. Though I couldn't tell if the latter was by birth or the work of the sun.

His hair and beard were black, though I thought they looked dyed.

When the soldiers escorted us in, a herald clapped his hands twice. The music stopped and the dancers moved to the sides of the room. Men to one side, women to the other.

The soldiers kept their crossbows on us the entire time. Even though the graf himself was armed, far as I was concerned. The bird leg he was currently gnawing on looked big and heavy enough to batter down stone.

He looked us over casually, while gnawing, before wiping his mouth and speaking in a rough, deep voice.

"What have you brought me, fist?"

Fist seemed to be his term for a sergeant.

"Scouts or spies, great one. Likely from Graf Cullen."

"We're neither scouts nor spies," I said. "We're travelers."

"Snail!" the fist said to me, thumping me in the back with his elbow. "You will not address the graf unless spoke to."

I was already in bad shape when that elbow hit. I staggered forward. Tiksdottir grabbed me.

And just that fast, we both were surrounded by the soldiers again.

"They claim to be travelers," the fist said. "But they could not name their destination."

"Traveling is its own reward," I said.

The fist raised the butt of his crossbow to punish me for speaking, but before it came down, I said, "I was answering you, not him."

The blow came anyway.

Floor, meet Volner.

I was starting to think that when I felt better, got maybe a better handle on my power, I was going to come back and clean this guy's clock.

In fact, I was getting downright angry about this treatment. Wasn't as though I'd done anything wrong. What right did they have to abuse me this way?

Me. A prince of the blood. A child of the Great Wolf.

How dare they?

That anger, it woke something deep down inside me.

Something that came out in a howl that carried me back to my feet. A howl so long and loud and terrifying that the dancers and musicians fled the room. Even the soldiers were staring wide-eyed, their crossbows dangling, forgotten.

And that howl gave my limbs a burst of power.

I seized the momentary advantage to grab my weapons again. I wasn't the only one moving, either. Tiksdottir had her weapons in a flash.

She turned to the soldiers.

I leapt over the table behind the graf. Before he could do more than budge his chair I had the point of my main gauche to his back, and the blade of my sword between his bird leg and his throat.

"Stop!" The graf called out. "Lower your weapons, men."

They did, though they didn't drop them.

"All right," I said, panting. That burst of power had cost me something, and I'd already drained my batteries pretty far that day. The world was growing red-tinged around the edges, and that wasn't a good sign.

And I didn't even want to think about the way my heart seemed to be staggering a bit as it sped.

"Let's everybody settle down," I continued. "Now, do you all agree that if I meant any harm to the graf, he'd be dead right now?"

Tiksdottir shot me a funny look, but went back to watching the soldiers.

"I agree," Graf Korga said. "Though you'd be dead a moment later."

"True," I said, "but wouldn't one of your own soldiers be willing to die, if his death bought the death of Graf Cullen?"

"Of course," he said, as though he had no doubts about his men. Made me wonder if they were really that devoted, or if the graf had a blind spot.

"So obviously we aren't working for your enemy, or you'd be dead. Right?"

"That ... does follow," he said, suspiciously.

"All right then," I said, lowering the sword but keeping my main gauche where it was. Just in case. "I hope you'll forgive this little demonstration, Graf Korga, but we really are just simple travelers. We planned nothing more covert than a night together on the beach before resuming tomorrow's portion of our quest to see the world."

"Well, that is a plan I can certainly imagine," the graf said, while managing to look both Tiksdottir and me over as though we were pastries on his plate. "Why didn't you explain that to my men?"

"I tried. They were too eager to insist that we were scouts or spies."

"You are fairly well-armed for travelers."

"The wide world can be a dangerous place."

"Very well," Graf Korga said. "Never let it be said that I am an unreasonable man. The two of you shall dine with me this eve, and share your romantic night together in my best guest room before going your way in the morning."

"Really," I said, "that's not necessary, great one."

"Oh, I insist," he said.

And just like that, all the soldiers were aiming their crossbows again.

Could I kill the graf before they killed me?

Yes. Unless he knew something I didn't know. Armor under his finery, perhaps? That might be, from a man who kept siege engines on his battlements.

The look in his eye was certainly unafraid.

I tried not to sigh as I sheathed my weapons.

"Then we really must accept," I said, forcing a smile.

As prison cells go, this one was pretty comfortable.

Oh, we weren't hauled away in chains or anything. Actually, we were escorted there by a page and only two of the soldiers, following a dinner that was ... filling, but uncomfortable as hell.

Tiksdottir and I were provided two simple fired-clay plates and a cup each, and seated on stools at the ends of the over-filigreed stone table. Which put us both in easy reach of the graf. A thought that was constantly on my mind, and kept me from paying any attention to the music and the dancing, when they started up again.

The food itself was simple, but pretty good. The cook knew his or her way around a spice rack, and had the timing down for roasting some six or seven kinds of meats.

The vegetables, on the other hand, were given all the attention of the afterthought that they were.

The pastries were all light, airy and too sweet for my taste, which was saying something. I mean, I was a kid who used to cover choco-late chip cookies with chocolate frosting from a can.

Food helped settle my system, though. And I went easy on the ale the graf provided. Didn't seem very strong, but I didn't want to chance that it just had a delayed kick.

While we ate, the graf didn't ask us questions about ourselves or our travels. Instead, he regaled us with stories about his victories in war. To hear him tell it, he was the supreme ruler of all the lands within a week's hard ride of the great ocean.

Of course, if he had a navy, he didn't mention it. Which suggested to me a serious martial lacking. At least, if anyone else in this world had a navy.

I did note that every story the graf told featured him leading from the very vanguard of his army. First to kill, and he claimed to boast the highest kill count in every battle he ever fought.

I couldn't help but wonder how much of that was trying to impress us, and how much was trying to make him feel better about the way we got the drop on him.

For that matter, he might have been trying to cover his own bout of Wolf Fear, which was what I came to call the terror that seized enemies when I howled just right.

By the time we were done, and the graf had ostentatiously selected five of the dancers to go to his chambers that night, I was convinced the we were going to the dungeons and not to the "guest room" he promised us.

Well, he was a man of his word, anyway.

What we were led to was clearly a corner guest room on the second floor, and likely the finest he had.

I noticed that the ascent to the second floor meant covering more stairs that I'd guessed. Two stories tall, this keep, but they were high-ceilinged stories.

The stone floor was well swept, and sweet smelling from herbs that hung from the ceiling. Sconces on the walls held candles, which the page lit with a taper from the impressively large fireplace.

And the fire was a good thing. The night air coming in through the windows, one on each of two walls, was pretty chilly. The page didn't close the wooden shutters on those windows, though. He moved as though he'd intended to, but one of the soldiers cleared his throat and the page changed his mind.

Two of the walls had no windows. Only tapestries depicting forest scenes with rivers. One where lovers locked in an embrace. The other featured a man (who looked suspiciously like Graf Korga) receiving pledges of love from a kneeling couple, dressed in finery...

Huh. That looked as though the couple should have been kneeling to offer wedding vows before a priest. But by their expressions, their words of unspoken adoration were aimed at the graf, not each other.

Quite an ego, this guy.

The room also had a good-sized bed with a mattress that seemed to be filled with down. As were the four pillows. The sheets and blankets were fairly soft.

I didn't actually want to use that bed, but I had to make a show of being impressed by it. So I oohed and aahed for the page, and Tiksdottir managed a faint blush, as though at the implications.

Apart from that, the only furniture was a basin of water, with three towels, a bar of what smelled like lye soap, and a small vial that looked like perfume of some sort.

We thanked the page — and through the page, the graf — for his hospitality, and made a show of raving about the room.

The last soldier out of the room closed the door. We heard a bar slide into place.

"Yeah," I said with a sigh, "I knew guests meant prisoners. Think he plans to execute us in the morning?"

"What was that stunt with the we-could-kill-you-if-we-want-but-we-don't, sire? With him as hostage, we could have escaped."

"I wasn't sure I could hold up my end of the fighting if it went wrong. Besides. How would we escape? You aren't ready to lead a Journey, and I'm certainly not."

"Did it ever occur to you, sire, that in my line of work I might know a thing or two about hiding from guards?"

"I..." I shut my mouth. Sighed through my nose. "I didn't even think about it. I'm sorry, Tiksdottir."

"Thank you, sire," she said with a slight bow.

"How bad is it?" I asked, walking over to the window, where she was scoping out the grounds.

"Sixty ... five foot drop straight down. No guards in the courtyard, but there are guards on the walls. Slow-moving patrol. More of those nasty-looking crossbows, though."

"Definitely rather not get hit by one of those," I said.

Tiksdottir huffed out an amused breath, her eyes on the patrol. Looked to me as though the patrol itself was only one guard per wall, though at the corner was a small, lit room.

The outer walls ran parallel, more or less, with the walls of the keep. So from our corner windows, we had decent views of two walls, and a good view of one corner. To see two more, we'd have to crane out the window, which might draw unwanted attention.

I was pretty sure, even without looking, that the other corners had more lit rooms, like the one nearest us did.

"More guards at the corners," I said.

"Yes," Tiksdottir said, not sounding concerned about that. "But no officers on the wall tonight. Or at least, if there's an officer in that one" — she pointed to the corner ahead straight ahead from our room — "he should be reprimanded. The two patrolling guards we can see aren't paying much attention, and they're movements are slow. Unhurried. As though sure they won't see any trouble tonight."

"Will they?" I asked, one eyebrow high.

"Of course not, sire," Tiksdottir said with a smile. "Perhaps it's time I show you what a royal messenger can do."

By the time I turned away from the window, Tiksdottir had a small, matte black crossbow in her hands. The bolt at the end was spiked, and it looked at though a kind of slender cable was tied to the back.

At the other end of the line was a small, folding grappling hook.

"Where did you get that?"

"Had it with me all along, sire," Tiksdottir said, but from the look of mischief in her eyes, she was enjoying showing me what she could do.

I nodded, accepting and respecting her secret, though I'm sure my smile told her how much I wanted to know how she did that, and what other tricks she had up her sleeve.

She carried the crossbow to the window on our righthand wall, but kept it low and safely out of sight. Why that window and not the other I didn't know, longed to ask, but knew better. This wasn't a time to bother her.

She waited until the guard passed the center of the wall.

She waited until he was three-fourths the way to the corner we could see.

She hefted the crossbow to her shoulder, took aim, and fired.

The bolt whizzed through the air, letting cable out behind it.

It slammed into the stone atop the wall. Not on the side, as I'd expected, but what looked to be a good stride in from the edge.

Tiksdottir attached the grappling hook to our window, and pulled out two short lengths of strong wire, with steel grips at each end. She handed one to me.

"You first, sire, and be quick about it."

I lost a moment giving her a puzzled look, but she shoved me toward the window.

I shook my head, drew a deep breath and — heart pounding so loud I was sure every guard in the keep would hear me — sat on the window with my legs out.

I felt as though I were about to be pincushioned by every soldier the graf had.

Just before Tiksdottir could complain that I was moving too slowly, I looped the cable over the grapple's wire, and hopped off the window.

The angle was a good one. Maybe forty-five degrees. Fast enough to keep us moving down at a good rate of speed.

Too good.

Yes, I liked the feel of the wind in my face, and blowing my hair hither and yon. But I didn't like the speed at which that very big and very thick wall was coming at my all-too-fragile person.

I wanted to yell. Or scream. Or maybe howl.

I didn't dare do any of it.

Faster and faster I went. Why?

Oh. I'd lifted my legs. That explained the bunching-muscles sensation through my core, and my glutes. I mean, the tension all through my arms was expected. But—

Here it comes!

My body was smarter than I was, it turned out.

By raising my legs that way, I didn't just slam bodily into the wall, but caught myself on my legs. I think my knees may have cracked in the process, but I was pretty sure all the tendons were holding.

I might just live to see the end of this craziness yet.

My lungs were now going so fast I thought they were trying to keep up with my heart.

Have to admit, though. I wasn't terrified. I was exhilarated.

I managed to scrabble quickly to the top of the wall, and lie down up there, keeping my eyes on the retreating guard. True to form, he hadn't heard or seen me.

Good thing I didn't tarry there on the cable. Tiksdottir was only a moment behind me, and rolled over onto wall with her weapons drawn.

"How do we retrieve the grapple?" I whispered.

"We don't," she said, giving me a look that made me think it was a stupid question.

The wall was about thirty feet tall. An improvement from the sixty-five feet of our window, but still not exactly an easy drop.

"Got another?" I asked.

"Yes," she said, "but I'm saving it. This way."

She turned and, keeping low, moved swiftly down the wall away from the retreating guard. I did my best to follow her, but I won't pretend I was even close to as graceful as she was.

Just as we got to the room at the corner, a miniature tower, if you will. Only one little story tall, but it had a scorpion on top, to make up the difference.

She pointed for me to mount a crenelation. I did, without giving it much thought. She knew what she was doing, after all. She'd been proving that pretty effectively.

She slipped up to the open doorway. Snuck a glance in.

Slipped inside.

I heard a couple of muffled thumps.

She leaned out of the doorway. Gestured for me to come in.

I did. There were three dead guards on the floor, each in a pool of his own blood. A table with some cards and coins, and a trapdoor that doubtlessly led to stairs.

She opened the trapdoor. Turned back to me.

"We're not going down?" I whispered.

She shook her head. "We're going to make them think we did. If we did, we'd have to deal with the guards at the gate, and they'd sound an alert. This way, they'll think we're still inside. It'll buy us running time."

"But the drop."

She smiled at me. Pushed me back out of the door and onto the wall. Not the side we'd come in through, though. The other side, where her timing had meant that the guard was walking the other direction, and paying us no mind at all.

I looked over the wall, still not liking the idea of a thirty-foot drop.

Then Tiksdottir was lowering a long, black rope.

"Where did that come from?" I whispered.

She only smiled and fished enough so that when we reached the end, we'd only have a drop of a foot or two at the most.

The rest of the rope she tied quickly around a crenelation. That left a good twenty feet left over, which I thought was a waste.

I almost said something, I admit. But I wanted to see where she was going with this.

"Down you go, sire. Quickly please."

I shook my head, hopped onto the crenelation, and started sliding down the rope as quickly as I dared. I used my boots, not my hands, as brakes.

The wind on my face felt even better on the way down. Felt like freedom. Smelled of sand and good sea air, too.

I landed with as soft a thump as I could manage, then quickly moved aside for Tiksdottir.

She tugged on the rope, and the knot unknotted itself. The rope slithered down into a coil on her arm. She glanced at me, one eyebrow high.

I turned away.

By the time I turned back, the rope was gone, and she was grinning.

I chuckled, and then we were both laughing as we ran off into the night.

10

———————

Energized by our escape — and possibly by that protein-heavy dinner with the graf — Tiksdottir and I ran late into the night.

We ran along the dunes at first, and then up among the farms, and then finally out through pastures.

We ran nonstop until we came to a river. A wide, slow-moving beast that fed three nearby farms, and at least two pastures.

At the river, we stopped. Panting. Smiling. Chuckling when we could. I wasn't even sure we knew what was funny anymore, except that we'd just survived a brush with death out in some unknown world, where neither of us could have just name-dropped our way out of trouble.

A death that we hadn't even done anything to earn.

Honestly, it was the most sobering lesson about the dangers of Journeying that I could imagine running across. Tiksdottir didn't even need to say anything about it this time, or call attention to any particular aspect.

The lesson was clear. I'd survived it, yes, but largely because she had been with me.

Which I had no intention of forgetting anytime soon.

I turned, to check for pursuit. I was sure that the graf's mean had to have realized by now that we were missing. It was only a matter of time before mounted soldiers came looking for us.

I didn't see any yet, though, and I got distracted by the cows in a nearby pasture.

Well, they weren't really *cows* the way I was used to thinking of cows. These things were hairier, a darker shade of brown, and had twisting horns. But they were sloe-eyed, and didn't care whether we were there or not. They just stood there, chewing grass, or possibly their cuds. So they were cows as far as I was concerned.

"How are you, sire?" Tiksdottir asked. "Up for swimming the river? We can probably catch some safe sleep among the leafy trees of that grove on the other side."

I shook my head. "No. I was thinking we shouldn't sleep until we're worlds away."

"Sire," she started, but I didn't need her to finish her sentence and I waved away her words to tell her so.

I already knew I'd pushed my store of magic to exhaustion not all that long ago.

I already knew I wouldn't be able to get us very far.

Hell, I already knew that I might hurt myself trying this.

But I figured *she* knew as well as I did that the graf wasn't going to take our escape well. He'd send out soldiers to scour the countryside until they found us.

If his territory truly extended a week's hard ride from that keep, then sleeping in a tree was no way to guarantee that he wouldn't find us.

Then again, I wasn't sure what other unknown capabilities Tiksdottir might have to keep the graf's men from finding us...

I cocked an eyebrow at her.

"Well, royal messenger?" I asked. "Does this mean you have some trick up your sleeve to guarantee that they don't find us while we're *both sleeping* in the trees?"

I cocked the eyebrow higher, in case she'd been planning to keep watch while I slept.

She frowned, shook her head and looked away.

"For myself, yes, sire. But not for us both."

"Then it's settled," I said.

Tiksdottir didn't look happy about it, but she bowed her head all the same.

I focused once more on my awareness of myself as the Wolf. On feeling my way towards the battlefield where my uncle Karl died. On the sights and sounds and smells I remembered from that battle.

And I began to lead us on a Journey, through a tunnel of amber once more.

On we went, past rivers and hills. Past farms and towns. Past seaports with great wooden ships, and a floating cloud city, ranging past snow-peaked mountains.

We traveled as the sky lightened, darkened, then lightened again in turns.

And all the while, I pulled against an unseen weight. Perhaps not as heavy as before. Perhaps heavier. Honestly, it's hard to remember that second Journey with precision. My own tiredness made it difficult, but my damnably strong focus made it more so.

In fact, I wouldn't be surprised if I'd managed to take us farther on that second Journey than I had on the first. Despite my exhaustion.

Not that I had any easy way of determining how far we'd traveled, in terms of worlds. It was just a feeling, really. Still. It was a feeling I could understand.

Part of it was that I'd recently called up the power of the Great Wolf within me, and that had restored my resources more than I'd originally thought, even while draining others of my resources.

I didn't understand how that worked. Not then.

Hell, to this day I'm not always sure whether calling the Wolf will give me more power or take more power from me when it leaves.

If it leaves.

The Wolf and I are one, but that oneness ... is strange and unpredictable at times. I know there's a balance to it. I'm just not sure how that balance works, exactly.

In fact, I think that's part of the reason that most of the family prefers the modern forms of Journeying over greatest grandpa's old method of walking the Wolf's trail.

The modern methods are more predictable in what they take out of us.

Another reason I might have carried us further across the worlds was that I'd regained a not inconsiderable amount of power, thanks to that roast meat I'd snacked on. The slices Tiksdottir had fed me while I lay exhausted at the foot of that sand dune, back before the soldiers found us.

That meat is special. It's restorative, in terms of the power of Journeying. It helps us recover quickly when we've pushed too far. And for one of the Wolf's blood, it's even more effective than it is for, say, a Tiksdottir.

I didn't even know all that for certain, yet, but I was making the right associations, and reminding myself to ask her about the meat later. Which I did.

Those were the two reasons I felt competent to try Journeying again that night, as well as the two reasons I may have taken us even further than I had on my first attempt.

It may even have been the benefit of experience. Having already done it once, I knew I could, and I knew what to expect in terms of difficulty.

The point is, I carried us as far as I felt I could go, through worlds and past worlds, surrounded by a tunnel of shifting shades of amber.

I stopped, though, before I would reach so dire a limit as I'd reached last time.

And when I stepped out of the amber tunnel and into a world once more, I found myself on a cobblestone street. A narrow street, between small stone houses with thatched roofs. Mountains rose high and dark in the distance, all around.

Torches burned at street corners, lighting up the dark night. Besides the torches, I could smell horses, though only tracers of their leavings. And none of the urine and other bad smells I might expect in a town that looked as medieval to me as this one did.

I also smelled woodsmoke from chimneys, which suited the chilly evening air.

The sky above was clear, and star-filled, with a crescent moon. The color of the night sky was tough to tell, beyond black. It reminded me of the night sky in the world where I'd grown up.

Why, I could almost have believed that a yellow sun would rise in a blue sky, come morning.

I heard the easy clopping of approaching hooves not too far away. Turning, I saw a pair of riders making their unhurried way down the street toward Tiksdottir and me.

One of the riders held a torch aloft. Both wore chain armor under tabards that showed a field of yellow-and-black checks.

They also carried cudgels.

"What do you think?" I panted to Tiksdottir.

She looked me up and down, a critical eyebrow high.

She didn't need to say anything, and she knew it. I was drenched in sweat, even with the *tlikswul* working for all it was worth. My muscles were strung out. My heart was going double-time, and so were my lungs.

If we were in for a fight, I wasn't going to be worth much.

I noted, though, that I didn't feel as enervated as I had when we reached those dunes.

"Hail," one of the guards said. As with the world of Graf Korga, they weren't speaking English, but I had no trouble understanding their speech, and responding in kind.

"Good evening," I said. "We've arrived in your town rather late, I fear." I shook my head. "We're both tired to the bone, but neither of us can spot an inn. Could you direct us?"

They looked at each other. Held a quick, hushed conversation.

"Have you come by way of the southern mountains?"

Was that a hint of suspicion in his voice?

"No," I said, hoping it was the right answer. "The pass was more westerly than that."

"From Honsbad, then?"

That might've been relief in his voice...

"By way of Honsbad, yes."

They nodded, a little more relaxed.

"Try the Cock and Crow," the one with the torch said. "Just one street over, and down two more to your right."

We thanked them, and — wonder of wonders — they went on their way without doing anything suspicious, or even trying to attack us.

The night was looking up.

———

THE COCK AND CROW WAS A LITTLE ISLAND OF HEAVEN IN A TRULY chaotic day.

It was a downright nice little place, in every sense of the word. Two story. With a solid stone foundation, but a softwood overlay that had been stained to a bright, cheery color. The same woods and stains had gone into all the furniture, from the bar to the tables and benches, to the frames of the beds in the bedrooms.

Very clean, the whole place, and staffed by a very friendly, smiling family of four. Two large parents, and two slender children, a boy and a girl. Though really, I should call them a young man and a young woman, because they looked to be almost as old as I was at this time.

The patrons were friendly, but Tiksdottir and I didn't pay them much mind, once we determined that none of them intended to fill us with crossbow bolts or stab us with, well, anything at all.

Except maybe kindness. They seemed the type.

We were quickly given two rooms, and each room had a big feather bed of its own, as well as plenty of water and a large copper bathtub.

Tiksdottir practically moaned with pleasure when she saw the bathtub. Me, I took one look at the bed and said goodnight.

I woke hours later, to find that someone had tucked me in — no, no one had stripped me, I was still fully dressed — and that a fire was going. Water was even heating for a bath, if I wanted one.

And I admit, when morning came, I wanted one.

I bathed with flower-scented soap. I shaved as well, and did my best to wash my hair without the kinds of shampoos and conditioners I was used to.

I donned fresh *tlikswul* clothing from my locker. A shirt of bright red, but tight pants of a dark gray. Kept the same boots, though. I was growing fond of them.

Tiksdottir, though, wore her same clothes when I met her in the hallway outside our rooms. Her clothes didn't smell as though she'd been wearing them through our misadventures the way mine had.

I wondered about that, but decided that, if I'd asked, she would only have answered with a smile.

Then again, she seemed to like giving me that smile...

I considered the question further, as we went down the wide stairs to the main room, to break our fasts. We were the only patrons at this early hour. In fact, we got the first loaf of morning bread, straight from the oven.

Oh, but it was delicious. Sweet and fragrant, and mixed with some kind of honey and nuts right in the dough. Barely needed anything to go with it, but they still gave us plenty of crispy bacon.

Of course, one reason for their speedy service might've been that we'd paid in advance, with gold. But I wasn't going to question it.

I was being waited on while we sat on our own at a long table, and I was going to let myself enjoy the friendly service before we took to the Wolf's trail once more.

So I ate my fill of bacon and bread, along with some cheese that was fresh, and reminded me of muenster.

And when we were ready to go, all four members of the family came out to wish us the best in our travels.

I had to stop and ask their names then, though they gave me only their family name. Fenk. Which was enough.

I had every intention of remembering this place. I would want to visit it over and over through the years. My own little haven of peace among the tumult of my life.

As we left, I commented to Tiksdottir, "Funny, how life works."

"Sire?"

"Well, look at this place."

I gestured first to the inn, and then to the clear blue sky. The friendly farmers just now carting their vegetables down the street to the town center, but still with enough time to give us a smile, a wave, and wish us good mornings.

"This place is amazing. It's like something out of a storybook. The kind of village where nothing bad ever happens. Oh, bad things probably happen one town over, or on the road through the mountains, or something like that."

I pointed to the cobblestones beneath us. "But not here. This is the place that hears the stories of wrongs, but doesn't have them happen here."

"Stories have places like that?"

"Of course," I said, chuckling. "You need a happy place to contrast all the badness that happens to the characters."

She frowned. "I guess I never thought about it that way."

"And here it is, come along just when we needed a break. Talk about coincidence."

Tiksdottir burst out laughing. Loud and clear enough that the nearest farmers turned and smiled, caught up in her humor without even knowing why she was laughing.

Come to think of it, I wasn't sure why she was laughing either. And I'm pretty sure my confusion was all over my face.

"I'm sorry, sire," she said, the picture of contrition. Although that picture was a little fuzzy, what with the smiling and the slight laughter still in her voice. "I assumed you meant that in jest."

"Why would I joke about that?"

"Because this is a waystation in a Journey, sire," she said, as though it were the most obvious thing in the world. A tone she took, I noted, with more frequency than I really liked.

I couldn't blame her for that. But I did resolve to do something about my stirring levels of ignorance. Though I could only learn so fast.

When she saw by my expression that her words were inadequate explanation, she continued.

"On a Journey, sire, barring interference from another power, everything is the result of the work of the Journey's leader. Those dunes in the graf's land, and his soldiers. I cannot be certain without knowing the depths of your mind, but we likely encountered those because of your fixation on a battlefield."

"We found a battle," I said, with rising understanding. "Or nearly one."

"Exactly, sire. And last night, though no doubt you intended your focus on that same battlefield, your need for rest" — she gestured to the Cock and Crow — "led us here."

"Then my subconscious mind is smarter than my conscious mind," I said.

"True for us all, sire."

And with that happy thought, I began the Journey anew.

———

MY THIRD ATTEMPT AT JOURNEYING WENT EASIER THAN EITHER OF THE first two. Maybe it was the good night's sleep and full belly. Or maybe it was just my growing power and experience. I wouldn't have a real sense of that until I had time to sit and re-read *Trails of the Wolf* to learn more about greatest-Grandpa's experience.

But I wouldn't have that chance for a while.

Anyway, as I led Tiksdottir through the tunnel of shifting shades of amber away from the Cock and Crow and towards the battlefield where Uncle Karl had died, I felt as though I were dragging less of a heavy weight behind me.

Instead of maybe five hundred pounds, it now felt more like maybe two hundred fifty.

And those curtains I seemed to be continually pushing through? Instead of weighing a good two hundred pounds each, they now felt closer to a hundred pounds each.

Easier going. And compared to the last two Journeys, this time I felt almost as though I were walking downhill.

We reached the battlefield that day. I wish I could tell you how long that took, but I told you I'd be honest as I went through this story. And I'm not going to start lying to you now.

So let me say something about time and Journeying.

It's difficult to keep track of time when passing between night and day in a series of steps. All those darkenings and lightenings of the sky outside the amber tunnel, far as I could tell, those were night skies and day skies of different worlds.

Which meant I was either traveling through time at accelerated rates while walking the Wolf's trail. Or different time flowed at different rates in different worlds.

Talking to Tiksdottir later confirmed for me that it was the latter. That each world had its own relationship with time.

Which meant that, while Journeying, the only chance I had at keeping time meant relying on my own internal time sense.

My *biological* time sense.

See, we have, each of us, a kind of internal clock. The beat of our hearts. It's not as simple as a timer ticking away the seconds or minutes or anything like that. It beats at an irregular rate.

Well, it's more or less a *regular* rate for most of us — excepting those with medically irregular heartbeats — but the point is that while it normally beats *steadily*, it doesn't beat *predictably*. Sometimes it speeds up because of excitement or effort, or it slows down for sleep. It speeds or slows little bits here and there for any number of reasons, but it does its best to be regular about it.

And that attempt at regularity means that, in a sense, we all have inside ourselves a personal timeline. The measure of our lives.

If the normal human lifespan is maybe eighty to a hundred years — as it was when I left the world where I grew up — then each beat of a person's heart is a sliver of that lifespan which could, in theory, be counted, measured, and have a value assigned in terms of a person's absolute internal clock ticks.

Got all that?

Good.

Now throw it out.

Yeah, I know. That sounds like I'm not playing fair. But I'm trying to explain all of this to you the way it occurred to me. And as I tried to figure out how to keep time while Journeying, I made the mistake of falling into this trap. Of thinking in terms of my heartbeat as the ticking of my personal clock, and what each beat might mean in terms of time.

Problem there comes down to one thing.

I won't die of old age.

See, in theory, I'm going to live forever. Unless I die on a battlefield someday, or unless someone decides they're sick of me being around, and is smart enough and focused enough to take my life.

So all those heartbeats? They have no time value for me.

In fact, the way my circulatory system works isn't *quite* the way it works for a normal human.

See, normal human beings, they have a cap for how fast their heart can beat before it seizes up on them in a heart attack.

Those of us who are children of the Wolf, though, we can't have heart attacks. So there is no theoretical upper limit to our heart rate. Depending on how hard we push ourselves.

And that brings us back to the practical limits of our bodies, beyond the theoretical limits.

See, we do have limits. But they have more to do with how hard we push ourselves and how fast. How much we train ourselves to do, and how well we maintain that training.

It is actually possible for us to work ourselves to death. I think. Certainly that was what Tiksdottir had tried to warn me about, back by the river.

Yeah, I could push myself to ridiculous lengths, as I came more into my power. But if I tried to do too much too fast, I could burn myself out. Or at least weaken myself to the point that someone would have an easy time taking my life.

Just as bad, far as I was concerned.

So, I'm afraid that gauging time while Journeying really came down to one thing for me.

How soon did I need to stop to eat?

Eating while Journeying just wasn't possible for me at that stage. I couldn't keep my focus on the Wolf's trail, while chowing down on bread or a piece of fruit, let alone a slice of meat.

No, not even a slice of that special roast meat we call *vulfaa*, or the Wolf's Gift.

So for me, a Journey's length was measured by rests and meals. Unless I reached the end of my Journey.

Frankly, between the two of us, I think that time issue is another reason that most of the family avoids the Wolf's trail approach. Because time gets ... fuzzy. Different worlds have different relationships with the flow of time, and most of the family keeps appointments. Either back home, or on politically important worlds.

Tough to keep an appointment, if you don't know how long it'll take you to get there. Or, worse, if you're traveling somewhere else first.

Anyway, this is why I don't know exactly how long it took me to reach the battlefield where Uncle Karl fell.

But I did reach the battlefield that day. In the sense that I reached it after leaving the Cock and Crow, but after only one short meal break, under the boughs of a great, spreading oak tree atop a small hillside. Hardboiled eggs and crisp pairs under a late evening sky, with the stars just starting to come out.

I do know, for whatever it was worth, that the sky outside the amber tunnel had gone from light to dark and back three or four times between the Cock and Crow and the moment when I stepped out of the amber tunnel and onto the remains of the battlefield where Uncle Karl fell.

It was late afternoon when we arrived. The sun was getting close to setting over a series of vicious-looking mountain peaks, maybe a half-day's march to the west.

Icy wind cut across us, coming from the west, and it still smelled of death. The skies above roiled with storm clouds, menacing that at any moments they might loose their heavy loads.

The field beneath us was covered in caked, dried mud. Redder in spots than it would have been naturally. Whatever grasses or whatever had once been there had long since been battered down by countless boots and hooves.

The battle was long over. The armies were gone. Their tents were gone. Even their bodies had been looted and carted away.

We stood there, alone.

Heat flashed through my head.

I could see him again.

No. Not Uncle Karl. I could see the last moments of his life. That knight on the huge steed. Both clad in gold, and both with golden unicorn horns as part of their armor.

That mace, so large the knight needed two hands to wield it.

The thunder of his hooves. The heft of his swing.

Closer.

Closer.

Closer...

I opened my eyes to discover that I was crouched and clutching my head, keening. My skin was hot all over, and my heart thundered like those hooves had...

Hooves?

"Sire," Tiksdottir said, voice warning, "we have company."

Men in plate armor, riding our way. Each armed with a lance.

And leading them, that golden knight.

I STILL HAD ECHOES OF UNCLE KARL'S DEATH ROLLING THROUGH MY head as I watched his killer approach. The ground beneath me seemed mud and blood soaked.

Except it wasn't. The mud and the blood had all dried and caked, even if the grasses that once grew here were a long way from recovering.

The smells of blood and offal had faded, though the smell of death lingered on the cold wind.

And the killer. The golden knight. He wasn't a mere dozen or so strides from me, hefting his two-handed mace.

He was riding towards me — the real, living me, not the past, dead Uncle Karl — from the west, with that icy wind at his back, as well as the slowly setting sun above him.

And this time, the golden knight was not alone. He was flanked by three more knights to each side. All riding warhorses — though none so big as the golden knight's — and all with lances pointed my direction.

And it was at me those lances pointed. Not Tiksdottir, standing beside me. A mistake on their part. Or at least, I thought so at the time.

I was torn about what to do. Part of me, the part still reeling from re-experiencing my uncle's death, wanted me to turn and flee back along the Wolf's trail.

Mind you, I don't know how easy that would have been to do. True, I didn't feel so spent and exhausted as I had the previous times I'd stopped for any length of time. I probably was capable of the Journey, magically speaking. But I wasn't sure how easily I could find the Wolf's trail in my current state.

My thoughts were too focused on my uncle's killer. Who was already riding my way. I couldn't have thought of anywhere else to go if I tried.

So the Wolf's trail was closed to me, far as I was concerned.

Which was just as well, because the rest of me wanted to draw down on this son of bitch and avenge my uncle.

I could already imagine drawing my sword and cutting his steed out from under him. I didn't have anything against the horse, but cutting that horse's legs away would send the golden knight tumbling, and give me one good, clear shot.

I wasn't mounted or armored. I needed every advantage I could snatch.

Mind you, though. Even with my blood burning for revenge, I knew this didn't sound like a smart move. There were two of us against seven of them, and they were already armored, with weapons in their hands.

So I tried to deny the fire in my veins. The racing of my heart. The clench of my jaw. The ready tautness of my limbs, and the itching in my palm.

Or, rather, I tried to let these things give me a haughty, even arrogant look as I crossed my arms and awaited the golden knight.

He didn't keep me waiting long.

"So," he said, and his voice came clear, though higher in pitch than I expected. And he wasn't addressing me, but his fellows. "It seems we've found a poor lost wolf cub, all alone."

Wow. An immediate slam on both my family and my companion. Not doing much to cool my thirst for vengeance.

"I've come to see about the death of my uncle," I said.

"Aw, listen to the wolf cub yip," he said, and his fellows chuckled. "He thinks he's fierce."

"Sire," Tiksdottir said softly, "now might not be the best time for this."

"Your insults do you little credit," I said, focusing on the golden knight. "And your arrogance even less."

"Truly?" the golden knight replied, amusement all through his voice.

His fellows chuckled. The tips of their lances never wavered.

"I had come here only to investigate my uncle's death," I said, "and learn the truths behind it." I shook my head. "And here I see his killer, acting not as though my uncle's death were a mere casualty of war, as it had seemed, but in fact an assassination."

"His yips *almost* mimic sensible speech," the golden knight said. "But I must be mishearing him. There's certainly no way he could be about to challenge me to a duel."

"As a matter of fact," I said, though Tiksdottir tried to stop me, "I *am* challenging you to a duel."

The golden knight *tsked* at me as though I were a foolish child.

"No," the golden knight said. "In another place and at another time, I might acknowledge your right to challenge me, wolf cub. But here, all the power is mine. And you" — the golden knight shook his head — "you are not worth my time."

"I am a prince of the royal house of Vol-Halá. I have every right to this challenge."

"And yet, I can tell by the look on your face that you do not know my name or my house." The golden knight shook his head. "Thus, your challenge is beneath notice. Take them."

And with that all six of the other knights moved their lances to within inches of my body and Tiksdottir's.

I didn't want to be taken. Damn it. Last time it was crossbows, this time lances, but I was getting sick and tired of wandering into packs of armed men who were only too happy to take me prisoner.

Unfortunately, I couldn't see any way to avoid it. And getting myself injured right now would only make the situation worse.

"Take the weapons from their belts," the golden knight said. "If they have others, leave them. I'm not so concerned about the wolf cub as all that."

The arrogance of the golden knight seemed boundless. To think that I would somehow be helpless without my sword.

Then Tiksdottir and I were disarmed and forced, at lance point, to mount behind two of the knights.

Their armor was thick, and I couldn't spot any good weak spots where I could thrust a dagger.

So ... maybe the golden knight had a point, once our longer blades had been taken from us?

I glanced over at Tiksdottir, to see if she had any great tricks in mind, for getting us out of this.

She shook her head. But she hesitated before doing so. And she bit her lip, just the slightest bit.

I'd come to know her pretty well in our travels. From what I could tell, those little tells meant that she did indeed have a weapon that could probably take down one of the knights.

She was right not to go for it, though. After all, there would be five others, plus the golden knight himself.

To make matters worse, they moved into a formation that left armed knights in front of us, behind us, and to each side. With the golden knight riding in the lead. Not exactly a great position for us, when it came to launching an escape.

They then turned their mounts about and began riding back toward those cruel-looking mountains.

"I told you," the golden knight remarked casually to the rider nearest him. "I sensed someone using the older style of Journeying. I couldn't believe it myself, of course. To think that anyone could be so foolish as to dare approach my home in so blatant a fashion."

The golden knight glanced over at me, though I could not see his expression, of course, behind his helmet's closed visor.

"I should have known it was just some wolf cub, newly into his power." To me he added, "Tell me truly, boy. That's the only way you know how to Journey, isn't it? To hike the old trails?"

I said nothing, but even that was the wrong answer, because the knight and his fellows all began to laugh.

At that, they sped their horses to a gallop, and spoke no more as they rode.

I DID MANAGE TO LEARN A FEW THINGS AS WE RODE TO THE FOOT OF those sharp, angry mountains, and along a pass between them.

First, the knights were following the lead of the golden knight. Not just that they obeyed his orders as commander, either. The golden knight didn't consider me a threat, so neither did they.

I didn't once spot any of them actually checking on me, the whole ride. Not that I could think of anything useful to do, other than study my captors.

All right, that's not quite true. I did slip a dagger from in my boot to up my sleeve. Just in case an opportunity to use it came up. But thick and well-made as their armor was, I doubted it would.

For travel, we rode in a top-heavy diamond formation with the golden knight at the apex. Five knights rode in the rank behind him. From left to right, was a knight, then the knight riding with Tiksdottir, then a knight, then the knight riding with me, then a knight.

Trailing behind us and forming the bottom point of the diamond was the last knight.

Not so tightly surrounded as we could be. Was that a sign of confidence in each other? Or an indicator of something else?

I wondered about the knight trailing behind. That *could* have been a rear guard position. Which would be respectable. Except this was the empty remains of a ruined battlefield. They considered themselves safe from all threats here, including us.

Not to mention that visibility in all directions was high. I could see clear to rolling fields to the east and north, and what looked like the start of a forest far to the south.

Nothing like a threat anywhere nearby.

Which meant that the trailing knight was being punished for something.

Interesting. And hopefully useful.

I noticed also that all the knights except their leader bore a unicorn heads sigil, done in gold and within a circle of gold, on the left shoulder of their armor.

So the unicorn had to be the sigil of this house. I wondered if I was supposed to recognize that. If the house with the unicorn was supposed to be important. One of the twelve major houses, maybe...

I thought back to meeting the high queen. I'd been in the room where the diplomats from all twelve of the other kingdoms gathered.

Each royal family had a tapestry in that room, with its royal sigil.

Was there a unicorn?

...I couldn't remember. I'd been too focused on meeting Garrison and my greatest grandmother. I just hadn't thought I'd need to study those tapestries.

The only thing I knew for certain was that Tiksdottir would recognize the unicorn sigil. I mean, that was part of her job, wasn't it? To know every major royal house, its crest, motto, and all that jazz? She was a royal messenger, after all. She'd need to know these things to avoid committing faux pas while operating in the name of the high king.

But what if the unicorn sigil didn't belong to any of the twelve?

What did that mean? Could it be the sigil of the royal house of Nulac O-Shantí?

I doubted it. In fact, the more I played it around in my head, the more I doubted that the unicorn was the sigil of either the Nulac or of any of the twelve.

Clearly, whatever house the golden knight represented, he wanted me to think that house was important. I had no doubt about that. But the more I thought about it, the more it seemed to me that the odds were, as far as Vol-Halá was concerned, the house of the unicorn wasn't a major house.

Yes. That tracked.

The attitude of the golden knight seemed to me as excessively dismissive of my family. That smacked of jealousy.

And yet, if Uncle Karl died fighting in a battle for the family — a battle against some major house — then where was his support? Surely the armies of Vol-Halá wouldn't simply abandon whatever they'd been fighting for, just because the enemy had managed to kill a prince of the blood.

If anything, that would be *more* reason to come back and wipe out the golden knight and his armies.

After all, my family could possibly afford to lose a battle now and then. And even the occasional prince.

But royal families that don't avenge their losses don't stay royal very long.

Back home, factions of the family were fighting for power. Which meant they didn't think they had to defend themselves from an outside threat.

Which meant the golden knight, whatever his house, was an unknown threat. Which excluded the Nulac O-Shantí, as well. The Nulac were a known threat.

Or had been, a long time ago...

No. Their return had to have been known about by the family.

At least, if their return hadn't been known about when Uncle Karl died, Tiksdottir would certainly have carried the word after Nulac assassins tried to kill me.

Had she told anyone at the royal castle?

No. She hadn't bothered. What was more, *I'd* mentioned them to Cassiel, who'd seemed impressed that we'd killed them — sort of — but he didn't seem shocked at the notion that I'd had to fight Nulac assassins.

So the golden knight couldn't have been Nulac.

Which meant he was something else entirely. A threat the family didn't know about. Either an old threat returning, or a new threat rising. And if the family was caught up fighting internal struggles, then the golden knight represented a greater threat still.

These were the things I thought about was we rode past waypoints and guard posts, and were waved on without the slightest check, past the foothills of those cruel-looking mountains and into the mountain passes.

I supposed we were simply waved on because if anyone managed to kill the golden knight and steal his armor, those guards at the waypoints and posts, with their chain armor and their swords and short bows, wouldn't have been a match for the killer anyway.

I counted the guard posts though. And the waypoints. I noted how many guards I could see at each, and how they were armed, and how much attention they paid to their duty.

Far as I was concerned, I was now officially the head scout in charge of surveilling of a new enemy for Vol-Halá.

I'D COUNTED TWO MAJOR WAYSTATIONS AND SIX MINOR GUARD POSTS — more than thirty soldiers on reasonably attentive duty — by the time we made our way out of the narrowest pass of the lot. A pass only wide enough for the horses to ride single file between high cliff walls.

Yeah, this was defensible as hell. Especially since I could spot ledges up above where a series of men with piles of rocks could hold off an army of weeks.

Still. How on earth did shipments of goods come and go? No way they could get a cart down this narrow, cragged, rocky pass. Let alone a whole caravan.

Something more to ponder as we came out of the pass at last. It opened onto a road that would lead us down along a series of switchbacks into valley.

The sky was bright blue overhead. Apparently the high, sharp peaks of all those mountains kept the storm clouds from menacing this beautiful little valley.

And I had to admit, it was a beautiful valley. Lush and green. Maybe twice as long as it was wide. Most of it dedicated to farmland and pastures, though I could pick out at least three towns.

The towns were located, naturally enough, along three rivers that came down out of the mountains to feed a large lake in the center of the valley.

Standing tall beside that lake, a gray stone keep that I felt sure was our destination.

All roads in the valley came from that keep. Out to the towns. Out among the farms. Out into the forest of ... some variety of deciduous trees at the west end. And most importantly, to the passes in and out of the valley, at the north and south ends.

Ah. There. I could see a wide, easy road leading out of the valley to the north.

Well, the road was easy. But a keep sat right at the entrance to the pass. In fact, it looked to have been built around the entrance to the pass, enabling its castellan to close off traffic entirely.

Looked fairly defensible. Though from this far away, it wasn't hard to look defensible. If I could get closer, I might spot a flaw, or an opening.

Lacking the chance to study that distant keep, though, I turned my attention to the valley itself.

I guessed the valley to be about three days long by no more than two days wide, at the cantering speed we'd been riding.

Without the icy winds, the air was pleasant, made more so by the fresh, sweet scent of some kind of grain growing from the farms nearest to where we came down out of the pass.

Practically bucolic, this valley. But that didn't make sense. The golden knight had recently fought what I presumed was a major battle. Certainly felt like one from my brief exposure to it. So where was his...

Ah. There.

Out on the other side of the gray castle beside the lake, I spotted the tents and fires of an encamped army.

So he had withdrawn from the field as well. After the death of my uncle, which, I assumed, was the last battle.

But the army my uncle had been supporting. Where had they come from? Where had the survivors fled to? Where they elsewhere in this world? Or had they fled by some Journey power?

The golden knight. He'd spoken of sensing my approach along the Wolf's trail. So he had the power of Journeying. But who else here did?

Too many questions, and not enough answers. For the moment, I had to settle for learning what I could on this ride.

Still. It was worth noting that, when I escaped — and I had to think of it as *when* and not *if* — I might be able to find aid without even leaving this world.

As we approached the gray stone keep, I wasn't all that impressed. Yes, it stood four or five stories tall, with a handful of towers going even higher, but it was nothing compared to the royal castle at Vol-Halá.

Further, it didn't look all that defensible. No wall. Not much in the way of parapets. Only a token guard presence, apart from the nearby army camps.

Seemed to me that if anyone managed to get past the keep at the north end, this castle would be ripe for the taking.

I smiled. Tiksdottir had emphasized before that how well she knew a place made a difference in her ability to Journey there. And now both she and I were getting plenty of opportunity to study the golden knight's home.

Which meant that either one of us would be able to bring forces straight here, bypassing that keep at the north end entirely.

Of course, the golden knight would know that. Which meant he wasn't likely to let us out of here alive.

Not by choice, anyway. Though our chances might've been better than I'd been crediting them. I'd noticed that the armor the knights were wearing had a flaw. When they raised their arms, there was a small gap at the edge of the breastplate.

A smaller gap than most plate armor I'd seen in my western martial arts classes, but more than enough to drive a dagger into. And a dagger of a decent length — the one hidden up my sleeve was the length of my hand — might even be able to reach the lung.

The question, now, was when to go for it...

Not anytime soon, alas.

As we approached the castle, more knights came out to meet us, filling out our formation, while the two at the wide ends of our line filled them in on who I was. If they mentioned Tiksdottir, I didn't hear them.

I was ready when the taunts and jeers began. I'd like to think I weathered them with stoic nonchalance.

By this point, I'd been hoping for a good look inside the golden knight's keep. Maybe his main hall. That would be a perfect place to pick for an endpoint to a Journey. Just skip the armies entirely and lead a squad straight into his home.

And I figured he might take us there. Show us off to his court. Maybe mock up some trial and convict us of something, so he could hold a formal execution.

Apparently he had something else in mind.

We rode around to one side of the keep. The only people near us now were armed. Mounted knights, as well as a handful of soldiers in chain armor and half-helms, armed with spears or halberds.

A knight cleared the soldiers away, loudly ordering them all back to their duties. I did, though, notice that men and women appeared to serve equally in this army. In fact, the knight who ordered the soldiers away was a woman.

Not a surprise, you understand. Just more information to bring back to the high queen. Or the high king, if he'd returned by the time I got back.

Around the side of the keep, toward the back, I could see a separate entrance that clearly led to the dungeons below.

The entry door was some thick, solid hardwood, with not only a key lock, but also bars available on both sides to keep that door shut.

Inside, cold, heavy stone for the tight stairs down. Already I could smell must, mildew, rats.

We went down there single file in the close conditions. Even the ceiling was low enough that I could have touched it without trying.

One knight — the knight who'd been trailing us on the ride here — took the lead, carrying a torch. Then me, with another knight one step behind. A dagger in his right hand and my arm in his left. Tiksdottir followed, guarded the same way by another knight. Then the golden knight himself. Finally, one more knight, with a second torch.

It looked to be a long flight of stairs. About halfway down I made my move.

The knight holding my arm had his visor up and was watching his feet on the stairs. When he was mid-step, I twisted my arm and whirled in place.

He lost his grip. Brought up his dagger, but his strike was slow. He was off-balance.

I grabbed his dagger arm and threw him down the stairs at the lead knight.

They had no room to dodge. As I turned away, drawing my dagger, I heard them crashing their way down the steps.

The shadows went wild as the lead torch went tumbling away with them.

On instinct I flattened against the wall.

Smart move. Tiksdottir dumped a dead knight down the stairs past me.

The dead knight's sword in her hand and my dagger in mine, we turned to face the golden knight.

He drew a short sword, and inwardly I moaned. His sword was

much better suited to these conditions than the one Tiksdottir had stolen from the knight.

"Keep him busy," I said, turning my focus on the huge, spreading oak where Tiksdottir and I had shared a meal what now felt like weeks ago.

I tried to reach for it. To open the Wolf's trail toward it here on the stairs.

But something seemed to be holding me back.

Blocked. I was being blocked. Probably by the golden knight.

All right, then. That just meant I needed more power.

I reached within myself for the Wolf. I drew breath to howl.

Before I could, the golden knight stamped his foot. And that had to have been the mark of his power from the Unicorn, much the way that howling was mine from the Wolf.

Because when he stomped on the stairs, the gathering power got knocked out of me. I staggered, barely able to avoid tumbling down the stairs myself.

I looked back to see the Tiksdottir disarmed, with the golden knight's sword at her throat.

"By all means, try again, wolf cub," the golden knight said. "I'll stop you again, of course. But this time the penalty for trying will be the life of this pretty woman. I trust you don't want that?"

"Escape, sire," Tiksdottir said. "My life is nothing."

Maybe she believed that, but I didn't. I sighed and surrendered.

11

———————

In many of the fantasy novels I'd read growing up, when members of a noble or royal house were taken prisoner, they tended to get treated well. Nice, comfy rooms, good food, a decent view. That sort of thing.

They didn't *always* get that treatment, of course, but often enough that when it didn't happen, it was clearly for a reason.

I'd been a prisoner twice now, during my short tenure as a prince of Vol-Halá. Once by Graf Korga, who thought I was a spy but imprisoned me like a noble.

And now by the golden knight, who knew I was a prince, but imprisoned me like a spy.

One of the knights I'd thrown down the stairs was dead. His neck had broken, either sometime during the fall or when he hit bottom. The other wasn't dead, but had several broken bones.

Tiksdottir's, of course, was dead.

Still, the golden knight didn't seem to hold the losses against us. If anything, I thought he was treating me with more respect now than he had been before. Taking fewer chances, and speaking without quite so much scorn as he told us to make ourselves at home, for it would be our last home.

And what a home it was.

A square room. Maybe fifteen feet across both directions. The dirty floor was covered with filthy straw that smelled as though it hadn't been changed for at least three occupants. And that they'd given up on using the bucket for their waste a good long time ago.

The straw rustled in places, suggesting that a family of rats now called the cell home, and would no doubt take our presence poorly.

The only window was in the thick, heavy, iron-banded door that closed us in. And that window was barred, and only opened from the outside.

One meager, tallow candle burned in a sconce along the back wall. It shed only just enough light for us to dimly see each other, and watch the movement in the hay.

The door was slammed on us with a sense of finality.

Tiksdottir and I stood together, just inside the doorway, while we listened to the receding boots of our captors.

When we could hear them no more, Tiksdottir said, "You should have left me, sire."

"I'm not sure I could have," I said. "He stopped me the first time."

"He never considered me a real threat," she said. "If you had drawn breath to howl, he would have gone for the stomp. With his focus on you, I could have thrown off his balance. Given you the momentary edge you needed. You could have escaped."

"I'm not abandoning you to die," I said, but before I could finish the thought, she spoke over me.

"Dying to protect you is part of my job, sire," she said. "If you risk your life for mine, I'm a liability, not an asset."

"You're not a liability *or* an asset," I said. "You are a friend and an ally, and I will not abandon my friends and allies for my personal safety. Is that clear?"

"Sire," she said, and I swear her eyes seemed to burn in the dim light, "I admit that my projection of the scenario might have been flawed. That you might not have been able to escape. That despite any distraction I offered, the golden knight might still have been able to stop you. But the day may come when my death *will* buy your life."

"I hardly think—"

"*When that day comes*, don't let me spend my life needlessly. Take the opportunity I give you. Escape. And live."

I wanted to refuse her, but the look in her eyes would brook no refusal. And if we were *both* going to make it out of here, we needed to be united. And strange as the idea was to me, that could only happen if she could trust me to leave her, if necessary.

I hated myself for doing it, but I nodded agreement.

"Good," she said. "Thank you, sire."

"So," I said, changing the subject. "Any idea what house uses the unicorn sigil?"

"None, unfortunately," she said with a sigh. "It sounds familiar, but only vaguely. Definitely not any of the major houses. Not the Nulac, either."

"What's the sigil of the Nulac?"

"Twin staves, crossed by lightning."

I smacked myself in the forehead. She'd already told me that, back when we were traveling to Vol-Halá.

I know. I'd been absorbing new information just as fast as I could. I could probably have been forgiven for letting a detail or two slip. But that wasn't how I saw it.

I had to stay sharper. I couldn't afford to let things like that slip past me. This wasn't a game. This wasn't a tournament. Lives dangled from my actions now. Not the least of them my own and Tiksdottir's.

"Guess that means these guys are a new threat, then," I said with a sigh. So no one at court would even know to worry about these guys? Oh, that was bad.

I shook that line of thought away and focused on more immediate matters. "Got any tricks for getting us out of here?"

"Maybe," she said, but she wasn't grinning this time. She really didn't know.

"Then I'll try first." I gathered myself, and focused on ... no. Not the oak. I needed to focus sharply on someplace I really wanted to go. Not the Cock and Crow, either. I didn't want to lead the golden knight there on accident.

So I focused on the platform above the courtyard before the royal castle at Vol-Halá. The mosaic pattern of dark reds and deep browns. The royal blue of the sky above. The twin rows of those leafy, bushy trees, each with its leaves a different shape and color.

I reached for that platform...

It was like trying to reach for the sky and finding the way blocked by a thick window.

"I ... can't ... reach..." I said through gritted teeth while frustration boiled within me.

"Stop, sire," Tiksdottir said, soothingly. "Stop then. The golden knight has blocked the Wolf's trail for you."

"How is that possible?" I asked, panting for breath.

Tiksdottir shook her head. "You'll learn all about it when you get your formal training."

"If we ever get out of here."

"Oh," Tiksdottir said with a lopsided smile. "And is my prince the only one present with the power of Journeying?"

I grinned back at her. "I should think not."

"We can only hope our host doesn't know that," she said, sounding serious now. "If he only blocked the Wolf's trail, I should be able to get us out of here."

Tiksdottir called her power together. Gathered it in her hands. Pulled it down by her side.

She thrust her power at the door of our cell.

The doorframe denied her. Her power didn't take, but bounced back at her. The feedback hit her like a mace blow to the head. I only just caught her before she fell.

"Thank you ... sire," she panted. She was sweating worse than I was, but got back unsteadily to her feet. "That way ... is barred as well."

I heard an inquisitive squeak.

Tiksdottir huffed out an impatient breath, drew a pair of daggers, and killed every rat in the cell in the next twenty seconds.

"I can't abide vermin," she said. "In fact..."

She shook her shoulders and hands, then called together her

power again. Not so much as last time, I noted, but only a fraction of what I'd seen her gather before. I hoped that was a sign of control, and that slamming her power against the golden knight's barrier hadn't harmed her.

She muttered something under her breath and flung her arms outwards. Her power swept over the room.

"There," she said, dusting her hands together. "Now we won't have to worry about lice, fleas and the like either." She gave me a quick, if tired, smile. "Much traveling as I do, sire, that spell is a necessity."

"I believe it," I said. "So the way is closed to us…"

I called forth my locker. Put it right back.

"All right," I said, "so I can do that much."

"I suspect it's only proper Journeying we've been cut off from," Tiksdottir said. "To seal us into this world completely, cutting us off from all power. That can't really be done, so far as I've heard. Not without sealing off the whole world from everyone. Which would trap the golden knight here too."

We leaned against the cleanest spots on the wall that we could find.

"Wait," I said. "You're a royal messenger. Do you have the power to send messages across worlds?"

Tiksdottir gave me a look, and I got the distinct impression that she wanted to say *If I could do that, don't you think I would have already?* Instead, she shook her head.

"Only the royal family has that power," she said. "And as you've not been trained to use it, sire, we have no…"

Her words trailed off because she saw me smile.

I brought my locker back. Dug into it for a certain dagger. A thin black stiletto, with a dark ruby on the pommel. I held it up with a grin.

"Sire?" Tiksdottir asked.

"A gift from dear cousin Cassiel," I said, as I put my locker away. "Along with instructions for how to use it to call him, should I need him."

With that dagger I carved the royal sigil into the door, then stabbed the center.

"Now what?" Tiksdottir asked.

"Now we wait," I said.

I hoped Cassiel didn't keep us waiting long.

WE FOUND IT DIFFICULT TO MEASURE TIME IN THE DANK LITTLE CELL we'd been consigned to by the golden knight. No one came to bring us food. No one even came to check on us.

For that matter, even though I thought I'd seen another three cell doors on the way to this one, at the end of the tight corridor, I hadn't heard a peep from any of them. And I'd tried spending a little while just listening at the door.

We still had light, though, because that little taper never burned down. Far as I could tell, it was based on the same principle as those torches in the hidden ways of the royal castle. Only instead of being bright, cheery torches, it was a single, dim, depressing little taper.

When we got hungry, we ate from the knapsack that Tiksdottir managed to pull out of nowhere in much the same way I could get to my locker. She also laid down a small, weatherproof tarp over the disgusting stone floor, so we wouldn't have to sleep on it. I grabbed us two sleeping bags from my locker.

Not that we needed two. We slept in shifts. The other standing ready guard. Still, it seemed polite to use two, since we could.

When it was my turn to stand guard, I didn't mess around. I donned my full armor, with my wolf helmet and had a good sword and shield ready.

I seriously considered taking a war axe to the door, but I wasn't ready to try that yet. It might draw not one guard, but a host of guards. Possibly knights. More risk and more fighting than I wanted.

Right now I still had hope that someone would come check on us. Someone with keys, and maybe not much armor. Which was why I stood my guard to one side, so anyone who used that little window in the door wouldn't see me, armored up and ready to fight.

That was also why I put my armor away again, to sleep. Tiksdottir didn't have any armor, so surprise was all she had on her side. Well, surprise, and a rapier from my locker.

After my third sleep, still no one had come to check on us. I was just donning my armor and giving serious thought to my war axe, when the window in the door slid open.

Crap! I was half-armored, and right in view.

I started clanking to one side, when I heard a hushed voice say.

"Way too noisy. Conditions like these, you need to armor yourself from the top down. Greaves last, of course."

A voice I recognized.

"Cassiel!" I stage whispered.

"Who else were you expecting?" he said, still quietly. "Now put the armor away. We need stealth more than steel."

Tiksdottir, by this time, had already come awake and rolled to her feet. She immediately began securing the sleeping bags, while I started removing my armor.

Cassiel was in and helping me before I knew it. He'd left the door open, too.

"The door," I said.

"It was barred, not locked," he said, and his fingers were faster with the armor's straps than mine were. "They'll notice the missing bar anyway. Might as well not let them just lock us all in."

I got all our extra equipment back into my locker while Tiksdottir filled Cassiel in on the golden knight.

"A unicorn?" Cassiel said, sounding as confused as I was. "None of the major houses use a unicorn for a sigil. Not since..."

"Not since," I prompted.

"Well," Cassiel said, frowning, "back when greatest granddad led the rebellion against Emerlaine and the Nulac, there was a great house that not only refused to aid us, but warned the Nulac of what we were doing."

"I remember something about that," Tiksdottir said. "The turn-cloak house. Pretended to ally, but ran to Emerlaine with everything they could learn."

"That's them," Cassiel said with a grimace. "House O'Berran. And their sigil was the unicorn. Don't remember where their homeworld was."

I huffed out a breath. "Pretty sure you're standing on it."

"Doesn't mean much," Cassiel said. "Their power was broken and their worlds split among the others. I don't think anyone in their royal family even survived."

"Pretty sure at least one did," I said, thinking of the golden knight.

So these were the ones who killed Uncle Karl. Perhaps to stop him from carrying word back that the Nulac had their old supporters rallying behind them once again.

"All right," I said, once everything was stowed, and I had a rapier and main gauche in my hands again. "Let's get out of here."

Tiksdottir lead the way, taper held next to her dagger, with Cassiel behind her and me behind him. All three of us similarly armed, and more than ready to fight.

The moment I passed through the door and into the tight corridor, I felt a *ping* of power pass through me.

"Move it!" I said, loud and clear. "Alarm just went off."

All three of us started running through the dim, tight corridor. Desperate to reach and mount those stairs before the fight came to us.

We made it to the stairs.

Tiksdottir was on the third stair when she clashed with a guard in mail armor. He was wielding a short sword, against her rapier and dagger.

She finished him quickly with a sword cut across his jugular. Another moved to take his place. Looked to be three more behind him, one of them with a torch in his free hand.

Cassiel pushed his way ahead of her.

He killed the oncoming guards so quickly they barely had time to fall. We had to push their bodies aside to keep climbing the stairs.

More guards came. More guards died.

I'd thought I was good with a blade. Cassiel made me look like a novice on his first day of class, still learning how to grip the handle properly.

Cassiel cut his way through those guards like they weren't there.

We made it out of the doorway and onto the grass outside the keep.

There were more guards here, but still the chain-wearing variety. These were still wielding spears, but we came out of the doorway too quickly for them. They didn't get to take advantage of their superior reach.

The three of us killed fifteen guards and bought ourselves a break in the action when we heard the real danger.

Hooves.

Good as we three were with our swords and daggers, we'd fall like a dead tree in a gale against those knights.

"Can you Journey us out of here?" I said, not sure of the proper way to ask that question.

"Help me," Cassiel said.

"I'll stall them," Tiksdottir said, grabbing up fallen spears and throwing them at the knights as they rounded the side of the keep.

They came in formation. A wedge of at least a dozen knights, the golden knight at their head.

"What can I do?" I asked Cassiel.

"The Way has been blocked," and he said "way" as though it were capitalized. "I'll need your power added to mine to punch through."

"Get behind me," he said, stepping in front of me. "One hand to the base of my spine. One at the back of my neck."

I quickly sheathed my blades.

When I had my hands in place, he said, "Good. Now try to reach through me with your power."

"Where to? I only know the Wolf's trail."

"Forget trails and destinations." He shook his head. "Howl."

I did, and Cassiel howled with me. I swear, the harmony of our howls called more power out of me than I'd ever felt before, and all of it rushed through my hands and joined with Cassiel.

He reached out and practically ripped a hole in the air in front of us.

It wasn't ... it wasn't quite so *visible* as that. And yet, I could feel the barrier between us and where we were going get shredded.

A moment later we were through, and standing on a ridge overlooking a beautiful river valley that extended as far as I could see by the setting sun. The sky was shades of red and yellow ahead of us, but darkening blue directly above.

The wind was cool, and clean enough that the only taste in my mouth was the dried beef from lunch.

"Good job," I said, to Cassiel, shaking his hand as he smiled at me. "Tiksdottir," I said, turning...

But Tiksdottir wasn't there.

I grabbed Cassiel by the collar of his dark gray, *tlikswul* shirt. "We have to go back for her."

"Volner," Cassiel started, but I didn't want his calm tones and I didn't want his explanations.

"She's saved my life over and over again. I'm not abandoning her."

"Volner," he tried again, but he still sounded calm and rational about leaving Tiksdottir behind.

And that would not stand.

"Fine!" I said, dropping my grip and turning away from him on the ridge. "I'll go get her myself."

Cassiel slapped me so hard the sound of it echoed all around the ridge. So hard I think he cracked away the kink in my neck that had come from sleeping on the hard stone of that cell floor. So hard that the shock of his slap seemed to resonate all the way down to my hands.

He definitely had my attention.

"Volner," he said, still infuriatingly patient, "we are not abandoning Tiksdottir."

"Too right we're not," I said, drawing my blades again. "Let's go."

"Volner," Cassiel said, "will you let me finish?"

I had to check myself from making about a half-dozen sharp remarks. But even I thought they would have sounded ungrateful to the guy who had just crossed worlds to break me out of a prison cell.

I nodded for him to continue.

"Thank you." He straightened his collar. "Now. Do you know where we are?"

I shook my head, fighting down a sigh.

"Of course not." He turned and started for a trail that looked to lead down from a ridge to a series of small, surprisingly modern-looking buildings. Maybe a two-story house and three other support buildings. Surrounded by the kind of neat, trimmed lawn I might have seen back in the Bay Area, complete with a handful of ancient looking oak trees.

The breeze was light, and carried only the smell of fresh, clean air that was more than welcome after too much time in that foul little cell.

I caught up with Cassiel a few steps later, fighting down my impatience. Even so, I couldn't help but notice how wide and easy the trail was down to those buildings.

"This," Cassiel said, gesturing to the world around us, "is my hidey hole."

"Your ... hidey ... hole," I said.

Seemed like a dismissive way to talk about an entire world. Especially a world that was no doubt inhabited by thousands or millions or billions or other people.

Cassiel gave me the kind of smile that I usually only saw on magazine covers.

"I know," he said. "I just can't help it. I find our powers to be too much fun to take them so seriously all the time, the way most of our elders do."

I sheathed my weapons. Clearly this was going to take a while. Quite possibly too long for Tiksdottir.

My impatience must have shown on my face.

Cassiel laughed. Not mockingly, but an open, honest sound.

"See?" he said. "I knew I'd like you. Some of our relatives, they look at people like Tiksdottir and see resources to be managed and spent. You and me, we see people."

"People who might be dying while we gab about hidey holes."

He sighed. "I knew you hadn't had full training, but I'd've thought they'd have at least…"

Cassiel shook his head. Pinched the bridge of his nose. Stopped walking and faced me.

"Volner," he said, putting his hands on my shoulders. "I need you to listen to me. Really listen."

I nodded.

"All right. Have you been told at least that time flows differently in different worlds?"

I nodded again.

"Good. Now. One of the joys of living as long as we do is that many of us continue to experiment with our powers, developing applications and approaches that were unheard of, back in the days of the great rebellion."

I bit my lip to keep my impatience in check.

"One of these applications, for example, is the locker. We've only had the locker trick down for maybe a hundred years. A hundred fifty, tops. But another innovation is quite recent. Uncle Karl was the one who came up with it, in fact."

"Uncle Karl did?" All right, he was winning his way past my impatience.

Nevertheless, Cassiel held onto my shoulders and spoke to me in a way that made sure I was listening.

"That's right. And I think he based the idea on the locker technique. Did you know that you can put an apple in your locker and it will never go bad?"

I nodded, cautiously. I was pretty sure Tiksdottir had said something about that.

"Meat kept there will never spoil. Flowers either," he said with a smile, "and personally I recommend keeping a few bouquets for times when the need might arise."

He shook his head. "Sorry. Point is, the locker exists in a kind of pocket space, outside of normal worlds and time. Uncle Karl found a way to extend that idea."

Cassiel took one hand off my shoulder and gestured to indicate the world around us.

"This valley is the whole of this world, and it exists outside of time. It is mine, and only I can access it."

I made some kind of low sound as the implications of this hit me.

"Officially, we call these things our personal retreats. Some have taken to calling them panic rooms or bolt holes. Personally, I prefer hidey hole." He grabbed both my shoulders again. "Only the family has this power. Even the royal wizard hasn't been told about it."

I started to ask why, then realized I knew the answer. It gave our family an edge. And right now we needed every edge we could gather.

"So," I said. "Right now those knights are all stuck mid-charge?"

"And right now, Tiksdottir is as safe as she can be." Cassiel started leading me down the trail again. "We could go back for her right now, true. But even if we armored up, we'd be little better off than we were before."

"Do you have horses?" I asked, assuming he'd probably start to regale me with the quality of the warhorses he bred here.

"No horses," he said. "No living servants either. Automata, robots, or enchanted servants only. Living beings wouldn't do well here."

"Why not?"

"How are you feeling after our fight?"

I frowned at the subject change.

"Fine," I said, slowly. "Got my wind back and—"

"Exactly." He gestured to the way the breeze lazily moved the leaves on his oak trees. "Time does pass here. After a fashion. But only in an absolute sense, not a relative sense."

"Lost me," I admitted.

"Mind you," he said, "this is only current theory. Testing is..." He frowned, and hung his head through a deep breath. "...*was* still being done by Uncle Karl. Someone else will have to take that up later."

He shook his head. Continued, "So far as we know right now, the time ratio between a hidey hole and any other world is effectively infinite to one."

"So…"

"So in the time it would take for those knights' horses to take a single step, thousands, millions, maybe billions of years would pass here."

I had to stop walking to grasp that one.

"But … the grass. The trees. The sky…"

"I know, right?" Cassiel smiled. "It'll keep you up nights, if you let it. Point is, what we have here is a chance to get you more up to speed before we go back and deal with that golden knight and his friends."

"Get me up to speed?"

"Well," Cassiel said. "You still won't get proper Journey training, because we can't leave here. But I can actually explain how at least some of the techniques work. So you can try them on your own, later." He shrugged. "Better than nothing."

"Yeah," I said, not sure how this would help.

"More importantly," Cassiel said, "you need training time with weapons. Real training time."

"I hold my own all right. I took down my share of those guards."

Well, I knew that wasn't quite true. Cassiel and Tiksdottir had been responsible for taking down most of those soldiers.

"Oh, you're … competent," Cassiel said. "I'll give you that. But your movements are wasteful and you're slow to the kill. You fight like a man who's never left the tournament field."

Well. I couldn't exactly deny that.

"You can help?" I asked.

"Oh," Cassiel said with a slow smile, "I can help all right."

Cassiel and I spent weeks in that little hidey hole of his. Months, maybe.

To be honest, it's tough to judge how much time was passing, because no sun ever made its way across the sky. We never really had night, either. No moon or stars. No darkness overhead.

Every day was clear skies, gentle breezes and temps maybe in the low 70s.

And every day basically went like this: training, training, and more training.

I trained before breakfast. Sometimes during. I remember once Cassiel and I were sitting at his little wicker table, out behind the main house, eating cantaloupe and scrambled pepper eggs when suddenly he was coming at me across the table with a knife.

While I was awake, I was training.

I drilled with swords of all kinds. Bows and crossbows. Pole arms. Clubs. Maces. Flails. Axes. Eastern weapons like nunchaku and throwing stars. This kind of African weapon that had both curved and straight blades, but was also balanced for throwing.

If it had ever been used to fight and kill, I trained with it.

I trained in armor and out of armor. I trained while wearing *partial* armor, in case an attack came while I was still getting dressed.

I trained without shields. I trained with various kinds of shields. Bucklers, tower shields, bash shields and more. I trained with small off-hand weapons like parrying daggers and main gauches. With two sword styles that incorporated swords of the same length and swords of different lengths.

Then there were the great two-handed swords. Not just the *zwei-händer* and claymore, which I'd used before in class. No. Apparently there was also a kind of extra long katana called the *ōdachi*. I had to learn to use that too, as well as four other types of greatswords.

Apart from meal breaks and sleep, Cassiel worked me nonstop. Harder than any human being could work without breaking down. Which was the point.

My powers were still developing. And with them, strength, speed and resilience beyond anything a normal human being could develop. By pushing me the way he was, Cassiel was ... carbonating my development, if you'll pardon the turn of phrase.

Apparently, left to my own devices, I would grow into the full blossom of my physical power over the course of about two years. That time frame could be shortened significantly by pushing my body to its limits on a daily basis.

It wasn't just weapons work, either. All kinds of training. Acrobatics. Lock-picking. Anything Cassiel knew that he thought I might need to know to get out of a tight spot. And always under threat of some kind of attack.

Oh, and the feaking cardio.

I don't know how many times I ran the length of the valley, as well as along rocky paths and slopes along the edges. I had to swim the river, across the current, with the current, and against the current. To free climb the cliff faces, which came in ten different degrees of difficulty.

And I wouldn't be allowed to leave until I'd mastered all of them. And the weapons. And gotten my body into what Cassiel called "reasonably good shape."

The only break I got from physical training came during our meal breaks. Oh, I still had to be ready in case of attack — an attack with did come at irregular intervals, to keep me on my toes — but for the most part we used meal time for other kinds of training.

For example, we discussed family history. We discussed our strategies for how we would save Tiksdottir when we went back for her. And most of all, we discussed Journeying. Unfortunately, that part could only be theoretical. Any practical work would put us back in the time stream, and put Tiksdottir's life at risk.

But at least I had begun to feel and develop a sense of my powers. So when Cassiel tried to explain how to hop directly between distant points, or how to find and open the way to my own hidey hole — as well as several dozen other concepts related to Journeying — I could at least imagine how it felt to attempt them.

What was more, I took notes. Extensive notes. Every time he started in on Journeying, I started note-taking.

I wouldn't always be here in this hidey hole. And once I was out, and actually had a chance to do some practicing, I wanted to have a reference guide available that wasn't as dated as *Trails of the Wolf*.

I swear. I came to feel that when I'd first arrived in Cassiel's hidey hole I'd been half made of dough.

But the time I'd spent there had pounded out my impurities, and fired me into something hard, clean, and dangerous.

In fact, I'd just gotten to the point when I was really looking forward to the next day's sessions when they abruptly ended.

The sky was still bright blue overhead, and the breeze was still just a suggestion. Far as I could tell, the weather never changed here.

Cassiel and I were sitting down to dinner at the wicker table, dining on thick porterhouse steaks with garlic smashed potatoes and a medley of crisp vegetables. I'd just toasted the day's work with a glass of what appeared to be an excellent cabernet sauvignon, when Cassiel told me we were leaving.

"No after dinner session tonight," he said. "Get some reading in on the heraldry of the great houses, then hit the rack. In the morning we're going back to save Tiksdottir."

Jitters danced in my belly.

"You're sure I'm ready?"

"Ready as you'll get, here." Cassiel frowned. "I think there's a metaphysical level of development that can only happen in a proper timestream. We of the Wolf need real time to develop, after a certain point." He shrugged. "It's just theory, though."

That finally raised a point that had been bothering me for some time now. And if I could feel certain that Cassiel wasn't about to attack me, this might be the time to ask.

"My father knows how to make hidey holes, right?"

"Uncle Alvin?" Cassiel said, his eyebrows coming up. "Of course."

"It's been bothering me for a while, now," I said. "When Tiksdottir first told us that the Nulac were coming—"

"Why didn't your father take you and your mother into a hidey hole?"

I nodded.

"Princes don't run from assassins," Cassiel said. "Especially not when they have time to prepare. No three Nulac assassins could take down Prince Alvin."

"But…" I frowned. Set down my silverware. "He could have sat me down and explained things to me. Who I was. What my powers were. What it all meant."

"No," Cassiel said, gently. "He couldn't have."

I frowned, but before I could reply, he continued.

"Look. Family loyalty aside, I don't know how much Uncle Alvin let himself go during his self-imposed exile. Truth is, he may well have been worried that those assassins could've taken him."

I almost interrupted to ask about this self-imposed exile, but let him keep talking.

"If Uncle Alvin tried explaining all this to you, then told you about the threat, what would you have done?"

"Exactly what I tried to do," I admitted. "Grab weapons and help him."

"And gotten yourself killed. You weren't ready." Cassiel shook his head. "Coming here, it gives us time. But he needed you *not* to have time. He needed you to just *act*."

"He ordered Tiksdottir to get me out of there."

"Exactly. And Tiksdottir would then keep you from doing something stupid."

"She tackled me as I tried to go grab weapons."

Cassiel chuckled approvingly. "And then she dragged you off-world before you could object?"

I nodded.

"And got you introduced to the Wolf at the first opportunity?"

"Yes," I admitted with a sigh.

"Then she did her job right."

"But if Dad had taken me to his hidey hole, I could have trained like this."

"No," Cassiel said, cutting a bite of steak now. It dripped with juice. "You couldn't have. You hadn't met the Wolf yet. Hadn't awakened to your powers. Your body couldn't have handled it."

"So he did do the right thing, then."

"Well," Cassiel said with a smile, "I'll let the philosophers worry about right and wrong. But I can tell you he did the smart thing. The practical thing. Dare I say it? The *responsible* thing."

I relaxed some, after that, and enjoyed an excellent meal. I'd never once seen the thing that served as Cassiel's chef in this place, but it could cook and season a perfect rare porterhouse, and knew just how to handle the vegetables. Even the bread was fresh and perfect.

I ate well. And I turned in early.

I wanted to be ready when we went back.

———

THE NEXT MORNING WE BREAKFASTED LIGHTLY ON HARDBOILED EGGS and fresh strawberries, and drank good, sweet river water.

We hiked together up the trail from his house to the ridge, and as I cast my gaze back down into the valley, I realized that I'd only seen the inside of two buildings: his house and the one barn-like outbuilding that served as his gymnasium. There were three other little buildings down there I'd never been inside, in all the time I'd been here.

Then again, this *was* Cassiel's hidey hole. And he'd been more than generous in sharing it with me. Of course, he benefited from my being here as well, in terms of what I would now bring to the fight when we went back.

Still. Curious as I was about those other buildings, I didn't feel I could ask about them.

All the same, I whiled away the hike up to the ridge by wondering what they could have housed. Personal libraries? Magical laboratories? Robotics labs?

Then again, if one of them happened to be for ... entertainments of a more personal nature, maybe I didn't want to ask...

As we crested the ridge, Cassiel turned to me with a smile.

"All right, Volner. Here we go. Grab your locker and armor up. Grab the weapon and off-hand you're most comfortable with, along with something bigger, like a claymore or a *zweihänder*. Something that can take down a horse."

Nerves danced all through me. Jittering my knees and keeping my fingers moving constantly. My pulse seemed to beat harder in all my joints and limbs.

Focusing on the straps of my armor helped.

One thing that didn't help?

Yeah, I'd probably traded a good ten or fifteen pounds of fat for a good twenty or thirty pounds of muscle.

My armor didn't fit right anymore.

"Uh, Cassiel?" I asked, turning to him.

He took one look at the way my armor clung too tight in some places and hung too loose in others and laughed.

But damn the man if even then I couldn't take offense at his laugh. It always seemed to be showing such honest amusement that I had trouble taking umbrage.

"It's not a problem," he said. "Really. Just finish strapping in as best you can. Then put on your helm and howl."

I frowned at him.

He chuckled. "Yes, Volner, because I'm going to start misleading you now about your powers. You've caught me out. These last few ... however many weeks have just been setting you up so your armor won't fit."

I tried to pretend my face wasn't hot as I finished donning my armor. And once the helm was in place, with the visor down, I reached into myself for the Wolf.

The Wolf answered right away, and I howled.

When I did, the wolf shape of my visor morphed to howl with me. And my armor began to shift and flow. For a moment, I wondered if I were going to turn into a wolf.

I didn't. Though my armor shifted shapes to fit me perfectly again.

Cassiel howled when he finished donning his own armor.

His howl echoed within me, and I felt my inner Wolf stir in response.

"Always best to howl when you don your armor," Cassiel said. "Especially if it's been a while. Just in case the fit is less than perfect."

I had a longsword at one side of my belt, and a short sword and main gauche at the other, next to the bag of goodies Cassiel had given me. Daggers in my boots. And in my hands, a naked claymore, whose scabbard lay across my back.

Cassiel also appeared to favor the longsword, but for his off-hand he had a sword-breaker. And in his hands, an *ōdachi*.

"One last thing," he said. He handed me a small scroll, which had been sealed with golden wax. "I have a duplicate of this. Normally, I'd send this message home before the fight. But I can't do it from here, and I won't be able to afford the distraction after we leave."

"Message?"

"What we've figured out about the enemy. The high king and queen need to know. The whole family needs to know." He drew a deep breath and let it out. "I know I told you the theory of how to send a message across worlds. But if we both come through this intact, I'll get to show you how it's done. If not, and you're the survivor, get this home. At best speed."

"Right," I said, tucking the scroll away into my boot.

"Ready?" he asked me.

Was I ready? Readiness sang in my muscles. In every beat of my heart. In every drop of rushing blood within me.

I only growled in response, and the growl felt right. It also sounded more like a wolf's growl than a man's.

"That's my boy," Cassiel said.

He tore open the space before us, and just like that we were back on the grass outside the golden knight's castle.

The air stank of blood and death from the more than twenty soldiers we'd slain moments before. Their blood made mud where their bodies littered the grass. The sky above us was a stark contrast — pale blue and too cheerful for all that death.

Tiksdottir stood a pace before us, sword and long knife in her hands. Her head whipped back and forth, looking for someplace, anyplace to flee from the oncoming slaughter.

The hooves of the approaching mounted knights shook the ground with their thunder.

The golden knight rode at the center of their wedge. Six knights to either side of him. All with lances couched and ready.

This was an absolutely terrible place to meet them. They had every advantage.

Or at least, they had every reason to expect so.

"Tiksdottir," I said, sharply. "Get behind us."

"It's my job to—" Her words cut off when she realized that Cassiel and I were both much better armed and armored than we'd been moments before.

At least, what had been moments before, for her.

"Yes, sire," she said quickly and got behind us.

As we'd discussed, Cassiel and I took strong stances. Sword blades high and ready to sweep like scythes at the harvest.

The knights rode closer.

In the background, at the nearby army camps, I could see soldiers just starting to wonder at what all the fuss was about.

Boy, were they about to get a surprise.

Closer the knights came. No more than a hundred feet now.

"Now?" I whispered.

"Hold," Cassiel said back softly.

Seventy-five feet and closing.

"Hold," he said again.

Fifty feet and closing.

"Now!"

We both dropped our greatswords and dug into the goody bags for small, pot-bellied bottles.

We each pulled a bottle, aimed and threw.

I hit the knight behind and left of the golden knight. I hit that man square in the chest.

Cassiel hit his target, too. The knight just behind and to the right of the golden knight.

The bottles shattered.

Fire blossomed, bright and orange and liquid. It caught the

knights and their horses, and spread to the nearest knights behind them.

Four knights fell screaming to the ground atop dying horses.

Whatever was in those bottles, it was every bit as deadly as Cassiel had told me, back in his hidey hole, over a dinner of roast chicken with asparagus.

"In the world where you grew up, did you have sticky fire?"

"Napalm?" I'd asked, and it had been gratifying to watch the way he went from not knowing the word to understanding it. I knew just how that felt. I continued. "Greek fire, maybe?"

"Something like those. There's an alchemical formula for it. Nasty stuff. Spreads and burns worse than anything this side of dragon fire."

That was what we hit those knights with.

We each had time to throw one more, accurately, and still grab our greatswords before the knights were upon us. And we each accounted for two more knights that way.

Thirteen knights had begun the charge.

They were five now, and the line of their charge was broken.

I tossed my remaining bottle to Tiksdottir as I took up my claymore. I think she had to drop her long knife to catch the bottle.

Cassiel threw his last even as he was taking up his *ōdachi*.

The golden knight aimed his lance at me, and I wondered if he had some means of knowing which one was me, or whether he was simply choosing the target to his left.

Muscles tight and heart pounding, I let him close. Even though my legs begged me to run from the giant armored animal and the evil thing it carried.

The bottle I gave Tiksdottir went flying past and took down the last two knights on my side of the golden knight.

More screams of men and horses. More fire spreading on the grass.

But right now. The golden knight's horse, trampling the fallen bodies of his soldiers. The tip of his lance coming for my head.

I didn't just duck. Cassiel had told me any experienced knight would be ready for that.

Instead I slid forward, just outside the horse's speeding hooves. And I slashed my claymore across the horse's unprotected underside.

I didn't have a great angle, but the sword was razor sharp and the horse did most of the work. I not only cut loose the straps of his barding, I slashed his belly open. Not deep enough to spill his entrails, but deep enough that the horse stumbled, bleeding to the ground.

As I turned, fighting to my feet, I saw that Cassiel had taken down one more knight with his last bottle of sticky fire, though it cost him a chance to take down the remaining knight's steed.

That knight had abandoned his lance for a huge, three-headed spiked flail.

Meanwhile, the golden knight had managed to leap free of his falling horse and was coming to his feet with that oversized, two-handed mace of his.

The weapon that killed my uncle.

I tossed the claymore aside. I wasn't going to try to match strength with strength. Instead I drew my longsword for my main hand and a short sword for my off hand.

"Come on, then," I said.

He came forward in silence, leading with a powerful swing. I parried, trying to only redirect and not fight the power of that mace.

Didn't help. Magic sparked green out of that mace as it snapped my short sword in two.

I didn't even think. I just drew forth a howl beyond anything I'd done before. This wasn't just a howl that called up the Wolf within me. This howl reached through me, through my family, and all the way back to the Great Wolf himself.

It was a howl that shook the ground, and echoed all up and down the valley. I swear, it even caused avalanches up in the peaks of those cruel-looking mountains.

That howl came forth with power unlike anything I'd wielded before.

And all of that power shunted down through me onto the edge of my great fang — I mean my longsword — and into the blow I struck then across the golden knight's stomach.

I cut right through his armor, as though I were cutting mist.

I don't know how deeply I cut. He might already have been dying. I knew the golden knight fell forward, prostrate on the field. His mace fallen beside him.

But the world, it was fading on me. I don't mean in a Journey, way. I mean, everything was starting to go black.

I'd drawn too deeply from my power and spent it all at once. I didn't leave enough to keep me going.

But I had to make sure he was dead.

My arm was dangling by my side, but it still held my longsword.

I yanked off the man's helm. Saw his pale, sweaty face. His shock of short red hair and beard. His blue eyes moved. Dying, perhaps, but not dead yet.

"For ... my uncle..." I said, and drove the tip of my longsword up through his chin and out the back of his skull.

I fell to my knees then, and the world went black.

12

———

I found out later that while Cassiel and I were busy with the knights, Tiksdottir had managed to save and steal two of the fallen knights' warhorses. They were singed a bit, by all accounts, but healthy enough to ride.

We rode out of there on stolen horses while the soldiers of the nearby camp were still figuring out what had happened. Cassiel on one horse, Tiksdottir on the other, with me unconscious and sprawled across the horse in front of her.

Cassiel handled the Journey back to Vol-Halá. And while grooms were seeing to the poor, mistreated horses, Cassiel and Tiksdottir reported where we'd been, what we'd done, and what we'd learned. For my part, I was taken to the family healers for treatment.

There may or may not be limits to what the Great Wolf can do. But there are definitely limits to what we Ulfsons can do.

In fact, as I was lectured later — at length, let me tell you, first by Tiksdottir, then by Cassiel, then by greatest Grandmother, and then, well, you get the idea — I shouldn't have been able to call forth as much power from the Wolf as I had. Not at my level of development.

In theory, I shouldn't have survived.

In practice, I almost didn't. Apparently Tiksdottir had helped a bit by stuffing torn pieces of *vulfaa* into my mouth and making me swallow, as we rode along the Journey home. Even that, though, shouldn't have been enough.

Or so everyone said.

Personally, I think they were just trying to keep me from doing something that stupid again.

Point is, once again, I did wake up. Even though I hadn't been sure I would.

This time, the bed was much larger, more comfortable, and had sheets of royal blue. I was in a room painted an antique white that was almost yellow. The room had three large windows, open to let in fresh air with a slight tang of the sea, and fine paintings of gentle still lifes, and soothing land and seascapes.

I'd been stripped naked, but my armor stood, waiting for me, beside the bed.

On the other side, Tiksdottir sat in a large, comfortable chair of royal blue, smiling to see me awake.

I was weak, though. Weak enough that I wasn't sure I could even reach the glass of water on the nightstand beside her, much less the crystal pitcher of water beside it.

I did manage a weak smile though.

"I understand you wouldn't let Cassiel abandon me," she said.

Now, my body was weak, but my mind was working just fine. I was trying to figure out how to explain that Cassiel hadn't wanted to abandon her either. About how we hadn't wanted to leave her in the first place, but how we needed me to be more of a warrior to survive that battle.

Before I could get my dry mouth to even consider saying any of that, Tiksdottir arched an eyebrow at me.

"That was foolish, sire. But thank you."

She heard me trying to speak. Gave me some water. I tried to take the glass from her, but I wasn't at that point with the workings of my arms and legs.

She must've known that, though, because she poured a tiny

amount of water past my dry lips. Just enough to wet my tongue, until it could handle a little more.

By the time I could speak, I realized I couldn't possibly get enough words out to really explain to her what had happened. So I had to settle for one word.

"Welcome."

That word got me a bright smile, though.

Tiksdottir visited me daily, during my recovery. Cassiel visited me often, as well, and made sure I knew that, when I was strong enough, the high king himself wanted to talk to me.

By this time, I was strong enough to be expressive with my face, if not really yet with my words.

Cassiel chuckled at my look of surprise.

"That's right," he said, smiling. "You hadn't heard. Well, it seems that the O'Berrans had managed to grab hold of dear old greatest Granddad when he was off wandering. But when you killed the golden knight, they felt his death. Gave greatest Granddad the opening he needed to escape."

He clapped me on the shoulder. "Thanks to you."

The thanks felt good, but an implication of what he'd just told me sent cold shivers down my spine.

Cassiel read that expression too.

"That's right," he said. "One of the O'Berrans had to have survived the great rebellion, and managed to have a few children. And possibly grandchildren. All with the power of Journeying. Though remaining hidden will have cut them off from most of the recent developments, which will still give us an edge."

He tilted his head in thought, adding. "Likely, that golden knight was the first one of them to die since the great rebellion." He shook his head. "I can tell you that the death of a prince wouldn't be enough to stun *us* into a lapse like that."

He frowned. "Then again. Greatest Granddad wouldn't exactly need much of an opening. He's a scary kind of powerful."

I frowned, trying to grasp all the implications of what Cassiel was saying, but couldn't. I just didn't know enough yet.

"Hey," Cassiel said, giving me a smile. "This O'Berran thing isn't your problem. You and me, we heroes right now. Enjoy it. Greatest Granddad's certainly been taking advantage of having most of the family home. Sure, they'd been here for their power plays, but now he can easily order a few of our aunts and uncles and cousins go digging around across the worlds to find out what they can."

I managed a nod.

"You rest now, all right?" He gave my shoulder another pat. "You did good."

I THINK I SPENT TWO WEEKS IN THAT BED. MOST OF THE FIRST WEEK, from what I understand, I hadn't even been conscious. Or at least, I have no memory of being conscious during that time.

Apparently part of the survival response to drawing too deeply on the power of the Wolf is to withdraw. Shut down all "unnecessary functions" until we recover enough to begin turning the lights back on, as it were.

Recovery is more a matter of time, than anything else. Although slices of *vulfaa*, given in moderation, helped.

On the first day that I was up and about, and allowed to go farther than the bathroom — yes, the royal castle had indoor plumbing — or down the long hall and back, I was presented to the high king. Well, *presented* makes it sound as though I had to walk past a crowd to ascend a dais or something.

That wasn't how it happened.

I wear wearing only the pale blue pajamas they'd given me, during my recovery. The day was warm. The bright sunlight brought out all the yellows in the antique whites of the room's paint. And the breeze coming in through the three windows of my recovery room was downright sultry.

Plus, it smelled of cinnamon pastries. A smell so good it set my mouth to watering and my stomach to rumbling. And that, more than anything else, had made me willing to go wandering.

Enthusiasm was one of the last things to come back, during this kind of recovery. And the doctors had warned me that when I felt enthusiasm, I should encourage it. Always in thought, while recovering, and in action if feasible.

So I took advantage of that enthusiasm to attempt something I'd been meaning to do since I woke up.

Put my armor away.

This meant calling forth my locker. A use of my powers, for the first time since that battle with the golden knight. But I felt ready. Or at least, ready enough for the attempt.

The locker was slow to answer my call. It felt like...

Once, when I was a kid, I'd broken a bone in my left forearm. Had a cast and everything. And the day I got my cast off, I tried to pick up a textbook with my left hand.

My arm shook with the effort.

That was kind of what calling my locker felt like.

But it answered. I was even able, panting and sweating, to put my armor away. And when I fastened the clasps on the locker, it went back smooth and easy.

Sure, I was shaking and covered in cold sweat, but I felt good. I felt as though I deserved a cinnamon pastry.

I then slapped myself in the forehead.

I'd just had my locker open.

I had real clothing in that locker. Hell, I'd been wearing real clothing underneath my armor, though I had no idea what the castle staff had done with it. All I could find in the room were pajamas.

Ah, well. Pajamas it was.

Barfoot then, I started across the floor for the door, to go in search of cinnamon pastries.

The door opened before I reached it.

It was that pretty, brunette serving girl. Thala. The one who brought my meals, fetched me books, and would otherwise answer if I rang the bell on my nightstand.

At least, if I rang the bell before dinner. After dinner a portly servant named Kadore would handle my requests.

"Sire," Thala said, looking surprised to see me out of bed. "Did you need—" She stopped herself and shook her head. "Excuse me," she said with a curtsey. A curtsey she held as she continued, "Sire, may I present his royal majesty, High King Ulfgar."

She moved to one side then.

In came the high king, and the family resemblance was uncanny. He had my blonde hair (even wore it long, the way I did, though his was back in a ponytail), my blue eyes, my cleft chin. He was even just about my height, though he had more muscles.

Scariest part? This man was millennia old, but he barely looked older than me, if at all. He could have called himself my brother and no one would have batted an eye.

They might even have asked which of us was the older brother. Then again, he wore the full beard and I stayed clean-shaven, which I suspect would have made more people guess him older.

High King Ulfgar was dressed in fashionably tight black pants, tucked into knee-high black boots that looked to be soft calfskin. His shirt was a dark brown, with the sleeves rolled up and the top two buttons undone. He smelled of leather and the deep woods.

He wore no obvious weapons, but I didn't doubt for a second that he was armed.

Four fully armed and armored guards stayed behind him, waiting in the hall.

He wasn't wearing a crown. But then, this wasn't some big, state event.

"Grandfather Ulfgar," I said, bowing no more than my head.

He smiled, and I hope you'll forgive me for saying so, but it was the most wolfish smile I'd ever seen.

"Good. You remember what Delfina told you about how to address us." He looked me up and down. Paced around me. "So you're are Volner. The child Alvin tried to keep hidden from us."

When he stood in front of me again, he shook his head. "Can't imagine why. You're certainly nothing to be ashamed of." He smiled and clapped me on the shoulder. "Hell, you've barely awakened to your Wolf and already you've accomplished more than half your cousins."

I wasn't sure how to answer that, so I concentrated on standing still and shaking as little as possible. Apparently using my locker had taken more out of me than I'd thought.

"Then again, he probably worried that if the rest of the family knew about you, they'd worry about your potential place in the line of succession."

I got as far as opening my mouth to ask about that when he told me with just a smile that no, he wouldn't answer any questions about it.

I asked something else instead.

"I had the impression that some of the family thought you might be dead."

"Hoped, more like," he said with a chuckle. "Now sit, Volner. It's clear you can barely stand."

Relief spread through my body as I eased down onto the soft, firm mattress.

"But..." I started, then needed a few breaths before I could continue. Thrice-great grandfather let me have them. "But wouldn't we have all sensed you die?"

"Not necessarily," he said. "Only death by violence sends strong shockwaves of the experience through the family. Other forms of death — death by poison, for example — might not merit a blip on the radar."

I smiled to hear him say "blip" and "radar," even though I knew full well he'd been to worlds with more advanced technology than anything I'd ever seen.

"It's good to finally meet you," he said, smiling again as he looked me over. "When you see Alvin, tell him to at least send a message now and then, if he won't come visit."

"Yes, grandfather."

"Now." He rubbed his palms together. "From what I can gather, you have an adventurous spirit. This is good. Because I can't spare Ganna to give you your proper training right now."

I hung my head forward. When was I going to get to learn how to use my powers properly?

"However," he said, chuckling at my hang-dog look, "Cassiel can show you the ropes well enough. And since the two of you get along well enough, that's what he's going to do as soon as you're ready."

He frowned, looking at my condition.

"*When you're ready*," he said again. "Not before."

"Yes, grandfather."

"Good," he said with a nod. "After that, take some time. Go exploring. Get used to learning how to do what you can do."

I already had an idea or two about that...

"*However*," he said quickly. "You will do nothing that will bring you into conflict with the other royal houses, or risk your falling into the hands of our enemies."

"How am I going to accomplish that, exactly, grandfather?"

"Because I'm going to send Ulna Tiksdottir with you. She'll keep an eye on you, make sure you don't get into too much trouble. And more importantly, make sure you don't get *me* into too much trouble."

He laughed then. I wished I felt up to laughing with him.

"Now," he said. "I should let you rest. You clearly need..." He frowned at me. "You used your powers, didn't you?"

"I called my locker, grandfather. Put my armor away."

"I'll send the doctor in when I leave." He shook his head, but he was smiling as he did it. "Next time, talk to the doctors *before* attempting anything like that."

"Yes, grandfather."

He started to turn away, but turned back with a curious expression on his face.

"Where were you going, when Thala opened the door?"

"I smelled those cinnamon pastries."

"Ah," he said with a broad smile. "The crullers." He addressed the serving girl without turning away from me. "Thala."

"Yes, your majesty?"

"Bring Prince Volner a plate of cinnamon crullers."

"At once, your majesty."

She quickly left on her task.

"Thank you, grandfather," I said, easing myself back into a prone position.

He smiled as he patted me on the shoulder, then turned and left.

Thala wasn't long fetching those crullers.

They were terrific.

———

GETTING OUT OF THAT BED AND THAT ROOM FELT EVEN BETTER THAN I would have dreamed. Then Cassiel and I spent about two months traveling to various kinds of vacation places.

Tours among the stars, tropical beaches, forest cities of elven beauty. Bright, elaborate gambling dens, quiet, soothing canyon hikes, tours of aquatic cities where we could somehow speak underwater.

A whirlwind of glorious sights and leisure activities. Though he did find us a few fights, as well, to keep in shape among all the relaxing.

And most of all, he finally had a chance to show me, and teach me all the tricks of Journeying that he'd told me about back in his hidey hole.

By the time we finished our tour, I was handling all our Journeying myself.

Then it was time for Cassiel to get back to his own activities — and despite traveling with me for two months, he'd managed not to tell me what those activities were — and time for me to go exploring. Tiksdottir by my side.

And the first place I went was home.

Er, *home* home. The home were I grew up, not the royal castle I was coming to think of as home.

I mean I went back to the Bay Area in the world where I grew up.

The first thing I did was help Diane.

One of the little tricks of Journeying is the ability to find things we want to find, even within a world. So I found the best attorney practicing in the Oakland area, and I paid her a lot of money to two things.

The first was to take care of that legal snafu that Diane was in over the theft she didn't commit. She hadn't been kidding about how slowly the courts worked in cases like this one. But with enough money and the right kind of attorney, I was confident that the matter would get resolved in Diane's favor, and that even the firing could be expunged from her employment record.

The second was to mock up a "scholarship fund" that could pay her college costs. She'd already finished up at community college, I could help with her four-year degree at San Jose State.

Damn it, I had some power now. And though Diane and I needed to go our separate ways — I understood that now — that didn't mean I was going to leave her twisting in the wind.

I had the means, and I was going to help her.

Then, it was time to go home. See Mom and Dad and Lynn.

When I went back to Long Pine City, it was October of the year following the year when I left.

The weather was cool, but the skies still clear of any hint of rain. The smell of fall was in the air, though. Woodsmoke from a few nearby houses, and fallen leaves.

Mom and Dad were waiting for me at the purple table in the kitchen when I came through the garage door. Mom had more worry lines on her face. Dad ... Dad looked the same as when I'd left. Though that sameness still made him look like a man in his forties.

His look was a lie. I understood now, how we could make the worlds lie for us about such things.

The kitchen looked the same. The oak cabinets, the granite counters, the Mediterranean style of the floor tiles.

The smell of Mom's lasagna was thick in the air as I came through the door. Slices of it sat on three plates, at the table, along with three glasses of tap water. A basket of fresh garlic bread sat in the center of the purple table.

I was barely through the door when Mom was out of her chair and hugging me just as hard as she could. Of course, at barely five feet tall and weighing next to nothing, the hardest she could hug wasn't very.

I hugged her back all the same.

Dad stayed seated at the table, though he nodded to me. His expression was cautious.

Not at all the homecoming I expected from him.

"Where's Lynn?" I asked, after Mom and I had finished saying hello.

"Off at Harvard," Mom said with a smile, "and already causing trouble. If her grades weren't so good…"

"But they are," Dad said, "as always."

He sounded as though he should have been smiling. He wasn't. He still had that careful look on his face.

"We've been so worried about you," Mom said, then shoved my plate closer. "Eat. Eat."

I tucked into a bite. The cheese and beef were perfect as always, and the sauce just tangy enough. The noodles, I swear, were just there to provide a delivery system for the beef and cheese.

"How'd you know I'd be here?" I asked.

"I'm surprised Tiksdottir isn't with you," Dad said.

Mom looked back and forth between us, frowning. "Alvin," she said softly. "Don't make this about politics."

"Everything is about politics," Dad said. "It's who we are."

"You haven't answered my question," I said, and Mom frowned at the suspicion on my face and in my tone.

"I still have my resources," Dad said.

I dropped my fork and stared at Dad in slack-jawed shock. Mom started to say something about Lynn, but I cut in over her.

"You aren't going to tell me what this self-imposed exile is about, are you?"

"Self-imposed exile?" Dad said with a bitter laugh. "Is that what they're calling it?"

"What do you call it?"

"No," Dad said, frowning. "You're too young, yet."

"Dad," I started, but he shook his head.

"They told you something, I'm sure. It'll do for the truth for now. You're not ready to hear my side of things."

"You said I wasn't ready to learn about the family," I said. "Not telling me almost got me killed."

"Not telling you kept you safe from the family's games for twenty-two years."

"And dropped me into the middle of them with no guide and no idea who I could trust, or even what the hell was going on." I stood up. "You should have prepared me."

"What difference would it have made? Look at you," he said, smiling bitterly and almost mocking with his tone. "A perfect little prince of Vol-Halá." He shook his head. "At least your sister will be spared."

"That's enough," I said. "If all you're going to do is offer me cryptic bullshit, don't bother. I'm leaving."

"No," Mom said, reaching for my arm.

"I'm sorry, Mom." I shook my head and grimaced at Dad. "You talk about the family's games? Well what the hell are *you* doing right now, but playing games, Dad?"

"I won't go back," he said. "You can't make me. And don't you dare take your sister."

I started to say something spiteful, but stopped myself. There was a look in Dad's eyes. It was a haunted look. The things he wasn't telling me. I was starting to think he *couldn't* talk about them for some reason.

Maybe he wasn't just *acting* cryptic. Maybe on some level, he had no choice.

"I'm not the one who's not ready," I said, wonder in my voice.

Dad started to say something. Stopped himself. Shook his head, a series of short, rapid shakes.

Mom looked back and forth between us. Clearly not sure what to do or say, but desperate to do or say something.

I couldn't be here without trying to talk to Dad. But he couldn't talk about ... whatever it was that was eating him up inside. All I'd accomplish by staying would be hurting both of them.

I wasn't going to do that.

I kissed Mom goodbye. She was crying, but I think she understood. Dad wouldn't stand up to hug me, so I clapped him on the shoulder.

That was a mistake. He must've associated it with the rest of the family. He got an expression on his face as though a pipe had burst and started pumping hundreds of gallons of sewage right into the room.

I turned to leave. At the door, I looked back to say one more thing.

"Oh," I said. "Don't know if your 'resources' told you this, but I killed the man who killed Uncle Karl."

"Man?" Dad said, frowning. "Son, the golden knight who killed Uncle Karl was a woman."

"No..." I started to say that I'd killed the golden knight. Except that I realized that Cassiel and I had identical looking armor. Likely the exact same look to the armor of every prince and princess of the Ulfson family.

Which meant that the O'Berrans were likely the same way with the golden unicorn look.

"How do you know?" I asked.

"That's right," Dad said, softly. "You hadn't awakened to the Wolf yet. You probably missed a detail or two, when Karl died."

Dad looked up at me.

"He said his killer's name. Shalla."

I left then, wandering almost aimlessly among the calm, suburban streets of Long Pine City until Tiksdottir picked me up in our rented Cadillac.

"What's wrong, sire?" she asked as I eased onto the leather seat of the passenger seat.

I looked at her. I wanted to tell her. But if I did, she would have to report this information. It would become part of the war effort. A war effort I was not ready to participate in.

I had more training to do. More to learn. More to practice. I had to become the man who could find and defeat this Shalla.

Because I wasn't going to let anyone else do it.

So I quirked a sad smile at Tiksdottir and told a truth that was only half an answer to her question.

"Things didn't go so well with Dad."

"I'm sorry, sire."

"That's all right," I said. "Let's go." I stared off into the distance. "I've got a lot of practicing to do."

SIGN UP FOR STEFON'S NEWSLETTER

Stefon loves to keep in touch with his readers, and loves to keep you reading. The best way for him to do both is for you to sign up for his newsletter.

Sign up at http://www.stefonmears.com/join

If you sign up for Stefon's newsletter, you get...

- Monthly updates about his publishing and travel schedules
- His latest news, in brief, and answers to reader questions
- A free short story for signing up
- List-only offers and occasional specials
- Plus a free short story every month!

ABOUT THE AUTHOR

Stefon Mears had a couple of classes with Volner at Cal. Stefon has more than thirty books to his credit, and he never stops writing. He earned his M.F.A. in Creative Writing from N.I.L.A., and his B.A. in Religious Studies (double emphasis in Ritual and Mythology) from U.C. Berkeley. He's a lifelong gamer and fantasy fan. Stefon lives in Portland, Oregon, with his wife and three cats.

Look for Stefon online:
www.stefonmears.com
himself@stefonmears.com

ALSO BY STEFON MEARS

Cavan Oltblood Series

Half a Wizard

The Ice Dagger

The Spell in the Blade

Spells for Hire

Devil's Shoestring

Zombie Powder

Spirit Trap

Dragon's Blood

The Rise of Magic

Magician's Choice

Sleight of Mind

Lunar Alchemy

Three Fae Monte

The Sphinx Principle

Double Backed Magic

The Telepath Trilogy

Surviving Telepathy

Immoral Telepathy

Targeting Telepathy

Edge of Humanity

Caught Between Monsters

Hunting Monsters

Power City Tales
Not Quite Bulletproof
No Money in Heroism

Sects and the City

Prince of a Thousand Worlds

Longhairs and Short Tales: A Collection of Cat Stories

Devil's Night

Portal-Land, Oregon

With a Broken Sword

Twice Against the Dragon

The House on Cedar Street

Stealing from Pirates

Fade to Gold

Sudden Death

On the Edge of Faerie

Confronting Legends (Spells & Swords Vol. 1)

Uncle Stone Teeth and Other Macabre Poems

The Patreon Collection Vols. 1-5 (Vol. 6 coming soon)

The 30-Day Novel and Beyond!

www.ingramcontent.com/pod-product-compliance
Lightning Source LLC
Chambersburg PA
CBHW021319190726
48288CB00003B/887